Extinction List

Extinction List

Jon Prinz

John Smiley Publishing
Philadelphia

Published in the United States by John Smiley Publishing
PO Box 2062
Riverton, NJ 08077-2062
U.S.A.

smileypublishing@johnsmiley.com

The characters and events in this book are fictitious. Any similarity to real persons, living or dead, is coincidental and not intended by the author.

Extinction List
ISBN: 978-1-61274-011-9

Printed in the United States of America.

10 9 8 7 6 5 4 3 2 1

First Edition: February 2011

Dedication

I wish to thank my wife, Dawn. If it was not for all your words of encouragement this book would not have been finished.

About the Author

Jon Prinz has been in the Civil Engineering/Construction industry for the past 26 years since leaving the Army.

In the Army he served as a base armorer and forward observer while in Germany.

He is currently Chief Estimator of JPC Group, one of Philadelphia's leading Civil and Site constructors.

Prologue

It was a warm balmy morning in the sub-tropical forest of what is now Montana. This is the time of the Tyrannosaurs and to modern day Paleontologists this is the time of the evolution known as the Late Cretaceous period.

During the Late Cretaceous period the world has assumed most of its present day appearances, though some shallow seas still flood low-lying areas. The dispersal of the continents has separated communities of both plant and animal life to some extent, but intermittent land connections allow migration to occur. With temperatures still warm, forests predominately cover most of the northern latitudes such as Montana and the territories of Canada.

The terrain at this time would have resembled a wetter version of the modern day Serengeti Plain in East Africa, except there would be no grass. It had not evolved yet. Other flowering plants, known as Angiosperms, which first appeared in the early part of the Cretaceous period, have dominated plant life. Angiosperms have seeds inside a fruit that the dinosaurs and small mammals found to be tasteful and a potent form of nutrition. These plants were fast growing and could be fertilized by wind, flying insects and animals, enabling the flowering plants to spread rapidly thus creating a vast food supply.

Also present during this time were water lilies, groves of magnolias and sycamores that helped support a very diverse group of small mammals and browsing dinosaurs in the time of the tyrannosaurs.

As the forest begins to come alive the unique trumpeting sound of the Triceratops can be heard at a distance as the herd starts their daily browsing of the angiosperms and magnolia flowers. The Triceratops is a medium size herbivore dinosaur that is protected from predators by a short neck frill and three facial horns and is about thirty feet long. The triceratops pause from feeding momentarily as a high-pitched cry is heard in the distance, alarming the herd it may be time to browse elsewhere.

The cry heard in the distance was not that of an injured dinosaur or small mammal, but that of the feared Velociraptor. This lightly-built, fast moving dinosaur which is only six to seven feet long, has grasping type hands, a stiffened tail for balance and a very deadly sicke-shaped claw on the second toe of each foot. This dinosaur is feared greater that the formidable Tyrannosaurus Rex because of its fearlessness and ferociousness when hunting. The velociraptor usually hunts its prey in packs like modern day carnivores such as Wolves and Lions. When velociraptors are on the move, the forest usually erupts in a frenzy of activity, from the burrowing of small mammals to the flight of large butterflies, interrupting their meal and thus pollinating other angiosperms in return.

Just as the Triceratops thought their new foresting area was safe they sensed light movement in the ground of something very heavy coming their way. Just as panic was starting to set in amongst the herd, the surrounding forest erupted with crashing trees and the hurried flight of birds. Most of the triceratops herd had managed to run for safety except for the youngest member of the herd who had an injured leg due to a previous aborted attack by a lone velociraptor. As the injured triceratops limped for the cover of the forest the largest of the carnivorous dinosaurs known as Tyrannosaurus or nicknamed by Paleontologists T-Rex emerged from the forest into the clearing. The T-Rex is a massive dinosaur which measures forty-five feet long and can weigh as much as seven tons and is the only predator of the velociraptor. Unfortunately the injured triceratops could not protect itself from the massive, but quick T-Rex. In the time of a few seconds the T-Rex had managed to overcome the injured triceratops and was quickly tearing about its prey with large saw-edged teeth set apart in its powerful jaws. Just as quickly as the drama had begun the T-Rex was finished feeding on its prey and would once again roam the forests and marshes searching for new prey. The triceratops carcass was left behind for the scavengers and insects to feed on. This is the way of the dinosaurs in the late cretaceous period.

One

65 Million Years Ago

Since the dawn of the dinosaurs during the Triassic period 165 million years ago when early dinosaurs evolved from primitive reptiles. They continued to evolve through the Jurassic to the early Cretaceous period 75 million years ago and scientists have pondered the question how did the dinosaurs get so large? Especially the herbivores since both modern grasses and flowering plants had not evolved yet.

During these periods the herbivore dinosaurs would eat conifers, ferns and Bennellites. Most of the ground foraging dinosaurs would eat the ferns and especially liked the Bennellites. The Bennellite plants had a bare trunk with a layered bark that resembled diamond shapes with hairy edges like a coconut. The trunks which stood between one to two feet tall were topped by a crown of leaves with about twenty stems with multiple leaves on each stem. The stem and leaves resembled a modern day palm plant.

Each plant had several seed cones located within the center of the trunk, which protruded a few inches above the leaves. The seed cones were about three inches long and two inches in diameter and resembled a stubby version of today's pine cone. During the slightly cooler fall and spring seasons the seed cones would emit a small amount of syrupy sugar that insects and some dinosaurs found to be tasty. During the fall and spring seasons the dinosaurs would chew up the Bennellite seed cones to get to the sweet syrup and break up the seeds which were then dispersed within the area. Once the seed cone was gone the Bennellite plant would generate a new seed cone on the existing stalk. This basic process of seed dispersal and seed cone regeneration helped the plant to produce more seeds and start new plantings. The Bennellite plant helped feed and sustain a large portion of the dinosaurs diet.

From the early Cretaceous period 75 million years ago to the late Cretaceous period around 65 million years ago, early flowers evolved call Protoanthus. The Protoanthus plant was around two feet tall with as many as thirty large lily-like leaves coming from a single plant. Each plant could have as many as twenty large three inch flowers which would turn into oval shaped fruit the size of a small cantaloupe. Each Protoanthus fruit contained over two hundred seeds and contained both citric acid and natural sugars. This fruit quickly became the herbivore dinosaurs food of choice and became a part of their regular diets.

The leaves of the Protoanthus were a dark green color and if eaten were extremely bitter tasting. This helped protect the plant from both insect damage and from being totally devoured by the dinosaurs.

The Protoanthus seeds were either digested by the dinosaur or discarded when eaten and this enabled the plant to propagate very quickly and in mass quantities.

The Protoanthus were fertilized by the wind and very often by flying insects and other animals. This enabled the new plant to spread very rapidly and in conjunction with the sub-tropical weather the Protoanthus grew to maturity very quickly.

As the landscape evolved to include a multitude of Protoanthus flowering plants the dinosaurs preferred the much more tasty fruit and flowers of the Protoanthus to the bitter and bland Bennellite leaves and seed cones. It was during this time that the Bennellite plant seeds were not released and thus the plant disappeared from the earth, replaced by the Protoanthus.

Along with the evolution of the flowering plants came the Butterfly. The group of insects classified as Lepdioptera included moths, skippers and now butterflies. The butterflies that had evolved during the Late Cretaceous period were much different from today's butterflies. Unlike the early books on pre-historic insects, which depicted the butterfly as an enormous insect with a foot long body with enormous wings, these butterflies were smaller than moths. The late Cretaceous butterfly had a body no more than a quarter of an inch long with wings less than a square inch. Unlike today's modern butterfly these pre-historic butterflies had cocoons which were the size of a small pea. The butterflies favorite plant to feed on was the Protoanthus plant. As the butterflies fed they would also pollinate the plant in return. At this time in the late Cretaceous period both plant and animal life prospered in the sub-tropical environments of what is now the North America and Asia continents.

During this time of the late Cretaceous dinosaur period, nature was in complete balance evolutionary speaking. Insects would feed on plants and pollinate them, herbivore dinosaurs would feed on the flowers and fruit of the plants, then the carnivore dinosaurs would feed on the herbivores and both would leave droppings which the insects would then use to incubate larvae and cocoons and thus the cycle was complete.

But this cycle did not last very long. In addition to the evolution of the Protoanthus flowering plants and butterflies came the evolution of a deadly and fast growing form of fungus.

This new form of fungus called Rogattus was blue-green in color and had the look of velvet when mature. Another sign that the fungus had fully developed was the strong odor that can best be described as concentrated cat piss. The fungus found the Protoanthus plant and some ferns to be an ideal host to grow and develop on. But instead of helping the plant prosper like the butterflies did, the fungus destroyed the Protoanthus plant. The Rogattus fungus would cover the leaves and stems of the plant thus preventing any photosynthesis and would breakdown the outer stem layers and disrupt the flow of water to and from the root system. Once the fungus was attached to a plant stem or leave the fungus would fully cover the plant and start killing it within a few days. This fungus also thrived from plant to plant by the very pollinating process which allowed the flowering plants to flourish. The deadly fungus was transmitted to other plants by wind, insects and other animals. Not only was the Protoanthus plant starting to die, but the dinosaurs stopped eating them because of the bitter taste and terrible smell.

One unusual aspect of the Regattus fungus was its ability to become dormant for long durations without oxygen. In some cases the fungus was not affected by stomach acids or other digestive enzymes when eaten. This fungus was able to start going again from piles of dinosaur dung.

This new deadly Rogattus fungus first evolved in the sub-tropical region of Asia of what is now Mongolia. This tragic reversal of natures cycle started when more and more Protoanthus and ferns disappeared from the forest creating a environment more like an semi-arid desert area like modern day New Mexico than a sub-tropical forest paradise.

As food became scarce the herbivore dinosaurs like the Homalocephale, a thick skulled species that grew to around ten feet long with a flat head studded with bony knobs started starving. In addition to these dinosaurs starving to death, they would fight each other to the death by charging each other at speeds over twenty miles per hour from over thirty feet away slamming each other with their heads. The Homalocephale would normally butt heads during mating times, but in these times they charged to kill. During this time herbivore dinosaurs had to worry as much about large carnivores eating them as other herbivores killing them for the same food source.

As most of the Homalocephale dinosaurs disappeared the carnivorous dinosaurs would hunt the nimble, but yet fragile Hadrosaur. The Hadrosaur was also known as the duck-billed dinosaur and had long powerful hind legs and small delicate front legs. These herbivores were not equipped to navigate a desert like environment because the Hadrosaur would use its powerful hind legs to jump from tree stumps and partially swing from hanging vines using its front legs. In desert conditions the Hadrosaurs balance was off and the creature was left very exposed. The Hadrosaur either starved to death, was quickly killed by the carnivorous dinosaurs or succumbed to the elements.

At this time in the late Cretaceous period the continents were divided similarly to today's geologic formation, but there still existed some land bridges along with shallow waterways. The largest land bridge that still existed linked what is now Alaska and Russia. Besides early migration of primitive birds, large herds of dinosaurs and small Mammals would migrate long distances from the southern Asian Continent to the North American Continent by way of this land bridge.

This was how the Rogattus fungus was transported by butterflies, birds, mammals and other insects northward from what is now Mongolia. The fungus eventually was spread over the northern land bridge linking the Asia continent with North America.

Other parts of the globe without land bridges were not immune from the deadly fungus. The fungus was sometimes transported within Archelon dinosaurs. The Archelon was a large carnivorous sea turtle which could grow to the size of an average car. The Archelons would feed on smaller herbivore dinosaurs who were searching for food close to the shoreline. At this time the starving dinosaurs had already eaten considerable amounts of the fungus and had undigested portions still in their stomachs.

The Archelon sea turtle would migrate from ocean to shallow sea stopping to feed, rest and lay eggs. During their migratory stops the Rogattus fungus was transported and spread to other regions from the sea turtle dung.

Within a few months of the evolution of the Rogattus fungus, over seventy-five percent of both Asia and North America was transformed from a sub-tropical forest ecosystem to a semi-arid desert and in some areas there was total wasteland.

In what had taken millions of years to evolve and prosper was decimated in less than fifteen years.

As the earths sub-tropical forests were transformed to semi-arid desert environments by the Rogattus fungus, the Protoanthus and some ferns were totally eradicated and the dinosaur population was decreasing rapidly.

As with the dinosaurs the Rogattus fungus was starting to die off with the elimination of the Protoanthus, which was the fungus main carrier and food source. The Rogattus fungus quickly killed off its host and food sources and just as quickly died off.

This was the end of the late Cretaceous period known by scientists and Paleontologists as the K-T boundary which was the end of the pre-historic time of the Dinosaurs.

The dinosaurs were not wiped out by a giant Asteroid that blocked out the sun which in turn killed off the plants and caused mass starvation.

The dinosaurs were not wiped out by a cataclysmic climate change caused by Volcanoes or a shifting polar axis.

The dinosaurs were not wiped out by a epidemic of disease or plague.

The dinosaurs became extinct by a common fungus.

Two

New Haven, Connecticut – Fall 1981

It was cool for an early October day at the famous and scenic
campus at Yale University located in New Haven, Connecticut. But Maxwell
Hamilton was much acclimated to cool weather having been born and raised
in north central Montana. He would have loved to be home in Montana but
he only had to finish his doctoral thesis to obtain his PhD from the famous
Yale University Graduate School of Arts and Science in the field of
Paleobotany.

Maxwell Harold Hamilton, known as Max or "Ham" to his closest
friends was born in 1967 in Montana to Edward and Judy Hamilton who are
wealthy cattle ranchers. Max has three brothers – James, Ed Jr. the oldest
and Tim the youngest. Max comes from Irish-German ancestry that had
traveled to the West to farm and to prospect for gold. His ancestry accounts
for his blonde hair, blue eyes and tall slender build. His family now owns
one of the largest cattle ranches in Montana called "Wolf Creek Ranch".
This ranch comprises over ten thousand acres of land located outside the
town of Denton, Montana which is about eighty miles east of Great Falls.

Max's family ranch has almost five thousand head of cattle in a county that has a population of less than fifteen thousand people.

Max had graduated from the University of Montana at Missoula with a bachelor's degree in Paleontology and then had completed his master's degree in Paleobotany. During his studies in Montana, Max would go home on the holidays to help with the ranch and would also write a scientific article each week for the Sunday edition of the "Missoulian", the local Missoula, Montana daily newspaper. It was because of these articles as much as his grades and grade point average that helped Max get accepted for graduate studies at Yale. It was one article in particular that had caught the deans attention. This article dealt with the possible theory that starvation of the dinosaurs lend to their extinction versus the theory of a sudden cataclysmic extinction caused by a meteor. The latter theory is the most common and widely believed. This is also the theme for Max's doctorial thesis.

Over the October weekend he would have to put off working on his thesis because he had offered to help prepare a local horse for transport across the country. Actually he had been volunteered to help an old friend of his fathers who lived back east. He was asked to prepare a horse for travel to Texas to attend a national rodeo event. Max had always loved riding and being around horses all his life. He was often called upon to help with the family horses because of his six-foot height and one hundred and ninety pound weight and because of his natural ability to both soothe and communicate with horses. Max is usually in good shape and can keep up with a runaway horse at least for a little while. Max would help out this horse because his father had asked, but he really cannot stand rodeos or any horseman who partakes or works at one. Max definitely knows about rodeos – both his oldest and youngest brother's ride and work for the National Rodeo Association. He really hates what they do, but still cares for them, since they are family. Max does not hate sports, he just does not follow any or play any sports, he just loves the outdoors, especially hiking and horseback riding. His other major dislikes besides rodeos is office and clerical work.

Early in November Max had completed his thesis title "The mass extinction of the Dinosaurs – By starvation, not a meteor". My mid-December he had received his doctorate degree from Yale and also had a portion of his thesis published in the "Journal of Paleontology" the most respected and influential journal for paleontologists and paleobotanists. Shortly after receiving his PhD he was offered a position at the world famous "New York Museum of Natural History" in New York City. He probably would not have accepted the position and traveled back home to Montana had he not met the likes of one Monica Lisa Caldwell who was an undergraduate student at Yale studying Biology.

Siberia – a land of death and chains

- Maxim Gorky

Three

Yakutsk, Siberia, USSR – August 1982

The day started out like any other summer morning in the northern hemisphere for Boris Panov except for the fact that his rented bungalow had sunk into the ground and was tilted at a twenty degree angle. This movement of Boris's house happened within the last twenty-four hours. This often happens to buildings without pilings, those wooden poles often seen at ocean front homes that protect them from high seas. Except in this case the pilings are used to anchor buildings deep within the permafrost. Permafrost is basically earth that remains frozen year-round to depths that often reach one hundred feet or more. This makes for easy travel and hard digging during the lengthy Siberian winter months. But often during the brief summer the top five or six feet of the permafrost thaws and can turn into a marshy swamp making roads heave, railroad tracks buckle and houses tilt. Boris felt lucky today because his stove still worked and he could still make his morning coffee.

Boris Panov is a heavy set but agile man of forty-five years of age. He is going bald besides his hair starting to grey. Boris is unmarried and has only dated a few times in his life, due to his travels and his all consuming work. Other than waking up to a tilted house, Boris felt eager to start his day and would do so as soon as he finished his American brand coffee, a luxury his splurged on, bought on the Russian black market.

Boris left his tilted house and walked along the rutted street fronting other tilted housing towards the Yakutsk University. The University was the newest building in town and was constructed with the latest permafrost and cold weather technology. The University building was built on pilings that were drilled into the frozen ground using a steam auger machine and then topped with a durable concrete frame.

Besides the University, Yakutsk is basically a river town, like most Siberian towns. Besides being one of the largest towns on the Lena River, Yakutsk is one of the coldest towns in Siberia. Fortunately for Boris, Yakutsk had a science university and one of the best natural history museums in Russia. The Yakutia Museum which contains ancient weapons, a mammoth skeleton and a mummified body of a ancient Yakut woman, was a favorite stop for Boris when not occupied with his work.

As Boris walked he began daydreaming of his youth on the outskirts of Moscow as he hummed an old peasant farm song his grandmother had sung to him. He started wondering when he would be able to return to his home in Moscow and sleep in a level house with running water and central heat. Boris's thoughts were interrupted by the shouts of several men down by the Lena River. Boris asked one of the men, a muscular and weather beaten man.

"What's all the shouting about?"

"A couple of mine boys are still drunk from the bar and are fighting over the only bed still available at the Hotel Lena"

"They could use my place".

"You could suggest it, but I would not get involved" the weathered man bellowed.

The Hotel Lena was a large two-story frame hotel which also had started to tilt. The hotel was rented mainly by miners who were looking for work or who had time off each month. By this time a small crowd had gathered and were all shouting encouragement for the two drunks to continue fighting, since entertainment in this part of Siberia was hard to find and police were even harder to find. The two drunks would have continued their fight, but they were quickly broken up by one of the mine foreman heading towards the mine train going north.

This part of Siberian Yakutsk is basically a stopping off point and lodging area for mine workers and university staff. Yakutsk is the only town south of the mining towns and is the only town to have a river port facility on the Lena River that is available for supplies all summer long. The Lena river called "Elueneh" in Yakut, the unofficial language in Siberia besides

Russian, is one of the longest rivers in Russia begins some three thousand feet above sea level near Lake Baikel, then runs north through mountains and taiga for almost two thousand eight hundred miles until it reaches the Artic sea. Besides providing a vital water link with the mining towns, in winter the river serves as a frozen highway for truck convoys carrying tools and materials from the south, like the ice roads of Alaska. These methods of transportation were preferred to traveling hundreds of miles along rutted and buckled roadways along with either washed out or damaged bridges. This part of Siberia is also known as the Yakut Autonomous Soviet Socialist Republic or Y.A.S.S.R. and is almost as large as all of Western Europe. This area is known for its mining and natural sciences. The Yakutsk University has several scientific departments, but the Archeological department is the largest and most funded department by the Soviet Academy of Sciences in Moscow. This is where Boris Panov works and this is Boris's life. For the last three years he has traveled to and from the mining towns of Mirny and sometimes to the gold fields of Aldan.

The town of Mirny, which means "peaceful" in Russian, is both the youngest town in Siberia and the largest diamond mine anywhere outside of South Africa. The town of Mirny was built for mining diamonds and consists of drab modular apartment buildings which once housed nearly forty thousand people and a circular diamond mine over a mile wide and over five hundred foot deep. The mine looks extremely barren except for two very large excavator machines located on the bottom of the mine and the movement of large dump trucks that ride up the sides of the mine where they deposit the diamond ore onto conveyors to enriching plants. The mine operation works twenty-four hours a day, seven days a week. Near the edge of the top of the mine, Boris has unearthed several archeological sites and sometimes gets in the way of the mining operations. Within these sites Boris has discovered many fossilized remains of Dinosaurs.

Boris often tells his comrades.

"This archeological site could be larger than the Dinosaur fossil area located at Dinosaur Provincial Park located in Canada".

But he is often teased and reminded by his comrades.

"Boris, your fossil discoveries are only available if the government mining company permits it to stay and who would want to visit such a location with temperatures that average -50 degrees below zero in the winter, not to mention mosquitoes the size of small birds in the summer".

Boris knew this was a reality, plus the fact the Russian government would never allow any western scientists anywhere near the mines or the University. One day he vows to write in the leading American and British Archeological Journals about his past discoveries and especially his latest fossil finds which have him puzzled.

Boris Panov's latest archeological fossil site is located within the Mirny diamond mine property and could easily be the size of a football field. During his weekly trips to the archeological excavation, he has unearthed fossils dating back to the late Cretaceous period some 65 million years ago. This was the time of the T-Rex, the Velociraptor and a multitude of large carnivorous and herbivore dinosaurs. What has intrigued Boris is not the late Cretaceous period of fossils, but the layer above this excavation. Boris has noted in his field journals that the dinosaur fossils were covered with many layers of fossilized mammals and plant life. He figures most scientists know that the dinosaurs became extinct at the end of the Cretaceous period, but he often lectures to the University students and staff about the lack of any evidence depicting an Ice age, cataclysmic volcanic activity or shifting of the polar axis. Boris usually starts his lectures with the comment.

"One day I will speak with scientists around the world and we can one day answer the age old question – What happened to the dinosaurs".

After the brief encounter with the young drunk miners, Boris continued on his walk once again daydreaming of fame and fortune. A couple of miles later Boris realized that he had daydreamed himself in possible missing the morning train to the Mirny diamond mine. He knew that this train would not depart again until the evening shift and he had classes and lectures the rest of the week. Boris knew he must excavate the area just east of the T-Rex site before it gets too cold or the mine engineers decide to dig for diamonds in his archeological area first.

Boris knew he was in no physical shape to run to the train platform near the Lena River. But luck was with him today. He was able to flag down an old Volga taxi, one of only five that still was able to navigate the rugged and twisted roadways and terrain in and around Yakutsk. Plus Boris happened to know the taxi driver named Vladimir, who's son attended the University and had taken classes taught by Boris and had sometimes helped his father drive the taxi. Vladimir asked Boris after a hurried greeting.

"Where are you going today Professor"

"I need to make this mornings train to the mines to get started on an important archeological excavation".

Vladimir who was only educated to a primary school level was not very interested in learning about old bones or about prehistoric creatures. He only needed to know enough to keep his taxi running and how to keep it warm in the winter. Vladimir listened to Boris, but only managed a short quip.

"Sure thing Professor Boris Bones"

Vladimir laughed for ten minutes all the way to the train station.

After arguing with Vladimir over accepting his normal payment of one hundred rubles, Boris had just enough time to run to the train and stand in the aisle with the rest of the young miners. He normally went to the train early enough to get one of the few seats not taken by mine foreman, geologists or KGB. But today he would have to endure the two hour train trip to the Mirny diamond mines standing.

Looking at the faces of the young miners who were probably only twenty to twenty-five years old but looked over thirty years old, Boris was thankful he had been chosen to attend science school instead of becoming a laborer. At this time in Russia, children were still divided up and given their prospective career paths by the Director of Children's Development at each primary school by the age of ten. Some students were natural athletes, some gifted in the arts and others were either selected for secondary science school or became day labor. After riding the train for a half hour, Boris again felt thankful for a science career and especially one he truly loved. Boris felt this way since most of the young miners were at one time promising athletes.

By the time the train arrived at the Mirny Diamond mine train station it was already near eight o'clock in the morning. This did not worry Boris since living at this latitude in Siberia, a summer day may last to nearly two o'clock in the morning. Upon leaving the train station, Boris was able to find his mine "contact", a man named Yanov Khudenko, a small, but stout man in his late forties with a receding hairline and wire-rimmed glasses. Boris looked at Yanov and thought out loud "Yanov is probably KGB, but a guy who generally stayed out of his way and who was friendly with the mine manager, an engineer named Viktor.

Boris made the half mile walk to his archeological site where he quickly surveyed his surroundings, unlocked his wooden shed and then gathered up his tools, consisting of a shovel, pick and an assortment of small implements including dental picks and spoons. Once he gathered his tools, Boris figured he would start digging at the area near his T-Rex site that where he had previously uncovered large concentrations of fossilized plant material. Boris wondered if he could arrange to have a Paleobotanist come to the site, since he was a Paleotologist which studies pre-historic animal life and Paleobotany studies pre-historic plant life. Just as quickly he realized that funding was becoming scarce from Moscow and they certainly would not spend any more money on other scientists.

"Oh well, I'm no expert, but I know enough to get by" Boris said to himself just as the mine manager Viktor was approaching.

Viktor did not bring good news for Boris.

"If the current area the miners were excavating for diamonds did not start producing as planned they would have to move the excavation over to where your archeological area is, probably this spring at the latest" Viktor told him.

This meant that Boris would have to complete his digging, collecting and mapping of this site in the next month or two before it got too cold to work.

"Would it be possible to borrow a young laborer from time to time to help with any heavy lifting and digging" Boris requested.

"Maybe" Viktor smiled.

"We can always arrange a trade professor" Viktor shouted as he walked away.

As Boris was carefully digging and mapping the yet unidentified fossilized plant life, he excavated another area which provided a lot of fossilized plant life followed by a layer of dinosaur fossils. Within the layer of dinosaur fossils, there little or no evidence of any plant life near the dinosaur bones. Boris photographed and recorded the findings and thought this pattern of fossilized material could very likely indicate evidence of mass starvation of the dinosaurs. Also noted by Boris was the lack of coprolite. Coprolite is fossilized dinosaur dung, basically the droppings of pre-historic animals. Boris could see the fossilized pattern at this site and wrote in his journal "no plants and no poop"

Boris finished his mapping and continued collecting dinosaur fossils. As he was finishing uncovering a layer of bone fragments, he started theorizing about the lack of any evidence showing a cataclysmic volcanic or meteoric activity associated with what appeared like mass starvation of the late-Cretaceous dinosaurs. The last journal entry Boris made for the day mentioned "check with KGB science advisor in Yakutsk and request the writings of a young Paleobotanist from Montana in the United States who's doctorate thesis wrote about the possibility of an organic virus or bug that could have caused the extinction of the dinosaurs.

The following week, Boris arrived at the Mirny mine site and was given two laborers and was told by the mine manager Viktor, that he would have no more than a few weeks to take care of what he needed from the archeological site.

In the next four weeks, Boris with the help of the mine laborers and a couple of University students he had borrowed was able to finish the collection, mapping and photography of the dinosaur site as best that he could considering the rushed process. The last week of work Boris started the fragile task of packing up all the collected dinosaur bones, fossilized plant material and coprolite. It was during the packing that Boris noticed a spec of light brown to yellow material in one of the fossils. This spec turned out to be "amber", which is basically fossilized tree sap. After closer examination he noticed that the amber was contained within a fossilized fragment of coprolite. Boris quickly grabbed his site maps and journal along with the student who had excavated this fragment of dinosaur dung. Later that day Boris determined the "amber" located in the piece of coprolite had been unearthed from the archeological layer within the dinosaur bones, the layer with little or no fossilized plant life. Boris had commented to the students and mine laborers.

"This is very strange. Why had the dinosaur eaten the tree sap, since it was widely believed they could not have been able to digest woody plant material".

"The only possible reason the dinosaurs had eaten the tree sap must have been because they were starving, and the million ruble question is? What happed to the plants?" Boris asked out loud. Boris then packed up his tools, arranged for transport of his collected specimens and thanked both the students and mine laborers for their help.

Later that night the couple of young mine workers who worked with Boris were drinking and talking to other mine workers at a local bar in Yakutsk about their work with the bone professor near the diamond mine site in Mirny. They had told their comrades about how excited, fascinated and perplexed the professor had been about this prehistoric tree sap material. The young miners had described a brown and yellow glass like material that the professor had taken from a piece of dinosaur poop. At this time the two miners along with their comrades started to laugh and began a long night of drinking and telling stories and jokes. But at the end of the bar neither drinking nor laughing was the mine "contact" Yanov Khudenko. He quickly mentally noted this information and had written down an instruction to himself to contact a KGB Science advisor from Moscow about professor bones latest discoveries. Yanov did not know a lot about dinosaurs and archeology, but he knew how valuable diamonds and gold were and he thought "maybe this amber material is also very valuable and I could get a big promotion for helping the state with the discoveries and maybe I could finally be transferred out of this inhospitable land of death and chains".

Later that month as Boris was preparing his lecture for his next class while sipping coffee in his tiny cluttered office, he was surprised to see Yanov Khudenko, the local KGB agent he had spoken to at the Mirny diamond mine. With Yanov was another man that Boris did not recognize. This man was introduced as Vasily Chekhov, a KGB Science advisor who had traveled from Moscow. Boris quickly asked if this meeting had anything to do with his trying to obtain scientific writings from America.

"Professor, we just need to see the glass tree sap stuff you got from the dinosaur poop" Yanov asked.

The KGB Science advisor Vasily Chekhov then introduced himself and requested Yanov leave them alone for a few minutes.

"No problem" replied Yanov in an upset voice. Yanov could not express his anger, since Vasily held the rank of Captain and he still held the rank of Lieutenant in the KGB. But he mumbled to himself out in the hallway.

"If I don't get promoted to Captain because of this, I will take some of dinosaur poop and sell it for more rubles then they are paying me. Maybe I could get hard currency like American dollars". The KGB Science advisor Vasily discussed with Boris the importance of his archeological find to the U.S.S.R.

"We will need to take this amber material and other fossil material to Moscow for further research" Vasily told Boris. Boris had started to protest.

"This discovery could help the great U.S.S.R. pass the Americans in pre-historic knowledge and would require you to come back to Moscow" Vasily added.

"Thank you, Thank you, comrade Vasily" Boris excitedly exclaimed. Boris took out a bottle of vodka from his desk, poured each a shot and they toasted to mother Russia. Vasily then asked to see the specimens and discoveries Boris had excavated from the Mirny mine site.

It was early in September in Yakutck and already there was a cold front that had come in from the northern artic circle of Siberia. It had already snowed a few inches and temperatures averaged twenty degrees Fahrenheit during the day. Boris was both glad to be leaving and sad to leave so many friends and gifted students. He knew Moscow had terrible and cold winters, but a Yakutck winter was just unbearable. So as the last boxes of collected specimens were sealed, Boris noticed that his detailed record of collected "amber" within the coprolite specimens did not match the packing slips attached to the shipping boxes and containers. Boris had asked around and was offered help from the local KGB mine agent Yanov Khudenko in searching for the missing "dino poop". As the laborers and students loaded the truck for transport to Moscow, Boris commented to his student help "I am either getting sloppy with my records or one of the mine laborers or one of you has kept a souvenir of my work". Unknown to Boris was that Yanov Khudenko the KGB mine agent had taken the "amber" specimen. He had hoped to sell it, since he had yet to receive a promotion or had received a transfer from Siberia. Yanov said goodbye to Boris and uttered out loud "Professor Bones and the dino poop are leaving for Moscow and we are still stuck here in the land of death and chains".

Boris rode the train for two days from Siberia and arrived in Moscow in the early evening in late September 1982 where it was a surprisingly warm evening for late September in Moscow. Considering that when he left Yakutck in Siberia, the temperature was below twenty degrees Fahrenheit and it was snowing. It had been over three years since Boris had been away from Moscow and he felt he would have to learn how to get around the city all over again. As Boris made is way to his government supplied apartment he noticed that he was sweating for the first time in three years.

Boris was given a medium size apartment on the eighth floor of the Moscow Science Housing complex, Building number 10. These apartments were basic one bedroom, bathroom and combined kitchen/living room units that were clean, furnished and were reserved for scientists, engineers and doctors. Once Boris had unpacked he realized his apartment gave him a good view of the building he would be working in, a classical pre-Tsar structure that was the headquarters of the Russian Academy of Sciences. The building was a large structure with several new wings and additions that had been built by the Soviet Union over the years. Boris pondered what it would be like to work with over sixty thousand other researchers and scientists in over two hundred different research institutes, all predominantly working in the natural sciences. Boris had also noticed he had a good, but partially blocked view of Red Square and the surrounding city of Moscow. This type of apartment was a rarity in both Moscow or throughout Russia. Boris turned on the older Television set which came with the apartment and he watched TV for the first time in three years. He watched the local Moscow news channel and listened to the local commentator. Besides television, Boris had not been able to listen to a radio in three years. Boris signed and spoke out loud.

"Even with over nine million people rushing about everyday, I still feel glad to be back in Moscow".

Boris started his research at the academy and started teaching at Moscow University while maintaining his records and filing in his small office located at the Academy of Sciences building. Boris had a good life compared to the common Moscow citizen and he felt blessed he had it so well. Unknown to Boris since his arrival in Moscow was that some of his excavated specimens, especially the "amber" filled coprolite was shipped to a top secret military laboratory in Rostov, about one hundred and fifty miles northeast of Moscow. Also during this time, Yanov Khudenko had resigned his post in Yakutck, Siberia as the local KGB mine agent and was over heard telling the mine manager that he was moving south to relatives in a village not far from the Afghanistan border.

Four

Rostov was once a prosperous town in the medieval times of European Russia. Like other nearby towns, Rostov was not destroyed by the German Army in World War II, but was destroyed by the communist government of the USSR. The communists believed that to build the future, you had to destroy the memories of the past.

It was just another routine experiment in a clean non-descript government building housing one of the USSR's most secret biological laboratories. This secret laboratory was known as Unit 57 and is located on the edge of Rostov about one hundred and fifty miles northeast of the capital city of Moscow. The area surrounding the laboratory building was mostly crop and livestock farm country.

The Chief Scientist of Unit 57, Dr. Dmitri Pochinkov, a fifty-five year old thin looking, slightly balding but strong looking man who wore round wire-rimmed glasses. Dr Pochinkov had carefully scheduled each experiment he had planned and then proceeded to a group of offices next to the personnel dorm facility. Dmitri knocked on office door number twelve and quietly heard "Come in comrade, What are your plans for today" asked

Vasily Chekhov, a chubby thirty-five year old KGB agent who was Unit 57's

KGB Liaison. It was only known to Dr. Dmitri Pochinkov and Vasily

Chekhov that Unit 57 was not only a viable Biological research laboratory,

but was also a top secret Biological weapons laboratory for the Soviet Army.

Dmitri often wondered if his dedicated staff of scientists and engineers

would work nearly as hard if they knew that they were not only looking for

cures for disease, but in creating the next generation of biological weapon.

Dmitri told Vasily "We are injecting a couple of rabbits with a new small

pox prevention serum that they were developing"

"Was anything done with the dinosaur poop from Siberia" Vasily

asked.

"We are going to attempt to isolate what appears to be insect larvae

located within a piece of 'amber' within the coprolite that was recently

obtained from Siberia" announced Dmitri. They had previously been able to

separate the "amber" material that had been embedded in the coprolite.

"Is there anything that Moscow should hear about" Vasily asked

without looking up.

"Not yet" Dmitri replied, knowing his conversation was finished

with Vasily.

Dmitri was interested in the encapsulated insect larvae, not for the

pre-historic studies like those of his comrade Dr. Boris Panov, who had dug up the specimens in Siberia, but for what may be contained within the insect larvae. Dmitri's position at the laboratory entitled him access to foreign scientific research and journals and this is where he had read that the Americans may have found a way to obtain DNA material from an encapsulated pre-historic mosquito located in a piece of "amber" excavated from a fossil field located in Canada. Dmitri and his scientific staff would like to beat the Americans at finding a use for any pre-historic DNA.

The "amber" scientific crew consisted of Aleksandr Belov – a young twenty-five year old Bio-Medical Engineer, the lovely Valery Kirichenko – a attractive thirty year old Genetic Engineer and Dmitri himself. Dmitri knew this was very important research and he wanted to keep the data between himself and just a few scientists.

Aleksandr Belov proceeded to slice the "amber" into very thin pieces that will be used for both microscopic and chemical analysis, while his laboratory partner Valery Kirichenko prepared some of the slices onto slides for further microscopic review.

"When do you think we may be able to isolate a strand of DNA from the 'amber' material" Dmitri asked Valery who was five years older than Aleksnadr and twenty-five years younger than Dmitri and was somewhat attractive, but was intimidated by Dmitri's power and closeness with the KGB Liaison. "It may take many weeks to process and even more time to try to isolate a DNA Strand, comrade" Valery replied.

"Valery my young engineer, we do not have the time since the Americans may have already isolated a strand and we must win this scientific race and unlock the dinosaurs secrets" Dmitri responded harshly. Dmitri would later tell KGB agent Vasily Chekhov "That his scientists will work as hard as it takes to beat the Americans and create a possible miracle cure or some mutant animal that they may show the world or for the USSR to unleash on the world, especially the West".

Later that day both Aleksandr and Valery would finish placing the thin slices of the "amber" specimens into a mixture of embryonic and protein fluids located in several laboratory Petri dishes that would be kept at various temperatures and light levels.

"Comrade would you like a shot of Vodka at my place or yours" asked Valery.

"Let's have a shot at both places" Aleksandr winked, since he was feeling good about finishing the latest experiments and knowing he had the next day off.

Later that week Aleksandr and Valery come rushing into Dmitri's office and with Aleksandr slightly out of breath said "Comrade doctor – Sorry for the interruption – Ah, and not knocking"

"Please sit down and tell me what you came here to see me about" Dmitri replied with a hint of irritation in his voice.

"We have some good news and some bad news Dr. comrade" Aleksandr replied after regaining his composure. "Well give me the bad, then the good news, please quickly – I have a lot of paperwork to get finished for Moscow". Aleksandr glanced at Valery waiting for her to start as Dmitri was starting to get angry.

"No wonder we are behind the Americans with scientists such as you" Dmitri shouted. Aleksandr was used to Dmitri's outbursts and then calmly explained "The bad news doctor – is we, I mean Valery has not been able to isolate a single strand of DNA so far". Dmitri could not wait for the good news and slammed his fist on his desk and told his scientists "Moscow expects results and is getting very impatient and very tired of waiting for results and spending a lot of rubles for nothing. This is making us and especially me look incompetent compared to other western scientists and if this continues you two will be shipped out to Siberia to dig for more dinosaur poop and I hope you freeze your balls and titties off"

"Do I make myself perfectly clear?" Dmitri said as he was fuming.

"Now tell me the good news please". Aleksandr proceeded to explain to Dmitri with Valery's help how a couple of the specimens that were placed in laboratory dishes filled with embryonic and protein fluids had started to grow a mold-like substance. They noted that the two samples were placed in conditions that would have been similar in temperature, humidity and light as that of the dinosaurs sixty-five million years ago. Just as quickly as Dmitri had gotten angry, he became joyful "Let me see these samples and give me a copy of all the data and records you have for these particular experiments, right after we toast our accomplishments". Valery and Aleksandr left Dmitri's office after a quick drink and then they proceeded to correlate their data for the current experiments.

Two days later Dmitri dropped in on Aleksandr and Valery to check on the progress of the "amber" experiments so he could prepare a presentation for the KGB Liaison and maybe a trip to Moscow. Valery was quick to tell Dmitri "We still have not isolated any DNA, but in the last couple of days a mold-like substance had grown from the two laboratory dishes to over twenty laboratory dishes, with no signs of dying off as long as it is kept in the nutrient fluid"

"Anything else out of the ordinary I should now about" Dmitri asked.

"We began placing various plant and animal cells within the mold-like substance and had just noticed today that the plant cells quickly died and were consumed by the mold substance, yet the animal cells were unaffected" replied Valery, Dmitri thanked Valery and then asked her to leave so he could have a private conversation with Aleksandr. "I would like you to place both grain and corn cells similar to the American and Chinese variety of plants into the 'amber' substance" Dmitri asked.

"Then start labeling this experimental substance 'Orange Agent'".

This was Dmitri's mixed up Russian version for the United States chemical defoliant called "Agent Orange" that was used extensively in Vietnam. Dmitri then quietly told Aleksandr "This is extremely top secret work and no one else is to know about this – not even Valery"

"Yes. Dr. Dmitri – you have my word"

Another couple of weeks went by when Aleksandr presented their finished experimental data called "Orange Agent" to Dmitri. Dr. Dmitri quickly read the outline and results sections of the report and gasped "Aleksandr – you and I will definitely be promoted to Moscow and should both receive state accommodations". Dmitri quickly excused Aleksandr and immediately called and asked to see Vasily Chekhov and asked him to schedule an appointment with his KGB superior as quickly as possible. Dmitri also asked Vasily to also arrange to have someone from the Science Ministry to attend and maybe a member of the Military chief of science.

After much anticipation, Dr. Dmitri was driven to Moscow and was escorted into the office of the Science Minister in Moscow. At the conference table was the General in charge of Military research and weaponry, the Science Minister, Vasily – his Unit 57 KGB Liaison officer and Vasily's boss, the assistant Commander of the KGB. The Science Minister opened the discussion and asked Dmitri to be seated.

"Please give us a detailed but quick overview of your secret report titled 'Orange Agent'" the Science Minister asked. Dmitri quickly explained the start of their experiments, the failure to extract any DNA and ultimately the results he has presented.

"gentlemen this new and unknown mold-like substance will not only kill off food producing plant cells that we introduced, but seemed to grow stronger after each sample was given plant cells. And the animal cells were completely unaffected" Dmitri added. After some hushed discussions, the Military General cleared his throat and asked "Doctor tell me in plain peasant Russian what does this mean to me and the great power the USSR".

"Sir, if we could make enough of this substance, we could introduce it to American crops located in their heartland and in a matter of months could cause complete devastation of America's wheat and corn crops and thus cripple them both economically and socially" Dmitri said softly.

"We could finally bring the American bastards to their knees without a single bullet, let alone a nuclear weapon" the General exclaimed as he leaned back in his chair. The room became very still and silent while everyone pondered the enormous consequences this could mean. The Science Minister broke the silence and offered "Dmitri at this time, what are the possible complications or other factors we should know about". Dmitri not wanting to sound downbeat, but he had to be realistic, so he told everyone in the room "At this time we do not have a way to kill off or stop the mold-like substance. We have tried killing it with other defoliant chemicals and have even tried using acid, but the substance still continued to grow if we kept supplying it plant materials".

"Doctor, in your scientific opinion, right now if this substance was released on a farm, when would it die or how do we stop it" the Science Minister interrupted.

"Sir, it would not die until it had killed most edible plant life. It is possible that it could spread from North America throughout the entire world and thus we would die also" Dmitri replied.

The Chief Scientist from Unit 57, Dr. Dmitri Pochenkov, his KGB liaison, the Science Minister and the Assistant Commander of the KGB and any other official who had access to or had reviewed any of the experiments, samples or reports about "Orange Agent" was ordered to never speak of these experiments or of the meeting ever again. Dmitri was ordered to preserve one sample of the mold-like substance he called "Orange Agent" and to store it in a safe location for future use of mother Russia.

In the next few months Dmitri was given new scientists for Unit 57. Both Aleksandr and Valery were transferred to other facilities. Unfortunately Aleksandr had violated his orders from Dmitri and the Russian Politboro to not tell anyone else about their discovery, not even Valery. Aleksandr could not help himself, because he was not only having drinks with Valery, but he was sleeping with her too.

Five

Moscow, Russia – July 1991

It was just a month after the election of Boris Yeltsin as the

president of the Russian SFSR (Russian Soviet Federal Socialist Republic)

which became the modern day Russian Federation after the collapse of the

Soviet Union. The mighty U.S.S.R. was dramatically changing since the pro-

independence movements within the Baltic States and the loss of its Eastern

European satellite states that had provided protection as a buffer from the

west. By this time the communist governments of Bulgaria, Czechoslovakia,

East Germany, Hungary, Poland and Romania had been swept up in a

bloodless revolution.

It was during this time in Russian history that both economic and

social unrest was flourishing within the once mighty U.S.S.R. Many state

programs involving military and biological research was impacted by the loss

of government funding transfer of key personnel or the complete closer of

some research facilities. Unknown to the United States government at this

time in Russian history was the fact that most top secret Soviet weapons

programs were either suspended or completely shut-down. Most of the

workforce at these facilities were either transferred to other facilities or were just locked out. Also most of the facilities were locked up or abandoned as they were left.

It was during this changing period in Russian history that Dmitri Pochinkov found himself working as a common research scientist at the Academy of Sciences in Moscow. Just a couple of months earlier he was working as the chief scientist at a top secret weapons laboratory known as Unit 57. This facility once provided research and development of both chemical and biological weaponry for the military within the U.S.S.R. Dmitri knew he would be transferred sooner or later, since most of his scientific staff had earlier been transferred or simply left, especially since pay, food and basic provisions were becoming harder and harder to obtain. The only people who were doing well at this time were the pheasant co-op farmers in the area, which during the communist regime were among the poorest group of people in this particular region of the Soviet Union. With supplies so short the farmers have been able to trade goods for services from unemployed factory and laboratory workers in exchange for bread, cheese and other provisions.

Just prior to the closing of Unit 57, Dmitri Pochinkov had to carefully record and pack up all of the laboratory equipment, supplies and experiments that were not already taken back to Moscow or stolen, and then sold by previous scientists and other staff members. It was already widely known that you could make a months wage if you could sell off a microscope or other experimental laboratory device on the black market. Most of the ex-KGB or local police did little to investigate these crimes since they were either too busy getting their slice of the black market pie or were busy investigating larger thefts such as tanks and missiles stolen from the collapsing Soviet military, not to mention nuclear materials.

It was during his inventory that Dmitri noticed that in the High Security Biological Hazard vault there were several missing containers and vials that could contain both biological and chemical agents. Dmitri quickly took out his experiment records log book to ascertain what the missing containers and vials held. He was able to conclude that none of the vials of Anthrax or Small Pox were taken and the no containers of nerve agent were missing. This was no relief to Dmitri, because the entire super ex-foliate they had developed which he had named "Orange Agent" was missing. Back in 1983 Dmitri and a couple of scientists named Aleksandr and Valery had accidentally developed a very potent form of ex-foliate that was obtained from a Pre-historic insect larvae trapped in a piece of "amber" which they had tried to extract a strand of DNA from the sample. He remembered that they had obtained the "amber" sample from a piece of fossilized dinosaur dropping called coprolite and that the sample came from a excavation in Siberia. Dmitri knew he had to find the missing vials of "Orange Agent" and he would have to contact the Paleontologist who had supplied the "amber" sample so he could locate another possible sample to try to replicate the experiment if required.

Dmitri knew he had to report the loss of the vials as stolen to the ex-KGB or whatever they called themselves now, so they could take over the investigation or they probably would simply place this incident into a "wait for it to disappear" file. If he could tell them the true power and the potential for destruction this experimental material could cause they would probable put over fifty men on the case. Dmitri wondered it he was maybe mistaken in his inventory or maybe the vials were relocated to another laboratory facility without his knowledge or maybe one of his top level scientists had taken the vials to sell on the black market. Dmitri would investigate the theft on his own for now and maybe contact Moscow in the future.

Upon going through his experimental inventories and notes, including the required experimental log sheets, he realized that the only people who had access to the top secret vault were himself, the KGB Science Advisor Vasily Chekhov and a Bio-Medical Engineer named Aleksandr Belov who had worked for him a few years ago at the Unit 57 laboratory facility and who had helped develop the ex-foliate material. If Aleksandr had taken the vials, he would not have any idea of how potent and dangerous and potentially deadly this experiment was. This experimental ex-foliate substance was then quickly stored away and any further experimentation was concluded, Dmitri and Vasily Chekhov were sworn to secrecy and told to end all experimentation of his named "Orange Agent". This is why he did not suspect the KGB agent, since he also knew the consequences of this deadly substance. It was during Dmitri's presentation of the experiment to the Minister of Science that they realized they had discovered a substance that could kill off all known food sources for both man and animal. Dmitri would have to find Aleksandr and his secret girlfriend Valery and get the "Orange Agent" back into storage or destroy it. Then he would have to locate Dr. Boris Panov, the Paleontologist who had originally discovered the sample and take any additional samples and destroy them just in case any of the experimental notes and logs was copied.

Dmitri decided he would not tell his superiors at the Academy of Sciences at this time and he would certainly not inform the ex-KGB. He would first try to located the missing substance on his own. He liked working at the Academy of Sciences and knew good scientific jobs were hard to find and keep, unless you able to sell your knowledge to black market weapon merchants or worse, you could work for the Arabs. His superiors knew the full danger of the missing vials and if they were not recovered the best job he could hope for at the Academy of Sciences would be to wash the floors.

Six

New York City – August 1991

It was now four months since Max Hamilton returned from his hometown of Denton, Montana where he had married his graduate school girlfriend Monica Caldwell. Monica is a good looking woman around five feet six inches tall with brown hair and hazel colored eyes. Monica met Max while they were both attending Yale University in 1983. He was finishing his doctorate and Monica was in her Junior year studying Biology and teaching.

Shortly after obtaining his PhD from Yale, Max took a position at the preeminent American Museum of Natural History in New York City. This job would be close enough to visit Monica in Connecticut until she graduated. After Monica graduated she moved to New York City with Max and started teaching Biology part-time.

Max and Monica had just moved into their new home in Fishkill, New York which is an easy commute for Max to New York City and not very further from Monica's family in New Jersey. It had been a busy and joyful time for Max in the four months since marrying Monica. He had been given a promotion to Chief Paleontologist at the Museum, the youngest person ever at that position, which meant a large pay raise. Monica and Max then found a wonderful three bedroom house in Fishkill, New York just up the highway from New York City. This move was just in time since Max and Monica had just learned that they were expecting their first child.

Max arrived at the Museum just after eight o'clock in the morning on a normally routine Thursday in August. Max greeted the security guard Harry at the main door and in passing Max quipped "Harry, just think in another three weeks you will have bus loads of screaming kids coming through those doors each day"

"I hope to retire in another two months Dr. Hamilton, so I think I can handle it" replied Harry. Harry the security guard really loved children and would most probably miss the school trips.

"When is Mrs. Hamilton expecting your first baby?" asked Harry.

"Around January 10th" Max replied as he ran up the stairs towards the employee offices. Once in his office, Max sat down to catch up on some paperwork, which he hated as much as rodeos, when suddenly the phone rang. It was his boss, the assistant curator for the Museum, Martin Weston.

"Max, how is your presentation coming along for Friday's Alumni and Benefactor dinner".

"Fine just doing a little tweaking" Max lied.

"Good, I hope to see your lovely wife Monica at the dinner" and Martin hung up. Martin Weston was good at his job, but Max thought he was too much accountant and not enough curator. Max stopped checking his paperwork so he could get started and try to write up a presentation that he now remembered he was supposed to present at the Annual Alumni and Benefactor dinner held each year on the Arthur Ross Terrace. Max decided he would present his theory on the extinction of the dinosaurs, similar to his doctorate thesis.

Before he knew it Max was escorting his wife Monica through the VIP line for the dinner at the Museum. The American Museum of Natural History is a one hundred and twenty five year old building located in Manhattan, New York City and is home to one of the world's most preeminent science and research facilities and is renowned for its many collections and exhibitions of earth's evolution. Max and Monica were shown to the Arthur Ross Terrace when Max complained " Monica, I hope this does not last too long, I cannot wait to get this monkey suit off and get back into jeans and get comfortable again"

"Max you cannot dress like you are at a archeological dig all the time" Monica teased him.

The Arthur Ross Terrace is a public space at the museum with over forty five hundred square feet that overlooks the famous Hayden Sphere located in the Rose Center for Earth and Space. Normally this terrace would be filled with screaming kids running around followed by teachers yelling their names, but tonight the terrace was filled with men and women in formal attire talking and laughing while listening to a string quartet located in the back.

Among the alumni and other dignitaries were a group of Russian scientists who had come to the United States to tour some famous Museums, Research Institutes and to meet with a group of US government scientists down in Washington, D.C. Among the Russian scientific delegation were scientists, bioengineers, genetic engineers and a Paleontologist who had worked in many Russian museums, institutes and many top secret laboratories within the former U.S.S.R.

After dinner, Max was introduced and spoke almost forty-five minutes about his theory that the dinosaurs had become extinct from mass starvation, not from a giant asteroid, a cataclysmic volcano, or a shifting of the polar axis, but from the elimination of their food sources from other means. Max elaborated on his theory that something killed off the plant life that so many Herbivore dinosaurs depended on for life, which led to their demise, followed by the Carnivorous dinosaurs. Max finished his presentation to a round of applause and he quickly thanked everyone for attending. As Max and Monica were making their way through the crowd in order to quickly and quietly leave the terrace, they were approached by two members of the Russian scientific delegation. They were Boris Panov and Dmitri Pochinkov. Boris Panov, a top Russian Paleontologist and Dmitri Pochinkov is a noted scientist at the famous Academy of Sciences located in

Moscow and he was also the former Chief scientist at the top secret weapons laboratory known as Unit 57 in the old U.S.S.R. Both scientists congratulated Max on a wonderful presentation and had told Monica how lovely she looked tonight.

"Mrs. Hamilton do you mind if we have a few minutes with your husband" Dmitri asked in good but heavily accented English.

"We will not be long or take time with you" Boris added in less perfect English.

"Please take your time gentlemen, and Max just meet be at the T-Rex exhibit when you are finished" Monica replied and left the terrace.

"What can I help you gentlemen with tonight?" Max stated, hoping to make this very short so he could return to his wife.

"My name is Dmitri Pochinkov of the Academy of Sciences in Moscow and this is my colleague Professor Boris Panov, a paleontologist like you Dr. Hamilton"

"I am actually a Paleobotanist" Max interjected. Dmitri unfazed resumed.

"We will not take up much of your time Dr. Hamilton" and told him they had enjoyed his presentation and that Boris would like to speak to him about his extinction theory in much more detail and wondered if Max would accompany them to Washington, D.C. when they meet with the group of US government scientists. Max told Dmitri and Boris that he would love to talk about his theory some more, but he had planned a quiet weekend with his wife Monica, especially since they had recently learned they were expecting their first child. Dmitri and Boris both congratulated Max on his upcoming birth and interjected "Dr. Hamilton we are very sorry to have intruded on your evening and we hope to read more about your theories and research". Dmitri and Boris waved goodbye and quickly disappeared into the terrace crown.

Max had later that night expressed to his wife how nice the Russian scientists were and that he felt guilty for not getting more involved with their request. Monica told Max to relax, since it was a normal Russian custom to invite a qualified speaker to help them in their studies.

"I guess, but the Russian named Dmitri seemed to want to tell me something important and he looked worried. I think there is something very bad that he is involved in" Max expressed to Monica.

Seven

Moscow, U.S.S.R. – September 1991

Dmitri had tried to locate both Aleksandr and Valery, the two scientists that had participated in developing the "Orange Agent" substance and who had probably stolen the vials that had been kept in secure storage. Dmitri had no choice but to inform his superiors and the police about the possible theft of the experimental ex-foliate. His superiors were not pleased, but with the pending collapse of the Soviet Union they could not worry about something that was probably destroyed or maybe misplaced. Most of the scientists were too worried about their future employment than they were with any lost experiments. But in the spirit of cooperation that had started to exist between the United States and the Soviet Union, a delegation of scientists were gathered to speak with several US government scientists about the missing experiments from the Soviet laboratories. The Americans were told that a couple of vials of a very potent weed killer had been stolen from the Central Agricultural Research Laboratory and that the chemical could cause some contamination in small amounts when mixed with water.

Dmitri had arranged for a group of Russian scientists including the Paleontologist Dr. Boris Panov and himself to visit the United States back in August. At the request of Dr. Panov, they had arranged to attend a dinner held at the American Museum of Natural History in New York City and spoke with the chief Paleontologist about attending their trip to Washington, D.C. They were going to confide in this American scientist against their bosses in Moscow, but they went to Washington without Dr. Hamilton and had only discussed the "approved" soviet problem with the US government and they were told that the United States would be vigilant in checking for any suspicious vials and personnel entering the United States from the Soviet Union.

Dmitri and Boris returned to the Soviet Union just as a failed Coup attempt was taking place which would seal the fate of the collapse of the old U.S.S.R. Dmitri and Boris were now officially working for the Science Academy of the Russian Federation. Their new boss was the ex-state Biologist at the old Academy of Sciences and once Dmitri was settled from his trip back from America he was sent a urgent message to see the Science Academy directors.

By this time, Dmitri had told Boris the entire story relating to the development and search for the missing vials which he called "Orange Agent". When they had returned to Russia, they had thought that given the current state of affairs in Russia, the vials must surely be destroyed. As Boris and Dmitri made their way to the Science Academy Boris asked "What would happen if the terrorists in Azerbaijan or the Georgian Republic were to obtain this "Orange Agent".

"They would cripple and destroy what is left of Mother Russia and perhaps the World" replied Dmitri with concern written all over his face. Once in the Academy they quickly located the director's office and told his assistant that they were expected. The director greeted them both "Gentlemen, you went to America as comrades of the Soviet Union and come back as friends of the Russian Federation, welcome home".

"It is good to be back, comrade" Boris quickly responded. The director then asked his assistant to hold all calls and that he was not to be disturbed during this meeting.

"Concerning our problem with the dangerous ex-foliate substance that you developed Dmitri, we have some new information concerning your previous employees Aleksnadr and Valery" the director stated. The director then told Dmitri and Boris that they had located Aleksandr at a small chemical processing plant outside of Moscow. He explained that initially Aleksandr denied any involvement in any theft at the laboratory, but was persuaded to tell the truth once the ex-KGB agents arrived. Aleksandr had finally told the ex-KGB agents that he had stolen the vials and then had traded a vial of the "Orange Agent" to a local farmer. Aleksandr had told the farmer that the vial contained a super potent weed killer that the farmer could use to control any unwanted vegetation around his co-op farm.

Aleksandr apparently had received a couple of days food and provisions for the vial.

"Did they recover the vial from the farmer and find the other three vials?" Dmitri interjected. The director paused then continued to explain that Aleksandr had destroyed the other three vials and could not remember the farmers name or address. Unfortunately Aleksandr was supposed to take the police to the farm location the following day, but was killed in a car accident that evening.

"Was the other scientist Valery ever located" asked Boris.

"She was located and questioned outside of Berlin, Germany and only remembers growing the 'Orange Agent' cultures and about her failure to obtain any DNA strands from the sample"

"And she claims that she and Aleksandr had broken up soon after their transfer from Unit 57" the director added.

Eight

Kotovsk, Russian Federation – Fall 1991

About three hundred and twenty five miles southeast of Moscow in a small farming village with a full-time population of fifty called Kotovsk lived a modest farmer named Vladimir Voronov. In the early 1980's Vladimir and his fellow co-op farmers had planted over five hundred acres of privately owned, not communist supported farms within a days drive of Moscow. This part of Soviet society was widely accepted within the ruling Politboro, but was not well known to westerners. Farming was tough work in the 1980's especially without proper irrigation systems, good pesticides or reliable working tractors or implements. During this time Vladimir and the other co-op farmers were considered some of the poorest people in the Soviet Union. This was probably why the ruling communist party turned their heads to private land ownership and a free market type business.

It was during the collapse of the Soviet Union that many farmers were able to obtain better equipment, tools and supplies by way of bartering with city workers that were unemployed. The unemployed city workers would barter stolen property in exchange for breads, jams and other food and clothing provisions. Many farmers besides Vladimir had prospered.

Around the fall harvest season of 1991 the poor peasant farmer was now considered to be a upper middle class citizen with lots of land and in some cases had hard currency consisting of US dollars and British pounds. The only people making more money at this time in Russia were the drug dealers and the black marketers.

Vladimir often joked with other farmers at the old co-op exchange building located near the center of Kotovsk that he had traded two sacks of potatoes for a large generator that he had hooked up to his well. He then told them the man was a scientist at some top secret laboratory and that he had stolen the generator before it could even be inventoried. Vladimir listened to similar stories from his fellow farmers and friends and then added "This same man came back a couple of weeks later with what he called a top secret substance that would kill any weed that I needed gone".

"I felt sorry for the man and gave him some flour and bread for the secret substance, even though there was not a lot of it in the vial and it looked like it had become moldy or had some sort of fungus growing – some weed killer" Vladimir finished as the group roared with laughter at his story.

"What ever happened to the guy and his magic weed killer" asked a fellow farmer.

"I just put the shit on a shelf in the barn and I never saw the man again" Vladimir answered.

58

Nine

Kotovsk, Russian Federation – Spring 2004

Kotovsk was still a small farming community within the Russian Federation in 2004 as it had been with the Soviet Union. This farming area was locally known as the "Chernozeur" belt or Black-earth belt which stretched from the Ukraine through the Ural Mountains into western Siberia. Even with increased profitability and advancements in farming equipment, Russia was still the world's largest importer of grain, but crop yields have been getting larger each year. Most of the farms in the "Chernozeur" area are planted in grains, such as wheat, barley, oats and rye. The other crops were widely split between vegetables, fruits and other industrial crops such as cotton and sunflower seeds.

The farming co-op building located in central Kotovsk was a large open bay wood barn-like structure that was left over from the former communist times, but was still used to prepare crops for market. This process of preparation and transportation has been going on since Vladimir Voronov was a young boy, except now he used a truck instead of a horse and wagon. Most of his crops were transported to Moscow's large food processing factories or to the Cheremushki Farmers Market in Central

Moscow. This farmers market is the largest of its kind in all of Russia. Most of the vegetable crops grown in western Russia are transported here to be traded and shipped to such places as Central Asia, Azerbaijan, Georgia and sometimes Lithuania and Latvia.

Vladimir Voronov had just returned back from a long trip to the Cheremushki Market in Moscow where he had delivered a large shipment of grain. All he wanted to do now that he was home was to relax and have a drink of the expensive vodka he had just purchased while in Moscow. But Vladimir would not be able to relax just yet. Not until he had taken care of removing the large amount of weeds that were growing along the fence by the house and were threatening to take over his wife's prized flower garden. Vladimir said out loud as he was looking for weed cutters "The next trip to Moscow I should take my wife and trade her in for some more vodka, but I will probably only get the cheap stuff". Just the he noticed his wife had been working in the flower garden attempting to pull out the weeds, when she called out to him "Vladimir I am running out of patience with these weeds and with you not tending to them". Vladimir threw up his hands and stormed into the barn mumbling all the way in. Once in the barn he realized he had left the expensive vodka out there, so after having his long awaited drink, Vladimir grabbed the so-called "super" weed killer he had traded for a few years earlier for meager loaf of bread. He proceeded to empty the contents of the vial into a sprayer, which he filled up with water. Vladimir figured he would try and dilute the substance and make it last longer if it worked, especially if it was a "super" as the scientist thief had claimed it to be. He then started spraying the weeds along the fence, his driveway, entrance road and had accidentally happened to spray some of the weed killer on his wife's prized flowers after she had went into the house.

"That will fix her nagging ass" Vladimir said out loud with contempt in his voice.

"Suppers ready – Hurry up before it gets cold" his wife shouted out the door. As Vladimir was putting away the sprayer and headed for the house he uttered "If she continues her shit, I'll use the last of the "super" weed killer stuff to spray her entire flower garden".

Vladimir did not need to spray any more of the "super" weed killer. A few days later he had noticed that not only were the weeds dead along the fence and roadway, but his wife's entire flower garden had been destroyed, not to mention several rows of wheat plants were starting to wither and die. As he was putting away a few things in the barn and was just getting ready to have another drink of vodka he heard his wife screech very loudly "Vladimir you asshole, you killed my entire flower garden". He ignored her and had his drink of vodka then picked up the empty vial of "super" weed killer from the trash can and tried to find any markings or labels that would explain the potency and any of its ingredients. "This shit is incredible – with less than a liter of this stuff I could probably clear an entire field" Vladimir mumbled as his wife continued to yell at him from the house. The next day Vladimir told his wife "I will go to the market in Moscow and bring you back over two dozen flower plants and a bag full of seeds to replace the ones that had died".

"That would be nice Vladimir and if you have time could you pick up some spices I need if I give you a list" his wife requested. The next day Vladimir packed up his truck with several bags of wheat and a few bushels of vegetables to trade at the market.

"I will see you in a few days, maybe three or four depending on the weather" as he left the house and waved goodbye. As Vladimir was leaving his property near the end of his driveway, he noticed that a few more rows of wheat had died just overnight. He made a mental note to try and wash this weed killer away when he got back from Moscow.

It had been three days since Vladimir arrived in Moscow and he had decided to stay a couple of more days. He was able to find a local telephone and had called the old Kotovsk farm co-op building to leave a message for his wife that he was delayed for maybe two more days. He hoped one day there would be telephone service out to the farms. The man who had answered the telephone was an old blind man who had once managed the co-op building until he was accidentally blinded by a liquid fertilizer spill.

"Good day comrade, what can I do for you" the blind man answered.

"This is Vladimir Voronov and I wish to get a message to my wife"

"Vladimir, we are so glad you called. You must come back as soon as possible – something has happened on your farm" the blind man interrupted.

"Is my wife OK" asked Vladimir.

"Yes, but you need to come home and…" the telephone line went dead. This is common for most of the Russian phone system even with capitalism and the new Russian AT&T. Vladimir quickly packed up his truck and immediately left Moscow for Kotovsk.

It was very late in the evening when Vladimir arrived in Kotovsk and he was surprised to see a group of farmers and local villagers milling about the old co-op building entrance. He slowed down the truck to say hello and was waved down by a couple of friends.

"Vladimir, I'm so very sorry for your farm" one man said while another chimed in "It looks like the same thing has happened to the Petrovsky farm next door and it has started on the farm across the street". Vladimir told them he has been away in Moscow for a few days and does not know what they are talking about or what is going on.

"It is all dead my friend, all of it" his friend told him as he started to drive away. Once he had driven to within a half mile of his farm he started to notice large clusters of dying wheat along with a lot of dead corn stalks and even some dead shrubs along the fence lines. As Vladimir approached his driveway he saw nothing but what appeared in the halo of his truck headlights to be brown and yellow dead foliage from around his house and as far as he could see. His wife ran out of the house and it looked as if she had been crying a lot. She hugged him saying "It's all dead, our farm is all dead".

"I'm devastated, I don't know what to do" Vladimir whispered to his wife.

"Oh Vladimir, I don't want to be poor again" his wife said as she started to cry again.

"Something terrible has happened here and we need help from the government very quickly" Vladimir said.

"Especially since it appears to be spreading and nothing is stopping it" added his wife.

"I'm going to the barn and sit down and think" Vladimir said as he gestured towards the barn.

"Oh god what have I done and what was that shit that scientist asshole gave me" Vladimir mumbled to himself on the way to the barn. Vladimir proceeded to drink half the bottle of vodka he had hid in the barn and then he tried to destroy any evidence of the "super" weed killer vial and hide his sprayer that still had some diluted "super" weed killer left. Before

Vladimir could notify the local farm official in the village the next day, another forty acres of vegetation had started to die from what was left of his farm, right next to a natural wildlife area that contains a pond a large natural wooded area. This wildlife area is known for an abundance of birds and animal life, which Vladimir and his friends often hunted in, but this natural wooded area felt the effects a couple of days later.

The local farm official drove out to the Vladimir's farm with him and was amazed at the amount of plant loss and was equally terrified at the quickness in which the mysterious plaque spread. The farm official called his superiors in Moscow to report the incidents of crop loss and requested immediate scientific help. He was told that he was not the only farmland that had been affected. One area was around fifty miles from Vladimir's farm and the other area was over one hundred miles away. The Russian authorities knew they had a serious problem and thought it might be some sort of plant virus that could be spread and carried by the wind, insects, birds or other wildlife. So far, Vladimir had kept silent about the "super" weed for fear he would be locked up or worst.

The promised help from Moscow was slow to respond, especially since the government was still trying to get used to life without communism, plus people were still be hired and appointed to positions within the Russian Federation. A couple of days later two young scientists had initially come to the areas affected and had reported to Moscow that his plant virus as they called it, would probably burn itself out in a few thousand acres. The young

biologists should have taken plant, soil and other samples with them to

Moscow for testing, but they were too eager to leave the rural farmland area

to get back to Moscow and its night life and entertainment.

What Vladimir thought was just a "super" weed killer and what a

couple of young biologists thought was just a simple isolated plant virus….

Was not weed killer or a plan virus, but a super deadly pre-historic fungus

known as the "Regattus" fungus and was responsible for the complete

extinction of the dinosaurs over 65 million years ago.

Ten

Moscow, Russian Federation – Early Summer 2004

Dmitri Pochinkov was very busy today grading exams. Unlike in
America, students in Russia go to the University year-round. Dmitri liked his
job at the Moscow University teaching General Sciences and Biology, but
sometimes he missed his old job at the Science Academy and he even
missed the challenges of his earlier research position at the then top secret
Unit 57. It has been four years since he obtained his teaching position at
Moscow University and has since written a couple of Biology articles
published in several scientific journals and had a chance to visit the United
States for a second time almost a year ago. Dmitri wondered what had
become of Boris Panov since he had left the Science Academy. He heard
that Boris had went back to dig for more dinosaur fossils in Siberia and that
Boris had become very friendly with the American Paleobotanist Max
Hamilton at the American Museum of Natural History in New York. Dmitri
also began wondering again what had become of the lost experiments that
had caused him so much grief a few years ago. Just then his student aid
buzzed him and asked if he had time to see a student before his afternoon
classes. Dmitri quickly stopped daydreaming and told the student aid "only
for a couple of minutes, I have another lecture to prepare for next week"

"He said he would be very quick Professor Pochinkov" called out his aid on the antiquated intercom.

"Send him in right away" Dmitri replied and shut off the raspy intercom.

The student named Gory had come to see Dmitri about a letter of recommendation for future employers after he had graduated this fall with his Biology degree.

"Gory, do you have any job prospects lined up yet? Dmitri asked.

"No Professor, I was thinking about learning English and maybe studying in America" Gory confessed.

"I like America. I have traveled to New York City, Washington and Los Angeles in California. America is very different then here in Russia. Make sure you have enough money for a plane ride back to Mother Russia" Dmitri said and laughed.

"Thank you for your time Professor" Gory said.

"Is there anything else you need, Gory?"

"Just the letter if you have the time Professor" Gory requested as he was leaving, but stopped half-way out of the door and asked "Professor have you heard about the large crop losses they have had in the south"

"No I have not" replied Dmitri who had already started grading papers again.

70

"My uncle says there must be over ten thousand acres of crop loss around the Kotovsk area in just the last two months – some sort of plant virus or something" Gory added.

"Did you say ten thousand acres Gory?" Dmitri stopped reading and asked.

"Yes Professor and that was just in the last couple of months. My uncle says the local biologist within the farm ministry said the virus should have burned itself out by now, but its actually still spreading" Gory explained.

"Where did you say this is taking place?" asked Dmitri.

"Near the small farming town of Kotovsk about a half-hour southeast of Lipetsk and about three hundred and twenty five miles southeast of Moscow" Gory answered.

"Oh No" Dmitri mumbled as he dropped his paperwork on the floor, turned pale and struggled to catch his breath.

"Are you alright Professor?" Gory asked fearing the professor was having a heart attack or something.

"I'm fine, just a little heart burn, I'll be fine Gory" as Dmitri composed himself.

"Gory please tell my student aid that I need to cancel my classes for the rest of the day on your way out please" Dmitri requested.

"Did you uncle tell you anything else about the problem down south" Dmitri asked as Gory was about to leave again.

"Well, he said that the scientists who came to the area said it was probably a plant virus, but rumor has it that a local farmer had used some kind of experimental weed killer and it got way out of control" Gory explained.

"That will be all Gory – Thank you very much – and tell my aid to try and find a number for a Dr. Boris Panov. I think he may still work for the Science Academy" Dmitri said has he got up from his desk and closed the door behind Gory. It took him all of his strength to close the door because he thought he might pass out at any moment. Dmitri plopped back down in his desk chair and stared out of his window and mumbled out loud "What have we done".

It took two days for Dmitri to reach Boris Panov even though Boris had finished working in Siberia and had taken his old job back at the Science Academy here in Moscow. Dmitri had asked Boris to meet him at the new Border Café, a new American style bar near the Moscow University and Red Square. The café was quiet and had the best vodka in town, featuring both Russian and Finnish varieties. He needed a couple of drinks today, actually he has been having to many drinks since speaking with his student Gory the other day and having spoken to other colleagues about the crop losses near Kotovsk. Boris arrived just as Dmitri had finished his second shot.

"Boris, how good it is to see you again" Dmitri said sincerely as he hugged Boris.

"And you too, Comrade Dmitri"

"Please have a seat and a drink before I explain my reason for needing to meet with you, because you are going to need it" Dmitri exclaimed as they raised their glasses and toasted to their health in the traditional Russian way. Dmitri quickly told Boris of his student Gory's account of the massive crop failures around the farm town of Kotovsk and that it could be only a very strong plant type virus or that somehow the "Orange Agent" has been released accidentally or intentionally.

"I do not know if we should offer our assistance, Say nothing or just let our superiors know what we know" Dmitri announced to Boris.

"We should tell your old boss at the Science Academy and let them handle it"

"God help us all if you are right about the 'Orange Agent' stuff Dmitri". They each had a few more shots of vodka, paid the bartender and they quickly walked towards the Science Academy under the shadow of the Kremlin. They walked in silence, but at a very determined pace.

Boris and Dmitri had told Dmitri's old boss at the Science Academy about his suspicions of the crops losses in the south. His old boss then told his boss, who had suggested a meeting with the Federation Science Minister with a scientific panel made up of top Russian experts and of course Dmitri and Boris Panov. By the time the meeting date was arranged a week later, the area of plant loss in the south now stretched approximately twenty miles both west and south of Kotovsk and over thirty miles eastward. The plant loss was averaging over 750 acres a day and getting worse.

At the meeting Dmitri quickly explained the reason for the meeting and stressed the possible devastation of this substance and the possible worldwide catastrophe it would cause if the "Orange Agent" had actually been released. The scientists starting murmuring amongst themselves and the conference room became a noisy debate about Dmitri's experiment or just a terrible plant virus. After a few minutes of this debate the Science Minister cleared his throat and asked if anyone had any direct questions for Dmitri.

"Would you be able to identify this so-called "Orange Agent" if you saw it again" asked one of the scientists.

"I have all the notes and the experimental log books, but no actual living specimen to compare it to" replied Dmitri. Then the Science Minister spoke up "You did not answer the question, Dmitri".

"I could not be positive if it was the 'Orange Agent' unless I had a living culture to check it against" Dmitri replied feeling some frustration and anger about the questioning.

"If only we still had a specimen left so we could reproduce the experiment using the old notes and log books" Dmitri told the group of scientists.

"If only we had a similar pre-historic insect larvae within a piece of 'amber' we could quickly re-start the experiment process and possible make a viable specimen to compare to the crop loss area and to study". Dmitri added.

"Well, according to your own notes Pochinkov, I do not remember seeing any dinosaur poop just lying around Moscow" quipped a scientist who previously argued with Dmitri and did not like him very much. Just then Boris announced to the group of scientists that he had been the Paleontologist who had originally dug up and conserved the amber filled coprolite and that this was the fossilized material that Dmitri had used for his research at Unit 57. Boris then told the group he originally had two very similar specimens, but one had turned up missing either before shipping from Siberia near the Mirny Mine site or from the University at Yakutsk.

"This does not help us, Dr. Panov" the Science Minister chimed in

"No Minister, this does not, but I recently returned from a trip back to my original dig site in Siberia and I found this" Boris exclaimed as he dug into his briefcase and brought out a sample of rock the size of a goose egg with what appeared to be a amber colored glass substance inside. Inside the "amber" was what appeared to be small insect larvae or cocoon.

"Do you think this will work, Dmitri?" asked Boris to a stunned audience of scientists and politicians.

As the group of scientists was leaving the Science Ministry conference room, the Science Minister asked Dmitri and Boris to wait.

"Dmitri I want you to put together a team of the best scientists we have and start making cultures from this 'amber' specimen as quickly as possible and I want both of you along with some Federal Police to go to the Lipetsk region and help investigate this rumor of super weed killer and obtain the specimens you may need"

"And Dmitri – and you too Boris, this matter is top secret – we do not need any interference now from the Americans or Europeans at this time" the Science Minister added as he quickly left the room.

"I hope your 'amber' is like the other specimens" Dmitri whispered to Boris.

"And I hope we are not too late to stop the 'Orange Agent'" Dmitri added.

"See you tomorrow for the trip to Lipetsk" Boris told Dmitri as he departed the Science Ministry conference room for his office with the Science Academy. Boris was not looking forward to this trip, especially with any Federal Police, since he know that most of them were either ex-KGB or ex-Politburo Guards. Boris had suspected that his other original specimen in Yakutsk had been taken by his KGB Science Advisor but had not reported this due to reprisals from fellow KGB agents. As Boris returned to his office he pondered whether or not he should mention the theft of his specimen to the Science Minister and then he started to think that maybe he should ask his friend Max Hamilton in America for his help. Boris decided he would wait to say anything until he got back from Lipetsk just in case the crop loss was just a severe case of a virulent strain of plant virus. Boris thought that disobeying a direct order from the Science Minister could land him in prison for a simple plant virus, but if it was the "Orange Agent" then prison would look good compared to witnessing the possible end of the world.

Eleven

Wolf Creek Ranch, Denton, Montana – July 2004

After spending the fourth of July with his parents along with his wife Monica and his two children, Max Jr. now thirteen years old and his younger sister Stephanie who just turned five years old, Max began packing for their return trip from Montana to New York City.

Monica thought that Max was not happy with his job at the New York Museum of Natural History and that he did not really like the Northeast, but would not say anything as long as her and the kids were happy. "Max, why don't you stay a few more days at the ranch?" Monica asked as Max was slowly packing the suitcase.

"I must get back to the museum and catch up on some paperwork" Max replied without looking at Monica.

"I'm sure the paperwork can wait and the curator can manage a few days more without you, especially since you have not missed a day since Christmas" Monica interjected and before Max could respond Monica continued "You could help your father and brother with the horses or you could go up to the museums fossil site up in Canada".

"I guess I could help supervise the fossil classifications on the site, but I'm a paper jockey now, not a field scientist" Max said as he finished packing and closed the suitcase.

"It's not like you haven't been in the field the last ten years Max, what about the fossil find in Mexico two years ago, and besides even if you shuffle more paper now, you are still the museum's top field Paleontologist" Monica offered as they heard a low hum of a helicopter in the distance.

"Let's go and see who dad has invited for dinner" Max stated.

"Or maybe this is our ride to the airport" Monica added as she and Max walked down to the family room of the house.

As Max, Monica, his mom and the grandkids were enjoying a light snack before leaving to go back to New York City, Max's dad Edward came into the house followed by a couple of military looking men dressed in what Max later described as standard blue government suits.

"These men flew all the way from Washington, D.C. to see you Max" Edward Hamilton said.

"My name is Daniel McLean from the Department of Agriculture and this is Charles Sheets from the Army's Biological Research laboratory in Reston, Virginia" as Max shook his hand. Daniel McLean is a muscular but not large man in his mid-forties with salt and pepper hair and what appears to be a couple of scars on his neck and lower jaw.

"What can I do for you" offered Max.

"Could we have a few minutes alone to speak to you" asked Daniel McLean.

"Sure, but I only have a few minutes before we have to leave to go back to New York" Max stated as they walked to his dad's den for privacy.

"Mr. Hamilton I will get right to the point, there have been some massive crop and plant losses in the interior of Russia that the US government feels needs our attention" Daniel said.

"Please call me Max, Daniel I am a Paleobotanist not a Botanist – What help could I be, since I study fossilized plants, not living ones" Max answered.'

"Max, please call me Danny. Our sources tell us that the Russian's may have developed some secret defoliant and have been testing it and now it has gotten out of control"

"But what does this have to with Paleobotany or Paleontology" Max replied.

"Mr. Hamilton, some rumors have surfaced that the defoliate was developed from a piece of fossilized material" announced the younger man Charles Sheets.

"Please tell me more" answered Max.

After a couple of more minutes of explanation by the government personnel Danny McLean and Charles Sheets, Max stated "You guys are not from the Department of Agriculture"

"No Max, I'm actually with the CIA" answered Danny.

"But, Charles is actually from the Army's Biological Research laboratory" Danny continued.

"So what does the army and the CIA want a Paleontologist and in particular this Paleontologist for" asked Max.

"We may be in a position to help the Russian's if asked or maybe even if not asked and we will need to mobilize a quick group of experts if the need arises" answered Danny.

"I would love some field work, but my job at the museum plus my family…" Max was saying as Danny cut him off "We will take care of your position at the museum and have asked your father to help us in the family matters department". And before Max could say anything else Danny stated "Max this conversation is highly classified and if anyone asks just tell them we are planning a joint fossil dig with the Russians and may have you join us in the research"

"How do I contact you for any further news" asked Max.

"Just continue working in New York and I will contact you – but you could place a call to your Russian friend Boris Panov and see if he knows anything, since he is in the fossil bone business like you" Danny requested as he and the Army scientist were leaving.

"How did a veteran CIA agent like you land such an assignment" asked Max.

"I have a degree in Biology and I speak fluent Russian" answered Danny as they took off in their helicopter.

Twelve

Kotovsk, Russian Federation – Late Summer 2004

Dmitri and Boris had arrived in Kotovsk with a Federal Police

team. They were able to find a hotel to stay at in Lepetsk, about a forty-five

minute drive from Kotovsk from which they had to travel each day from

Lepetsk to Kotovsk in a unmarked Federal Police car. Once they traveled

for the first time to within twenty miles of Kotovsk they could see the start

of the devastation to both crop and native plant life. Due to recent rains in

the area, the landscape looked as if a flood had cascaded through the dead

vegetation and had caused areas of severe erosion, especially along the river

and stream banks.

Dmitri collected samples of both dead and dying corn plants along

with a sample of healthy plant tissue that they had collected along the way.

As Dmitri was in the field collecting and examining plant material, Boris

along with two Federal Policemen were at the local co-op building in town

interviewing farmers and town residents about the plant loss and to try and

locate any evidence of an accidental or intentional spill of a super

experimental weed killer, known only to Boris and Dmitri as "Orange

Agent". The Federal Police and Boris were referred to a farmer named

Vladimir Voronov who lived on the outskirts of Kotovsk. The farmer at the co-op told them that the plant loss had started at Vladimir's farm and that he had once bragged of having obtained a super weed killer in a trade for bread or potatoes.

When Boris and the Federal Police arrived at Vladimir Voronov's once prosperous farm all they could see was dead vegetation along with a barren and eroded landscape as far as the eye could see. Boris said to one of the policemen "The house appears to be vacant and abandoned"

"This is the Federal Police, please let us in" he demanded as he knocked on the door. Just then an old truck was driving up the Vladimir's old driveway. The truck stopped in back of the unmarked police car and the old farmer who was driving asked "What do want – Why are you here?"

"We are Federal Policemen looking for Vladimir Voronov" one of the policemen stated as they showed their badges and identification.

"Vladimir and his wife are gone. I'm looking after their house in case they return" the farmer said.

"Do you know where they went?" requested Boris Panov.

"I'm not sure, but I think they traveled south to Stalingrad – Vladimir's wife has a sister living there" the farmer replied.

"We will be looking around for a little while" the policemen stated as he kicked in the door to house. The farmer started to laugh as he climbed back into his truck

"What is so funny?" demanded the other policeman.

"The door was unlocked" the farmer quipped. As he started up his truck and was starting to back up, Boris yelled out to him "Do you know if Vladimir Voronov had used any powerful weed killer on this farm?" The farmer stopped his truck and replied "He used something right along this fence line and next to his house"

"Do you know where he may have stored the weed killer?" Boris asked.

"Look in the barn, that is where Vladimir kept his tools, fertilizer and hid his vodka" the farmer replied.

"You are not looking after Vladimir's house are you?" one of the policemen questioned the farmer.

"No, the rest of us still here plan on using the wood from the house to keep warm this winter, since that son of a jackal, Vladimir killed off everything and took away our livelihood" the farmer said as he got back in his truck and sped away.

Boris Panov and the police quickly searched Vladimir's house looking for anything that might confirm the use of the "Orange Agent" or an address to where Vladimir may be living now. They found nothing in the house and they now searched the barn and outbuildings on the rest of the farm. When Boris went in the barn it appeared as if someone had ransacked it. There were containers of chemicals thrown around, bags of fertilizer ripped open and what appeared to look like a partially burned up plant sprayer. Boris and the police started their examination of the barn near the burned sprayer.

"Why would someone try to burn a simple farm sprayer?" Boris asked.

"If this was a theft or a killing, a criminal may have tried to destroy any evidence – maybe this is the sprayer that he used to start the whole problem" stated one of the policemen just as the other policeman shouted "Look at all the broken glass over here near the workbench – it looks like broken scientific containers"

"Some of the glass fragments have writing on them and one piece has gradations like 60ml and 70ml" he added. Boris ant the other policeman hurried over and began looking at additional pieces of broken glass. They had collected a handful of broken glass fragments when Boris gasped and said out loud "Oh no – Oh no".

"What is it Dr. Panov?" asked one of the police. Boris held up a glass fragment to show them the marking "Unit 57". Boris quickly contacted Dmitri using the police phone and they both agreed that the "Orange

Agent" was accidentally released and is spreading at an alarming rate. They alerted the Science Minister in Moscow, who immediately informed the Russian President. Boris and Dmitri were told to collect some additional specimens and to get back to the Science Academy in Moscow as soon as possible.

By the time Boris and Dmitri had arrived back in Moscow the "Orange Agent" had wiped out almost five percent of the summer crops within the Black-earth belt region of Russia. This Black-earth area is equal in size to the country of Switzerland. The devastation to both plant and business was too enormous to hide and before long both the European and United States governments were quick to offer any help if needed. The Russian President was not a scientist or well versed in the sciences, so he agreed to let a contingent of foreign scientist's access to help and try and stop the plant loss. When hearing this news, Boris told Dmitri "This is the smartest thing the President has done for Russia"

"Do you think we can ask Dr. Maxwell Hamilton to be part of the foreign scientific team" added Boris. Dmitri who looked as if he had aged ten years in the last two days, just murmured "I hope there is a Russia here when they arrive".

Thirteen

Dmitri waited patiently as the British Air flight arrived one hour late

to Moscow International airport. As the airplane taxied towards the arrival

gate, Dmitri retrieved his sign which read "Dr. Maxx Hamilton". He could

not remember if Dr. Hamilton's first name was spelled with one or two X's,

but was pronounced the same anyway. Dmitri was posted to greet the

American scientific team headed by Max Hamilton, the Chief Paleontologist

at the American Museum of Natural History in New York City. Dmitri

hoped Max would recognize him even though he had only met him one

time awhile ago. Boris Panov was originally going to greet the Americans,

but he had obtained a lead as to the location of his missing "amber"

dinosaur specimen. Boris needed to find the missing specimen since his

latest find from Siberia had indicated no evidence of any fungus or other

prehistoric plant life. He had flown down to the Russian village of

Orenburg, not far from the Kazakhstan border accompanied by a Federal

Police escort. Boris and the Federal Police were looking for an ex-KGB

Science named Vasily Chekhov who had worked with Boris in Siberia

during his dinosaur explorations. Boris was going to meet Dmitri and the

American scientists in Kurst, located in southern Russia, not far from the restricted zone. This area was set-up and quarantined to prevent any entry to the affected area primarily thought to be affected by the "Orange Agent" substance.

Several passengers had already disembarked from the aircraft when Dmitri recognized the tall blond haired, blue-eyed man in old faded blue jeans as Dr. Max Hamilton. Dmitri shouted "Dr. Hamilton, welcome to Russia" as he held up his sign for Max to see.

"Nice to see you again Dr. Pochenkov" Max announced as he walked over to Dmitri and vigorously shook his hand. By this time the rest of the American scientific team had been swiftly escorted though customs and were gathered near the taxi entrance to the airport with Max and Dmitri.

"Let me introduce you to the rest of our team" Max stated.

"I would like you to meet Bob Fisher, Danny McLean and Barbara Steele" Max added. Dmitri shook everyone's hand before they were escorted to a waiting van to be taken to the Science Academy near Red Square in the center of Moscow. On the way to the Science Academy, Max went into more detail about his scientific team. He explained that Bob Fisher is the leading American expert in Botany from Columbia University and who specializes in plant disease. Danny McLean is a expert Biologist and Barbara Steele was on loan from the U.S. Army. Max told Dmitri she is a Major in the Army in charge of the Army Biological Research laboratory and is an expert in biological containment. Unknown to the Russians, Dmitri and the rest of the scientific team was that Danny McLean was actually a seasoned CIA agent who had previously served in the Army's Delta Force commando unit and who just happens to have a degree in Biology and speaks fluent Russian.

Once at the Science Ministry in the Science Academy, the Americans were ushered into a large conference room and were introduced to the Russian Science Minister, then to a group of Russian scientists and a group of European scientists who had arrived earlier. The Russian Science Minister quickly outlined the extent of the crop and plant loss and then turned the meeting over to Dmitri. Dmitri introduced himself and then explained to everyone how a Russian agriculture laboratory had accidentally created living cultures of a fungus like substance they had called "Orange Agent". The American Danny McLean had to fight to control his laughter at the twist of words used by the Russians to name what his sources had confirmed to be a secret experiment aimed at US farmland. Dmitri continued to explain that the "Orange Agent" was created when his scientists were attempting to obtain a strand of dinosaur DNA. Dmitri further explained how the culture would take over and kill any plant cells that they introduced and that they still were not able to extract any DNA. Because of the lack of DNA results the experiment was ultimately cancelled and the notes and cultures were placed in storage. Max then asked Dmitri "

How did this experimental culture wind up killing thousands of acres of crops and vegetation?"

"Unfortunately during the change over from the old Soviet Union to the new Russian Federation, many scientists and engineers were either not paid for weeks or were just simply fired. These lend to some thefts of scientific equipment and also lend to some scientists offering their services to highest bidder. Some even went to work for the Arabs" Dmitri replied.

"So this experiment was stolen and may have been released by terrorist elements" asked Danny McLean of the American scientific team.

"No, the experiment was stolen by one of the scientists and traded to farmer as weed killer for a bag of potatoes, we think" replied Dmitri.

"And I guess the farmer finally decided to use the weed killer and this is why we are here now" Dmitri summarized.

Dmitri showed the group of scientist's photographs and specimens of both affected and healthy plant tissue material. He had also prepared microscopic slides and other data for the group to view. Dmitri told everyone to please take a moment to analyze the material and data that he had explained from the origin to the process of the experiments. Dmitri then told the group of scientists how his colleague Boris Panov had obtained the original "amber" sample and then Dmitri proceeded to outline the original experiment note by note. After a couple of hours of examination, the group of scientists was given coffee, sweet breads and some pastries. Dmitri asked them to take a small break and meet him back in the conference room in a half hour.

Once everyone was gathered again, Max told Dmitri that the American Botanist Bob Fisher thought he had an idea about what may be causing the devastating plant loss. Dmitri introduced the American Botanist Bob Fisher to the group and said "Mr. Fisher, please let us know what you think about this substance". Bob Fisher explained to the group that the Fungi family includes Bacteria, Yeasts, Molds, Mildews, Rusts, Smuts and Mushrooms and that since fungus lacks any chlorophyll it must obtain its food from some other living organism or from the dead remains of organisms. He further explained that fungi are heterophytic or commonly known as parasite plants. One of the other scientists form the European group asked "Do you think this devastation is caused by a fungus?"

"Yes, As a Botanist and Plant Pathologist I am primarily concerned with parasitic fungus, for they are the organisms that attack many healthy and useful plants thus using the host plant to survive and prosper" Bob Fisher answered.

"Is this a form of Bacteria or a mold type organism?" asked Dmitri.

"I believe this is a fungus that belongs to the group known as Phycomycetes which is a water type mold. This is the common mold which causes bread to become moldy" Bob Fisher replied.

"The structure of this organism is very similar to some common types of algae, hence the group name of Phycomycete which literally means alga-like fungi" Bob Fisher added. Then the Russian Science Minister asked "How can you be so sure this is the organism responsible for killing the plant life?"

"This fungus seems to be attacking the plant and then occupying the intercellular space within the tissue of the host plant, therefore robbing the plant of both water and any nutrients, causing both the way in which the vegetation is dying and the quickness in which it dies" Bob Fisher explained.

"Have you ever seen anything similar to this before, Mr. Fisher" asked one of the Russian scientists.

"I have seen something similar on a much smaller scale and have been told that the potato famine in Ireland back in the 1800's may have been caused by this type of fungus, and to be honest, I have never seen a fungus like this or of the veracity in which it attacks and spreads form host plant to host plant" replied Bob Fisher.

"If this fungus is anything like the one that devastated Ireland so long ago, we have a problem with this fungus. It may be carried by wind, insects, birds, animals, not to mention carrying the fungus spores on our clothes and shoes" Bob Fisher added.

"I believe that this organism was caused by some sort of mutation caused by radiation or some other means. How else do you explain witnessing this fungus for the first time" the Russian Science Minister stated. This caused some murmuring within the group of scientists, then Max Hamilton cleared his throat and announced "This fungus did not mutate, nor is it a new variety of fungus"

"Then how to account for the fact that this fungus has never been witnessed or written about in any known scientific forum" one of the Europeans interjected.

"I believe this fungus was seen before – around 65 million years ago" Max added as the group of scientists started talking amongst themselves causing some to get into a short heated argument and caused Dmitri to feel sick to his stomach. Max asked everyone quiet down and told the room "This fungus was not witnessed by human eyes, but by prehistoric creatures – I think this is what caused the mass extinction of the dinosaurs!"

Fourteen

Orenburg, Russian Federation (near the border with Kazakhstan) – Late Fall 2004

Boris Panov had flown down to Orenburg with a Federal Police escort in a small government airplane that was normally used by members of Russia's Federal Parliament. The urgency and importance of this trip weighed heavily on Boris during the flight from Moscow. Just a week ago a team of top Russian scientists had failed to process a living culture from his recent piece of "amber" filled coprolite. The team of scientists had worked with his colleague Dmitri Pochenkov and they had worked around the clock to try and replicate the previous "Orange Agent" experiments from Unit 57, but no living cultures were produced. Both Boris and Dmitri had been devastated by the lack of results and were in the process of preparing a presentation to a group of incoming European and American scientists headed up by Boris's friend Max Hamilton. Also during this time the Russian Army had deployed restricted zones in the plant loss areas around Kotovsk. They set up a perimeter "restricted zone" boundary and were ordered to burn unaffected crops and forest areas around the "Orange Agent" zone to try and stop the loss of vegetation, like a fire break used to contain large forest fires.

It was just a couple of days ago that Boris received word that a undercover Federal Police detective was investigation a Russian mafia smuggling operation and had questioned a Kazakhstani truck driver about his role in shipping black market products along with weapons and drugs across the Kazakhstan/Russian border. During the interrogation of the truck driver they had learned that the local mafia group in Orenburg was headed by an ex-KGB man named Yanov Khudenko who had worked for the KGB at the Mirny mine area in Siberia. His name was entered into the newly acquired Federal Police computer system and that is when they found out that not only was Yanov Khudenko the local mafia kingpin, but was one of Russia's most wanted men.

Upon news of Yanov Khudenko's whereabouts, a large contingent of Federal Police descended upon and surrounded the local hangout of the Russian mafia in Orenburg and a deadly shootout took place. Two Federal Policemen were killed and another six were wounded with over a dozen mafia men killed and another six wounded. Among the wounded mafia men was Yanov Khudenko. He had received one gunshot wound in his arm and another had grazed his head. The other five mafia men were taken to the local hospital clinic in Orenburg for treatment, but Yanov was taken to an old secret and run-down building located in an old military base outside of Orenburg. Yanov's wounds were treated by an ex-Army doctor and he was sedated while they waited for the arrival of additional government officials and Senior Federal Police from Moscow. They had left word not to touch or talk to Yanov Khudenko until they had arrived.

Once Boris and the Federal Police had landed, they were quickly driven to the old military base outside Orensburg to meet with Yanov Khudenko. Once Boris and the other policemen were situated in the make-shift interrogation room, Yanov was brought into the room in a wheelchair with his hands cuffed behind him. The ex-Army doctor proceeded to administer a shot into Yanov's arm and he quickly perked up and became wide-awake.

"I am Boris Panov of the Science Academy in Moscow and these are my colleagues from the Federal Police Special Section along with the Organized Crime unit"

"Yea and I'm Yanov 'fucking' Khudenko and do you know who you are fucking with, comrade" Yanov spat.

"You may remember me from 1982 when you worked as the KGB Science Advisor for my dinosaur excavations in Siberia" Boris resumed.

"I remember you now. You were the dinosaur doctor who dug up all the dino poop" Yanov replied.

"What the fuck does a dinosaur poop doctor want with me" Yanov added. This response had earned Yanov both a slap in the face and a punch in the stomach by a Federal Policeman. Boris was a little shocked by the amount of force displayed by the Federal Police, but he needed some answers and he needed them quickly. He had no time to play games with Yanov Khudenko.

"Yanov, I do not condone such violence, but we have very little time and we need some information from you very quickly" Boris resumed his questioning.

"Again, Dr. Dino, What the fuck would you want with me" Yanov hissed.

"Yanov, back in 1982 I had discovered a couple of coprolite specimens which contained a substance called 'amber'" Boris stated.

"What the fuck is coprolite?" Yanov asked.

"Coprolite is what you referred to as dinosaur poop and back in 1982 I had excavated two specimens, but one was missing from the shipment to Moscow" Boris explained.

"And I believe you may have taken this specimen because of your lack of any promotion or credit that you did not receive from this discovery" Boris added.

"I took nothing from you or the fucking KGB pigs or from that hell-hole place in Siberia that they had sent me to" Yanov yelled as he was punched in the back of the head this time.

"Yanov, I do not care about the theft long ago, but I need to have that specimen back, it is a matter of national importance to all of Russia" Boris continued unfazed.

"Fuck you doctor and your KGB pig friends and fuck Russia" Yanov hissed again. Just as the Federal Policeman was about to slam his fist into Yanov's face, Boris shouted "Wait a minute, let me have a word with him alone. I used to work with him years ago". All of the Federal Police left the interrogation room except for Yanov, Boris and a very large Federal policeman nick-named "Banyh" which means "Rock" in English.

"I am starting to lose my temper Yanov. I do not care if you live or die Yanov, but I care about the millions of people who may die if I do not get the answer I need from you" Boris told Yanov in a calm, but serious tone.

"Fuck you and your million people doctor" Yanov yelled. Just then the large Federal Policeman called the "Rock" picked up Yanov from his chair and threw him over the table and into the wall nearly five feet away.

"Yanov, what did you do with the dinosaur specimen you stole twenty years ago?" Boris shouted. As Yanov was starting to reply the "Rock" quickly whispered something into Yanov's ear and Boris noticed that Yanov's whole demeanor changed from pure hatred to a more resigned composure.

"Doctor I gave the dino poop to a business associate from down south as a gift for his many and frequent purchases" Yanov stated.

"You gave it to a Kazakhstan smuggler" Boris asked.

"No, further south doctor" Yanov replied.

"No more games Yanov, where is the fucking dinosaur poop" Boris shouted at Yanov as he was getting very angry. Yanov looked up at an angry sneer on the policeman's face and then told them "I gave it to an Arab named 'Tarik'. His is a middleman that I use to smuggle arms through Afghanistan"

"Where in Afghanistan is 'Tarik' located. We can have the Americans look for him" asked the Rock.

"He is not from Afghanistan, he is Iranian and he operated from a fake shipping company located in Tehran" answered Yanov. Boris then had the policeman take off Yanov's cuffs and handed him a notepad and pencil.

"Yanov please write down everything you know about this Arab named 'Tarik' and I need it in fifteen minutes". As the Federal policeman escorted Boris out of the interrogation room, Boris asked him "What did you say to Yanov to make him cooperate?"

"We know from your sources that he thinks of himself as some sort of ladies man, especially with the whores he hires, so I told him that if he did not tell us what we wanted I would first rape him then cut off his dick and shove it up his own ass" the policeman told him. Boris was very thankful that these particular Federal Policemen were on his side.

Boris left the village of Orenburg with no "amber" filled coprolite specimen, but they were now a little closer to finding it as long as Russia still had "people" located in Iran. Boris started to think during his flight from Orenburg to Kursk about what would happen if the Iranian government knew what this "amber" could really be used for. He hoped that this Iranian named "Tarik" just kept the specimen on a shelf as just a Russian souvenir and nothing more.

Fifteen

Restricted Zone near Lipetsk, Russian Federation – Late 2004

Dmitri Pochenkov lend the group of European, Russian and American scientists to the affected area of devastation caused by the "Orange Agent". The restricted area was now the size of Pennsylvania and was still spreading at a rate of over one hundred acres a day.

Once Max Hamilton and the other scientists arrived at the once prosperous city of Lipetsk they noticed that the city was deserted. The Russian army had evacuated everyone from Lipetsk to nearby towns fifty miles east of Kotovsk. The city of Lipetsk just two months ago was a vibrant small industrial city within the farm belt and now was a virtual ghost town that lies nearly ten miles inside the restricted zone. As the scientists entered the restricted zone outside of Lipetsk they noticed the area was completely burned for approximately a mile. This area was followed by the area where the fungus had spread which was the start of the dead and dying plant life.

As the scientists left the suburban area of the deserted city of Lipetsk, they entered an area that resembled nothing they had ever witnessed. The massive erosion that was created by heavy rains had caused all the streams and rivers to turn muddy brown and what trees and vegetation that was unaffected by the fungus were either washed away or would ultimately die from the massive amount of chemical defoliate that the Russian Army was using to try and eradicate the spread of the fungus.

About twenty miles east of Lipetsk the Russian army had set-up a large military camp that had once housed a very large co-op farm complex just a few months earlier. The scientists would stay at the army camp for a few days and set up a temporary laboratory where they were to analyze samples and be able to confer with each other each day about any break troughs they may have to be able to stop the fungus. They now know that the fungus did not affect animal or human life other than to deprive them of their food sources. The scientists knew a little bit about how the fungus attacked and ultimately killed their host plants, but they have not found a way to eradicate the "Orange Agent" fungus or slow it down.

At this time the Russian army had burned an area around the affected area, like a fire-break for a forest fire and this has so far temporarily slowed down the spread of the fungus. Also the spread of the fungus may be slowing down due to the natural dying and dormancy of many plants in late fall and early winter, especially this time of year in Russia. The Russian army had also tried to isolate an area that had just started to be affected by the fungus and sprayed massive amounts of chemical defoliant on the plants to try and kill both the host plant and the fungus, but they only managed to kill off additional vegetation that was not affected by the fungus. The fungus had continued to maintain its spread but at a slower pace from host plant to host plant.

The scientists along with Dmitri's help were getting set-up in the make-shift laboratories that had been placed earlier by the army when Boris Panov arrived to meet everyone and to see his friend Max Hamilton again. Boris hugged Max and said in less than perfect English "It is good to see you again my friend, I just wish it had been better pleasant circumstances".

"It is good to see you again Boris" Max responded.

"Did you have any success in locating your other 'amber' specimen" Max added.

"Unfortunately no, but we have an idea where it may be" Boris answered Max and then elaborated in Russian to Dmitri "The specimen has been given as a souvenir from the Russian gangster Yanov Khudenko to a smuggler from Iran". The group of European and American scientists did not know what Boris had told Dmitri except for the Biologist Danny McLean who spoke fluent Russian. Danny had noted on his laboratory report form "amber in hostile hands, must make contact with friendly in Tehran".

At the end of a long day the scientists got together to discuss their laboratory work and analysis. Dmitri stated "I hope everyone is happy with their laboratory space and their sleeping accommodations".

"Dinner will be served in about an hour at the army mess area in the center of the camp and then I will make a satellite phone hook-up available for about five minutes for each person to phone home or work if needed" Dmitri added. Boris then asked if anyone had any questions or made any break troughs today.

"So far with my team we know that not all vegetation is affected by the fungus. The woody plants and trees seem to be immune from the fungus plus some flowering plants have not been affected" Max stood up and told the group.

"What impact does this have?" asked Boris.

"This pattern of plant eradication by the fungus is very similar to the type of plant loss that occurred during the time of the dinosaurs" Max answered.

"I noticed such an occurrence during my excavations at the Mirny Mine site. The fossils of dinosaurs were with many plants and trees and then there was a layer wit just dinosaur bones with a few plants and trees, then there was a upper layer in the excavation that had no more dinosaur bones" Boris added.

"If we could determine exactly how the fungus attacked the host plants and why some flowering plants and trees were unaffected, maybe we could find a way of stopping the fungus" Max summarized.

"Or we could obtain another specimen of 'amber' and try to recreate the experiments of Dr. Pochenkov again" Max closed.

"I hope we can get the specimen back, Max" Boris offered as the group of scientists headed for dinner.

Meanwhile in a seedy and not so religious warehouse area of Tehran, Iran, sometime after twelve midnight a lone figure was counting money on a desk in a small office within a warehouse building known locally as Warehouse 5. The man was counting and sorting piles of money by country of origin such as US dollars, British ponds and European Euros, making notes in a folder for each pile he counted. The man known as Tarek was a middle aged slightly bald and short man known within the criminal world of Tehran as "Tarek the shoemaker" for his collection of fancy foot ware from all over the world. Tarik was sweating profusely since it was still over ninety degrees in Tehran even past midnight and there was no air conditioning. This did not faze Tarik since when he finished he was going to the local café and buy a cold beer, a drink he had started to enjoy when in Russia. Religious law in Iran forbids the consumption of alcohol, but either hard currency such as dollars or pounds could buy most anything and anyone in Tehran, Iran.

Tarik was satisfied with his count and carefully put each stack of money into a small safe behind his desk as he sighed with anticipation of have some beer and maybe the not so shy or not so religious daughter of the café owner. Just as Tarik was leaving his office outside of Warehouse 5, a small group of Russian commandos were waiting for him. As Tarik walked outside of the warehouse he was quickly tackled, gagged, handcuffed and blindfolded by three commandos as a small Tehran taxi cab arrived driven by another commando dressed in Arab headgear and clothing. As the commandos were loading Tarik into the trunk of the taxi a small Chinese made police car approached them from behind the warehouse driven by a Tehran policeman. The Tehran police man jumped out of his car and shouted in Arabic "What is going on here. Do not move or I will shoot you!" as the policeman quickly pulled out his small 9mm pistol. Just as quickly another Russian commando located near the warehouse door saw the confrontation and fired a short burst silenced rounds that quickly and permanently ended the patrol of the Tehran policeman. The commandos then split up with one group remaining at the warehouse to hide the dead policeman's car and body, then to search the warehouse, while the other commandos went in the taxi with Tarik in the trunk. Both groups of commandos proceeded to search for any artifact called coprolite, which contained a "amber" substance. Their commander had given them a photo of the specimen and told his commando unit that they needed to find this substance as quickly as possible and at any means necessary, since Russia's very existence may depend on it. One group of Russian commandos searched within Warehouse 5 and another group had searched Tariks house, but found nothing. The commander told the commandos to change into Iranian clothing and bring Tarik and meet him at the Russian Embassy. The commander told them that someone in the embassy staff was an expert at interrogation techniques and they needed to talk to Tarik as soon as possible. Earlier in the evening Tarik was counting both his money and his possible pleasures and now he was counting how long he would live.

Back at the make-shift Russian army camp outside Lipetsk, Russia, Boris and Dmitri were told by the camp commander that the Russian army had raided the business and house of Tarik the smuggler in Iran and did not find the missing "amber" specimen, but added "We have him prisoner at our embassy in Tehran and he will talk or he will die"

"This is not good news comrade" Boris stated to Dmitri.

"I feel this is just the beginning of more bad news Boris" Dmitri said as they walked towards the scientist housing building in the camp. Just as Dmitri and Boris were about to enter the scientist's building a young Russian army soldier ran up to them and handed them a note from the Science Minister in Moscow. Dmitri read the note and passed it to Boris and stated "Boris I told you more bad news was coming, but I did not think it was this bad"

"We need to pass this on" Boris whispered as they entered the building. Boris and Dmitri had all the scientists gather and began to tell them that several other areas of severe and concentrated plant loss has been observed in both Russian and now in parts of the Ukraine.

"It appears that insects, birds, animals and even humans have been transporting the fungus all over by way of pollination, food or simply allowing the fungus spores to cling to shoes or clothing" Boris added. Max Hamilton stood up and asked everyone in his team along with both the European and Russian scientists to work as long and hard as they have to in order to eradicate the fungus.

As the scientists were headed back to the laboratory, the American CIA/Biologist Danny McLean overheard Dmitri tell Boris in Russian "If the army does not find the location of the 'amber' from Tarik, the Asian continent could become a wasteland void of plant and animal life in just a few months". Danny McLean stopped on the way to the laboratory to use the bathroom and to send a secure coded message from his mobile satellite phone to his superiors at CIA headquarters in Langley, Virginia. The message when un-coded at CIA headquarters read "Situation in Russia grave. Request immediate closure of borders from the Russian Federation. Request restricted air travel from Eastern European countries and from the Asian sub-continent. Spread of fungus substance not stopped or contained.

Possible use of force against Iran could be forthcoming from Russian forces. Further information soon. End"

Sixteen

Moscow, Russian Federation – January 2005

It had been three months since Max Hamilton and the rest of the

American and European scientific teams had arrived in Moscow to work

with the Russians to help in finding a way to eradicate the deadly plant

fungus. Max and members of his team had traveled back to the United

States several times except for Danny McLean, even though Max and his

team along with the Europeans with the Russian scientists were no closer to

finding a solution and were still working hard on the problem. The scientists

had figured out how the fungus developed within the affected plant life, but

still had not found any substance capable of destroying the fungus. The only

good news that Max was able to sent to the US Presidents Chief Science

Advisor in Washington was that the spread of the fungus had slowed down

dramatically in the last month, mainly due to the harsh Russian winter and

normal dormancy of many plant species. Max was directed by the United

States authorities to leave Russia for a few weeks with his team and to

report to Washington, D.C. to discuss the Russian situation with the

President, his cabinet and selected advisors and then Max and his team

would have a chance to visit family, take care of personal issues and grab

some much needed rest and relaxation before returning to Russia if needed.

Both Dmitri and Boris escorted Max and the American scientific team to Moscow International Airport for their flight to Washington. Again, the only scientist not to go to the airport was the American Biologist Danny McLean. He told Max that he would try to develop additional intelligence, besides he had no family in the states and had taken care of any personal business before arriving in Russia. He would stay in Moscow to work with the Russian scientists and government while they were gone. Once at the Moscow airport the Americans were escorted to a private area in the airport where they would board a United States government jet. This was the quickest and easiest way to travel from Russia via a airplane since most flights from Russia have had several restrictions in place for boarding and even tighter restrictions when arriving into the United States including possible quarantine areas. These restrictions were downplayed by both the Russian and US governments as only a precaution to avoid mass panic and total disruption of air travel throughout the world.

Even with flying on a private jet instead of a commercial airliner the scientists' bags and clothing were thoroughly checked for any signs of plant life and they were told to leave their shoes behind once they entered the boarding area. Max's team would go through the same screening once they arrived in Washington, D.C.

As the scientists entered the boarding area Max told Dmitri and Boris "We should only be a few weeks and I hope to get some fresh ideas from my colleagues in the United States, especially since we have been sending them data each week"

"Let's continue to speak while you are away and I will send you any updated data once we receive it from the field" Boris added.

"Our biologist Danny McLean is staying in Moscow for a few days before returning to the restricted area and he plans on assisting you any way he can" Max offered. As they were heading for the boarding gate, Boris yelled "Please be safe and come back soon comrade" as he and Dmitri began walking back from the boarding area. Boris the asked Dmitri "What is wrong my friend, you have not spoken two words all day"

"It has been too many months and we are no closer to stopping this fungus that I am responsible for – and if we do not find a way of stopping it soon, our homeland is doomed because of me" Dmitri mumbled. Boris was genuinely worried about Dmitri since he noticed that Dmitri was drinking too much and had recently talked as if he would not be around much longer. Boris hoped he was wrong, but both alcohol related illness and suicide was at a record high in Russia and was increasing at an alarming rate since the start of the plant and farm loss. Boris and Dmitri had just been notified a couple of days ago that the farmer who had accidentally started the fungus devastation had shot his wife and then killed himself. A note was found stating that the farmer could not live with the guilt anymore and would not allow his wife to bear the embarrassment for him. This note sounded similar to the way Dmitri was talking.

During Boris's trip to the Moscow Science Academy he was told the area of devastation by the fungus was now the size of both Pennsylvania and New York combined and was still spreading at a rate of twenty acres per day even during the harsh winter and plant dormancy.

Seventeen

Tehran, Iran – January 2005

Sometime in late December of 2004 Tarik was finally persuaded to tell the Russian authorities located in the Russian embassy along Nezami Ave. what he had did with the "amber" specimen gift that he had received from the Russian gangster named Yanov Khudenko. Unfortunately Tarik did not survive further questioning from the Russians and was taken from the Russian embassy and dumped in the salt-encrusted wastelands surrounding Lake Urmia, the great salt lake that spreads over two thousand square miles. But, before Tarik died he had told his interrogators that he had given the "amber" gift as a bribe to a high level officer within the Iranian Presidential Guard. Tarik said the officials name was Abdullah M. Tarik said he did not know Abdullah's last name and explained that he did not need the man's last name to conduct his business. It was during an extended interrogation session where the Russians were trying to help Tarik remember Abdullah's last name that he must have had a massive heart attack.

After investigation the information obtained from Tarik, an internal informant within the Iranian government had told a Russian diplomat that

Tarik's acquaintance in the Presidential Guard was either Abdullah Mafid or Abdullah Mohammed. The latter senior guard just happens to be the Iranian Presidents youngest brother. Based upon this information, Russian diplomats then tried unsuccessfully to use their past friendships and alliances with Iranian officials along with their diplomatic status to try to arrange question the named guards and ultimately have them turn over the "amber" specimen. The Russian diplomats had told their Iranian government contacts that gangsters had stolen this "amber" specimen from a Russian laboratory and it was vitally important to the Russian government that it was returned to Russia as soon as possible.

After a few days of failed diplomacy, a team of Russian commandos were dispatched to Tehran. The commandos staged a daring daylight kidnapping of the Iranian Presidential Guard named Abdullah Mafid as he was leaving a Mosque within central Tehran after morning prayers. The commando mission did not go as smooth as hoped and one of the Russian commandos was killed in a gun battle with Abdullah Mafid. During the gun fight Abdullah was hit by gun-fire but his wound was not life threatening, but the Russian commandos' body could not be recovered and taken back to Russia. Fortunately no Russian was spoken during the raid and the dead commando had no identification and his clothing was civilian and made in Germany. Even with no identification Iranian officials believed that the Russians had kidnapped a member of the Presidential Guard and they were also tipped off that the Russians would probably try to kidnap and question the Iranian Presidents' youngest brother Abdulla Mohammed. There was some debate within high levels of the Iranian government and the Presidents staff whether to give the Russians what they wanted. Some Ministers of the Iranian Cabinet had expressed support for this, since the Russians have been a ally to Iran for a long time, not to mention a loyal oil customer. But the Iranian President informed them that the Ayatollah himself made it clear that no deals or talks with the Russians would be tolerated and that there must be more to this missing specimen then the Russians were telling them.

After several hours of questioning by the same Russian interrogators as Tarik had, they determined that Presidential Guard Abdullah Mafid was not the right Abdullah and was not the recipient of the "amber" gift. Tarik's business acquaintance must be Abdullah Mohammed, the Iranian Presidents brother.

The Russian commando unit was ordered back to Russia and the Russian diplomats were given orders to assist a contingent being sent that consisted of both Russian and American agents, once they had arrived in Tehran. The Americans would be arriving posing as Russian Federal Security Service agents along side real Federal Security Service agents along with ex-KGB agents. During the next two days while waiting for the incoming agents to arrive, the diplomats at the Russian embassy in Tehran were busy trying to persuade their Iranian contacts in the Iranian Ministry of Intelligence to help set-up a high level meeting between both the Russian and Iranian Presidents, but they did not have much luck in their request.

A group of Russian Federal Security Service agents, Russian ex-KGB and American CIA agents posing as Russians arrived in Tehran, Iran and debriefed the embassy diplomats and then they formulated a plan to try and recover the "amber" specimen. Leading the American agents was the Biologist/CIA agent named Danny McLean who had previously posed as a biologist with the scientific team helping the Russians try to eradicate or stop the "Orange Agent". Danny McLean was quietly transferred from the scientific team to field operations with the Russians to try and help find and bring back the much needed "amber" specimen. Danny McLean was one of just a few people who knew first hand the deadly consequences of not recovering the specimen.

After the agents and diplomats were gathered into a secure second floor conference room at the Russian embassy, the embassy chief explained to everyone the basic government and political system within the Iranian government to the Security Service agents. He told the group that Iran's political system is based on their 1979 constitution called "Qanun-e-Asasi" which is comprised of the Supreme Leader the Ayatollah who is the head of the Army, Military intelligence and all security within the Islamic Republic. Second to the Ayatollah is the President of Iran who is responsible for the

Iranian constitution, government polices and decisions. Under the Iranian President there are eight Vice-Presidents and a Cabinet of twenty-one Ministers. The Russian embassy chief told the agents "We have been speaking to the Minister of Intelligence to try and set-up a meeting between the two Presidents, but we have not received any answer". The agents were then briefed on the exploits of the Russian commando raid and the subsequent interrogation along with the detention of the Iranian smuggler Tarik. Danny McLean asked the embassy chief in perfect Russian "Do you know if the Presidents brother Abdullah Mohammed still has the 'amber' specimen?"

"As far as we know yes, but he may now be guarded within the tight security of the Presidential Palace located on Sepah Ave. in central Tehran" the embassy chief answered.

"Is there a military option available if you cannot locate this Abdullah Mohammed or do we wait until Russia and the rest of the world is as arid as Iran's northern desert" Danny asked. Before the embassy chief could respond with an answer the Captain of the Russian Federal Security Service interrupted him and told the group "I am authorized to offer to pay for the 'amber' specimen from the Iranian government anything they want for it and if they do not agree, I am authorized to come and take it from them"

Meanwhile at the Iranian Presidential Palace in central Tehran a group of Iranian scientists comprised of experts in Organic Chemistry and Biophysics were busy examining the "amber" specimen. They were working under orders that came directly from the Ayatollah himself. Their directive was to find out why the Russians wanted this specimen back so bad and if this had any connection with the massive plant loss occurring within Russia and the Ukraine. The Iranian Minister of Defense had also requested a report as to the possibility of a Russian biological weapon gone bad as to the cause of the Russian plant and crop loss and maybe this specimen was somehow connected to this problem as their Iranian spies had claimed. The Iranian scientists did not doubt the Defense Minister's claims, since it had been rumored that he had previously worked as a spy with the Russians in the development of other biological weapons when the Minister was a general posted in Afghanistan.

Eighteen

It had been two months since Max Hamilton and his American scientific team had traveled back to the United States to see family and friends and to work with other leading American scientists concerning the Russian plant loss. During their time back in the United States they had not been able to help in either stopping or slowing down the deadly fungus called "Orange Agent". Also during their time in the States, Max Hamilton had enlisted the help of an old college friend from Montana who specialized in chemical analysis of previously obtained "amber" specimens from Canada and the United States. He had informed Max that the data he was sent from the Russian fungus was different from any other type of fossilized organism ever seen in "amber" and that if the other missing sample was recovered he would be happy to help in the dissection and chemical analysis.

As Max Hamilton and the rest of the American scientific team arrived back at Moscow International Airport, both Dmitri Pochenkov and Boris Panov were waiting for them. Max and the group of scientists were quickly escorted through customs and were ushered outside to waiting cars. Max joined Dmitri and Boris in the first car where they were driven to the

Ministry of Science near Red Square in central Moscow. Once everyone was settled in, they were told that they would be going to another affected field location closer to Moscow that had been set up for scientific research while working on a solution to the problem. Moving the scientists from the old complex near Lipetsk was facilitated because of the distance traveling to and from Moscow and also because of some recent political and military unrest in the areas around Lipetsk. The scientific team of Russians, European, Americans and now joined by a group of Chinese scientists were informed that the area of plant loss caused by the fungus now stretched from parts of eastern Ukraine to east of the city of Ufa, south to the city of Sartov and to within one hundred and fifty miles south of Moscow. The area of devastation is approximately the size of North Carolina to New York combined.

With no immediate way to stop the fungus and resulting plant loss, the Russian Federation was in crisis mode. If the plant loss and fungus continued to spread at this alarming rate, any future Russian farm crops of grain, corn and wheat could be eliminated in just a couple of months. The Russian economy was already on the verge of collapse with record unemployment rates, overwhelming welfare expenses and a very large and increasing trade deficit with the west, largely due to the loss of farms and plant life. Russia during good growing seasons still imported almost fifty percent of its grain and wheat supplies and now this percentage has jumped to nearly seventy five percent since the fungus devastation started. For the first time, both American and European governments have not burdened the Russian Federation for full payments on food supplies. Also at this time the Russian government could barely afford to pay the interest on its imports if it wanted to. The financial experts within the Russian Federation figured that if the government had to import from between eighty five to ninety five percent of its farm products, the Russian government would be bankrupt in a few months and the government would surely topple shortly after that.

The group of American, Russian, European and now Chinese scientists saw the devastation caused by the fungus in both plant destruction and economic destruction, both taking place near and within the city of Moscow. Boris Panov and Dmitri Pochenkov explained to the group that the fragile democratic government of the Russian Federation was in serious jeopardy because of the fungus, not to mention the severe environmental catastrophe taking place south of Moscow. What the scientists including Boris and Dmitri did not know was that a group of old hard line communists from the former U.S.S.R. government had already started preparations for a potential coup and had started both secret diplomatic and social propaganda aimed at the farmers and the poorer people within Russia's rural areas. They also targeted government officials in the Ukraine and there was secret diplomatic talks with several former satellite states that once made up the former U.S.S.R. Also unknown to Boris, Dmitri and the rest of the world was the fact that this group of ex-communist hard liners had already aligned themselves with key generals within the Russian Army. The hard-liners had told their supporters that a possible coup was likely within a few weeks.

Also during this time, Boris had noticed and confided in his friend Max Hamilton that his colleague Dmitri Pochenkov had been drinking too much in the last few weeks and had been talking and expressing some crazy thoughts. Boris told Max "I think that Dmitri has slipped into a deep depression over what has happened and I hope he does not do anything crazy".

"Do you think Dmitri may be suicidal?" asked Max.

"I do not think so, but he is very capable of some terrible things, since I know he has been involved in some terrible top secret weapons research in the past" Boris answered.

"Just keep an eye on him, since he has been such a big help in this crisis, regardless of how many bad things he has done in his past" Max responded.

To add insult to injury to the current government of the Russian Federation, the Russian president had finally tired of the religious rhetoric and stall tactics coming from the President of Iran. Because of these problems, he sent a personal message directly to the Ayatollah of Iran. The message simply read "Give us the 'amber' specimen back now or we will come and get it". This message was hand delivered to the Ayatollah in Tehran, Iran and then after reading it, the Ayatollah quickly sent a message back to Moscow with an attached letter from the Iranian President in reference to the Russian threat. The Iranian message read "Russia should not infer any threats to the people of Iran, since you were defeated in Afghanistan and you will be slaughtered in the Islamic Republic of Iran". In conjunction with the Iranian message, the Iranian Minister of Oil and Energy was ordered to stop all shipments of oil to the Russian Federation including any shipments of tankers and trucks already en route to Russia.

Not only was the government of the Russian Federation slowly starving from the massive crop loss, but now Russia's leading exporter of oil has stopped all exports to Russia. The Russian government had imported nearly fifty-five percent of its oil from Iran and now Russia's industry was threatened besides its agriculture. The Russian President now faced a possible coup, a war with Iran, an environmental catastrophe and maybe the total devastation of his once proud and mighty Mother Russia.

Nineteen

Tehran, Iran – April 2005

While the Russians were busy trying to keep its government running and trying to stop the spread of the fungus, the Iranians had figured out through spying on Russian diplomats that the "amber" material was responsible for the devastating plant loss in Russia. The Iranian government had also been able to buy copies of some of the original experimental "Orange Agent" data from the original "amber" specimen from a Russian scientist working in Moscow. Even though Russian scientists working on fungus projects were sworn to secrecy and were threatened with prison if they spoke to anyone about their work with the fungus or associated projects, the money paid by the Iranians was just too much to resist even with the potential prison or other penalties. Even with the purchase of scientific research, the Iranians were still missing parts of the experimental data of "Orange Agent", but they have been able to purchase many key sections of information, not to mention the ability to buy information about the recent attempts to kill the fungus.

The Ayatollah himself had directed all scientists including any from their nuclear program to try and re-create the Russian experiments that had formed the deadly fungus and he also wanted the scientists to determine a way to kill the fungus. The Iranian government figured if they could produce the deadly fungus and also find a way to kill it, they could essentially hold the world hostage. The Ayatollah would then be able to

create a "World of Islam" with Iran being the central leader of this new world. If the Americans, Europeans and other non-believing Muslims around the world would not do as Iran requested or pay Iran large amounts of gold and property, then the world would become a wasteland like the Sahara desert and they would all die.

Twenty

Moscow, Russian Federation – May 2005

During the first week in May the American scientific team led by Max Hamilton informed the United States government that there were no major breakthroughs in stopping the fungus and without re-creating the original Russian experiments with the same type "amber" material they would not be able to help at this time. Max then told his US contact in Russia that the American scientific team would like to go home, especially with the latest political turmoil and military crisis within the Russian government. The Americans were told they would be leaving by a US government chartered plane within a week and to make arrangements with Boris Panov and Dmitri Pochenkov so they may be able to assist them once his scientific team was back in the United States. They were told by the US embassy staff that the American scientists would have to wait a few days to leave unless the situation in Russia became worst.

Boris Panov met with Max Hamilton and confided in him just how bad things had become in Russia, both economically and politically. Boris told him "A friend in Russia's Ministry of Banking and Finance told me that the Russian economy is totally bankrupt and that it had been this way even before Iran had stopped exporting oil to Russia"

"Boris, I hope we can help Russia through this mess so you may enjoy a good taste of freedom and democracy not to mention a decent paycheck with food on the dinner table" Max expressed.

"Max, we have not been paid for a month now and if it was not for the Army's free meals in the ministry dining hall we would not have eaten" Boris sighed. As Max was leaving Boris's office to make final travel arrangements to go home, Boris had received a fax giving him the latest estimated amount of plant and crop losses as of the end of April. Boris told Max as he was leaving "The estimated area of devastation has now reached an area approximately ten percent of the Russian Federation tillable cropland"

"We are all dead – it is just a matter of time" Boris added. Max then reassured Boris that they will find a way to stop the fungus, but as he was saying this to Boris, he was thinking of spending as much time at home and in Montana with his family just in case.

Just as Max Hamilton and the other American scientists were packing for a private flight from Moscow to New York later in the day, a US embassy staff member informed them that the Russian President had stepped down as the leader of the Russian Federation to avoid a possible bloody and violent coup attempt that was in the works. Despite the Russian

Presidents attempt to avoid any violence and bloodshed, Max could hear some scattered gun fire in the city and heard what sounded like a couple of explosions not too far away. Max was later reassured by the US embassy staff that the Russian government change had been executed without violence and that the ex-president of Russia had negotiated with the new military leadership for a peaceful and quick transition of power.

As Max was watching a group of Russian soldiers smoking outside the Science Ministry housing building the phone rang. The call was from Boris Panov and he was extremely distraught and had briefly forgotten to speak English to Max as he spoke very quickly for a couple of minutes in Russian. As Boris calmed down a minute later he told Max "Dmitri is dead. He was shot dead a couple of hours ago".

"What happened, was he robbed or was he in fight" Max asked.

"No, Dmitri was drinking very heavily after hearing the news of the new government and decided to go out, but he went out with a AK-47 rifle".

"He got shot for walking around with a rifle or did he shoot someone else first" Max asked with sincere regret.

"apparently he was very upset about another communist government – he blamed himself for this and decided he would end the coup and end the new government by himself" Boris explained.

"So, Demitri tried to enter the main entrance of the Kremlin and demanded to speak with the President. The guards told him to go home and sleep it off, but Dmitri pointed his gun at one of the guards and again demanded entry into the Kremlin. In the confusion around Moscow a gun shot rang out nearby and that is when another guard shot Dmitri" Boris added. Max Hamilton was crushed, especially since he had gotten to know both Boris and Dmitri very well in the last couple of months.

"I will make other arrangements to go home, so I can stay for Dmitri's funeral, and by the way – how is Dmitri's family handling the situation" Max asked Boris.

"Dmitri has no known family and he will be given a basic Russian state funeral and will be buried in a military cemetery somewhere outside Moscow"

"Please let me know if there is anything I can do" Max asked as he hung up the phone. Max then called the US Embassy and told them he would like to stay in Russia for a few more days, but the rest of the scientific team would be going home as scheduled. The embassy staff member told Max that this should not be a problem, especially since the new Russian government has not only talked with the US President since the transition of power, but has requested both scientific and even military assistance if needed. Max thanked him and then asked the phone operator to connect him to the United States, so he could tell his wife Monica the bad news and that we would not be coming home for another couple of days.

The Russian Federation was now in complete turmoil. The government had just changed from a fledging democracy type government to a military type government led by a group of ex-hard line communist officials and Army generals. The Russian economy was bankrupt and their countryside was dying acre by acre. Both the United States and Europe have pledged both financial aid and loans. They have also pledged deliveries of both food and oil. The United States had arranged to have oil shipped from Iraq to Russia and has pledged several thousand additional tons of wheat and corn. Even with the added help from the United States and Europe, Russia's needs for food and oil are still more than can be currently supplied. In addition, the United States and Europe have agreed to delay any request for payments for food and oil, especially since the new Russian military government has again threatened to invade Iran for the "amber" and the oil that Russia needs to survive. The claim they would be able to sell the remaining Iranian oil to pay for its food imports.

The new Russian leadership must find a way to stop the fungus and a way to replenish its food and oil supplies before the harsh Russian winter in a few short months. Some officials within the United States government would not mind if the Russians went into Iran and kicked the Ayatollah into the Persian Gulf, but this problem could potentially trigger a World War, especially since Iran's largest importers of oil consist of China and North Korea. With the transition of power in Moscow, any new attempt to covertly steal back the "amber" material has been delayed. A team of Russian Federal agents along with United States CIA agents who were led by the American agent Danny McLean were told to stand down for a few days at the Russian embassy in Tehran until things settled down in Moscow.

Because the fact that the fungus may spread further, but in some cases not kill certain crops has created a surplus of some Russian crops, namely Cotton and timber. The surplus has created because of a worldwide ban on any Russian crop exports or plant products that went into effect a couple of months ago. This meant that Russian farmers could still plant to help eliminate erosion problems, but could not sell their products outside of the Russian borders. This has caused the Russian economy to fail even more quickly and had caused many farmers to just give up and to try and collect money and food from the government. Most of the devastated areas caused by the fungus in both the Ukraine and Russia looked like untouched forests to barren eroded landscapes closely resembled moonscapes.

During this time in Russia, because of both the fungus and the Russian government change, most travel including planes, trains and by car have been restricted from both the Ukraine and most of Russia. When travel is allowed, severe measures are implemented such as disinfection of shoes, clothing and automobiles and at some border crossings like the one into Lithuania for example the trains are stopped at the border, the passengers are checked and disinfected, then they are allowed to board a new train located on the Lithuanian side of the border. If traveling by car, you would need to have someone pick you up at the border crossing after disinfection, but you must leave your car on the Russian side of the border. When traveling by air with the limited number of flights still traveling from the Ukraine and Russia, the plane will be immediately disinfected upon landing, especially the landing gear while still on the taxiway. The plane will then be diverted to a isolated area of the airport where the passengers will be allowed to depart the plane and would then be taken to a disinfection area by a airport bus.

In addition to the extreme travel restrictions imposed by the United States and other countries, the lengthy border between Russia and China has been completely closed. This is the first time the Russian and Chinese border crossings have been closed since the fall of communism within the old U.S.S.R. To make it known that the Chinese border is closed, several thousand additional Chinese troops have been sent to the Russian/Chinese border area to discourage any travel between the two neighboring countries.

Twenty-One

Moscow, Russian Federation – June 2005

The Russian Federation is a very dangerous place in June 2005. With the Russian government virtually bankrupt, democracy replaced by a group of ex-communist officials and generals and now a staggering fifteen percent of all Russian tillable crop land essentially devoid of any crops and other food bearing plants. This has created chaos and turmoil. There are still forests and trees, but large areas have been so decimated that they resemble a moon surface or a volcanic eruption area more than a farm area.

Most American and European scientists, engineers and other non-embassy staff have left Russian, mainly due to the rising crime rate, lack of food and goods, daily demonstrations that have resulted in military action and mainly just the overall dread and mass panic that is starting to grip the Russian people in both cities and rural areas. The new military leaders have placed a night-time curfew in effect and have again like the former U.S.S.R. have taken over all television, radio and other news media outlets and have also taken control of several key manufacturing sites just like it was during the cold war with the former U.S.S.R.

Like the other American and European scientists, Max Hamilton made it back to the United States after attending a small and quick burial service for his Russian colleague Dmitri Pochenkov. He would miss his friends in Russia, especially his friend Boris Panov along with many other Russian scientists he had recently worked with, but Max missed his family more. Once back in New York City, Max was asked if he wanted his old position back at the Museum, but Max and his wife decided it was time for them and the children to move to Montana with Max's mom, dad and brothers. Max's wife Monica felt that with the current state of affairs in Russia and along with the fungus and the chance it could spread worldwide creating a global catastrophe or even another World War could be a definite possibility. She felt that Max and her family would be safer in rural Montana than in New York City or its suburbs.

While at the Academy of Natural Sciences, Max had arranged a position for Boris Panov and had asked him to come to the United States to escape the ever changing and dangerous conditions there. Boris called him back and stated "Max, you are a great man and your offer is probably the best thing that I could ask for, but Mother Russia needs me here"

"Boris you could work here for six months and work in Russia for the other six months each year" Max countered.

"That would be great, but I need to be available at a moments notice to offer my assistance with the 'amber' specimen if located" Boris answered. Still not taking no for a answer, Max continued "You are a Paleontologist not a Microbiologist, you can let the other scientists fix the 'amber' experiment, plus it is much safer here in the United States at this time"

"Your offer is very generous Max, but I am the only person still alive who could both identify and authenticate the 'amber' material if and when we get it back from the Iranians" Boris exhaled loudly on the phone.

"OK, I won't ask again right now. You take care of yourself and stay safe my friend and do not forget that you are welcome at our ranch in Montana whenever you want" Max expressed to Boris as he hung up the phone.

The new hard line military government of Russia wasted no time in their threats to invade Iran. Two Russian Federation Army divisions were sent from the southern Russian border area of Orenburg along the Ural River south into the sparsely populated area of Kazakhstan known as the Ust Urt Plateau. This semi-desert like land in Kazakhstan covers an area between one hundred and two hundred miles wide for most of the length of the Caspian Sea. Because of a lack of moisture and high temperatures in summer, much of this area of Kazakhstan is barren with plants that are mostly desert tolerant and were widely spaced. The Russian Federation Army chose this harsh route through Kazakhstan to avoid disturbing too many villages plus lessen the chance of accidentally spreading the fungus from Russia. Once through the Ust Urt Plateau the Russian Federation Army entered the country of Turkmenistan through the region known as the Kara-kum sand desert. Again this area has very few villages, plant life and also very few roads. The Russian Federation Army was planning on staging troops along the Kopet Dag Mountains along the Turkmenistan and Iranian border.

This is the first time Russian troops have been on foreign soil since the fall of the previous U.S.S.R. In addition to Federation Army troops traveling through the countries of Kazakhstan and Turkmenistan, the Russian military had ordered all Naval units and vessels to proceed to an area within the Caspian Sea just east of the Azerbaijan port city of Baku. The Naval fleet was ordered to set anchor in this area and wait for further orders.

Both Kazakhstan and Turkmenistan officials immediately demanded a withdrawal of all Russian troops and they called upon the United Nations along with the leadership of the European Union for help in turning back the Russian Federation troop movement. The Russian military leadership relayed a message to officials in both Kazakhstan and Turkmenistan that they will not harm any of their military forces or civilian population unless they try to stop the movements and advancement of the Russian Federation Army. All Russia wanted was to move troops safety to the Iranian border and to bring support and supplies from Russia to these

146

forward positions of the Russian Army units. Both the United Nations Security Council along with the chairman of the European Union voiced their opposition to the Russian's advance within Kazakhstan and Turkmenistan, but they offered no diplomatic or military assistance to these countries.

A few days into the Russian invasion, a United States backed diplomatic team had successfully negotiated a peaceful deal which included additional aid and also debt forgiveness to both Kazakhstan and Turkmenistan in exchange for a safe military corridor for the Russian Federation Army and a safe flight path for the Russian Air Force if needed to use during this current crisis. At first, officials of Turkmenistan thought that they would be targets from Iran if they helped the Russians, but with this deal they could say they had no choice, but secretly hoped the Russians would invade Iran and would eventually claim the area of the Kopet Dag Mountains as their own. The Russian military leadership also agreed to be very respectful of local villages and local people and would be especially careful to avoid spreading any fungus into any other farmland or anywhere else. To accomplice this, the Russian Army had implemented a state of the art decontamination facility designed and constructed by the United States military. This decontamination unit was originally designed for use in preventing both airborne and static microbes from being transmitted outside a human body.

Twenty-Two

Tehran, Iran – late June 2005

Meanwhile during the mini crisis in Kazakhstan and Turkmenistan involving the Russian incursion, the United Nations Security Council had sent a delegation to Iran to try and negotiate a peaceful return of the "amber" material to the Russian government. The United Nations delegation expressed the worldwide concern about the spread of the fungus throughout the world. The United Nations delegation also asked for the resumption of oil exports to resume from Iran to Russia. The Iranian President and his Cabinet of Ministers told the United Nations delegation that they did not have this so-called "amber" material and they have never had it in their procession. They also expressed to the United Nations that Russia had created a biological weapons substance that had gone wrong and that the Russians were looking to put the blame on another nation. During the meetings with the Iranians one of the United Nations delegates asked the Iranian Minister of Energy "Will you consider resumption of oil exports to Russia in exchange for other United Nations and worldwide payments?" This request was relayed by phone to the Iranian President and his replay was simply "Only if the Russian's formally apologize to the Islamic Republic of Iran at a special worldwide televised meeting at the United Nations headquarters and then they would have to remove all their troops along our borders and any advancing army or naval units headed towards Iran". The United Nations delegate said they would speak to the new leadership in Russia about Iran's demands.

Unknown to the United Nations delegation meeting at the Iranian Ministry building was the fact that three levels below them was a secret laboratory where Iranian scientists may have successfully replicated the "amber" experiments that had created the deadly fungus that has devastated such a large portion of Russia and the Ukraine. In fact the Iranian scientists had been able to make several specimens that appear to kill off some forms of plant cells when they first come in contact with them. Once the fungus specimens have reached full maturity, according to the purchased Russian scientific notes, the Iranian scientists would be able to conduct full scale testing of plant cell material from both European and American crops. This testing may be ready within a few weeks and they could have enough fungus material that could be prepared for shipping within a couple of months. Both the President of Iran and the Ayatollah had visited the secret laboratory and were very pleased with the scientists' progress. The President told his family and some key staff members about the successful experiments that had happed so far and that before long Iran would rule the world, a Muslim world.

Meanwhile a group of Russian Federal Agents with the help of the United States CIA and the help of a undercover source within the Iranian Ministry building were finalizing plans for a covert mission to retrieve the "amber" material from the Iranian Presidents youngest brother. Unknown to the group of Russian and American agents was that the Iranians have moved the "amber" material and have successfully recreated some of the experiments and have for the most part had to destroy most of the original specimen in the process of creating the fungus.

Later that week, immediately after morning prayer a small group of foreign agents consisting of Russian Federal agents, CIA Operative Danny McLean, a couple of ex-KGB operatives and an Iranian/Russian double agent drove out of the Russian embassy towards central Tehran. The agents were dressed like Muslim women, covering their faces and not speaking. They entered the Ministry of Energy through a side door that lead from the Mosque. So far the plan had been successful, but would be very tricky from here. Through their spying and informant network, the Russians had determined that the Iranian Presidents brother Abdullah Mohammed was staying on the fourth floor of the Ministry of Energy building within the guard quarters through an unmarked side door that led into the Ministry building. Once they entered the Ministry of Energy building they quickly removed their burkas and other women's clothing which they proceeded to hide in a nearby broom closet. The agents then went to a back stairwell now dressed in olive drab Iranian Army uniforms. The small group of agents quickly ran up the stairs to the fourth floor and they quietly opened the stairwell door that placed them in a wide hallway area that led to a small window at the end of the hall. The lead Russian Federal agent quietly asked CIA agent Danny McLean in Russian "We have arrived at the right place on schedule and without any alarms. I hope our informants have given us the right information so we can get this 'amber' stuff and get out of here"

"So far so good, we now have to go down the hall and find Abdullah Mohammed's room. It should be the last door on the left" Danny McLean responded. Just as the team of agents approached Abdullah's door a stray and unexpected Iranian Army guard had just finished his duty early and had come up the same stairs as the agents approached them. The Iranian guard saw them in their Army uniforms down the hall and asked in Arabic "What are you doing up here?"

"Shut Up" the lead Russian Federal agent shouted back in Arabic as a silenced 9mm round punched through the guard's heart. He mumbled a prayer in Arabic as he fell through the open stairwell door and fell loudly down the flight of stairs. Knowing that the dead guard could soon be found, the agents quickly slammed open Abdullah Mohammed's door to find him watching the American cartoon Tom & Jerry with Arabic sub-titles. Abdullah seeing the Iranian army uniforms had not yet registered who the agents were and shouted at them "Who are you and what do you want?"

"Shut-up, do as you are told and we will not kill you" shouted in Arabic from the lead Russian Federal agent.

"Do you know who I am and who my brother is?" shouted Abdullah.

"He is the President of Iran and I will kill him if you do not cooperate with us" the Russian agent shouted back. The Presidents brother Abdullah was quickly handcuffed and tied to a chair while a couple of other Russian agents checked the hallway and stairwell to make sure that they were still not yet compromised. The lead Russian agent then asked Abdullah "Where is the 'amber' material?"

"I do not know what you are talking about" shouted Abdullah.

"We do not have time to play games with you Abdullah. Now where did you put the 'amber' material?" the Russian agent said as he grabbed Abdullah by his hair. Abdullah started to answer again that he did not know what they were speaking of when another agent grabbed Abdullah's right hand and broke his pinky finger. Abdullah screamed out in pain and shouted in broken English "Fuck you American pigs". The lead Russian agent heard this and grabbed Abdullah's head, punched him in the nose and shouted in Arabic "I am Russian and if you do not tell me what I want to know you will pray to Allah to let me kill you quickly after we finish with you". Abdullah settled down and quietly told the agents that he did not have the "amber" material and that the Iranian government scientists have

153

already created a weapon form it that would wipe out Russia and its new friends the United States. After hearing this news from Abdullah, the agents tried unsuccessfully to get the location of where the Iranian scientists that were working on the "amber" were located. After a couple more failed attempts to gather more information from Abdullah, he was shot in the head from a silenced 9mm round from CIA operative Danny McLean's H&K submachine gun. He was shot after he passed out for the third time. Just as the agents were preparing to exit Abdullah's room the dead guard's body was found on the stairs by his roommate who had radioed to his supervising officer about his dead roommate. As the agents approached the stairwell, they were met by a small group of Iranian Army Police who thought they would be going to investigate a murder between a couple of guards fighting over a whore, but were met with a volley of silenced machine gun fire. A intense but short gun fight erupted between the agents and the Iranian Army Police which resulted in all of the Iranian Army Police killed along with two dead Russian agents and another one wounded. The rest of the agents ran down the stairs, retrieved their hidden women's clothing and somehow the remaining agents including the wounded Russian Federal agent managed to blend in with other women leaving the Mosque. The Russian and American agents were then able to return to the Russian embassy for a debriefing and reporting of the mission along with the unexpected incidents. They spend the next two hours telling the Russian embassy chief what they had learned from the now deceased Abdullah Mohammed.

Twenty-Three

Washington, D.C. – Late June 2005

Based on the news about the Iranian's "amber" claims, United States President Warren Baker had received from his intelligence briefing from Joe Stapleton, the director of the CIA, the President sent a message to the new Russian leadership requesting an urgent phone and video conference as soon as possible. The US President Warren Baker is a tall and slender man of fifty three with a full head of graying hair and a quiet demeanor. The President has now been in office since January 2004 and has had no major domestic or international crisis events until now. The President asked his CIA director Joe Stapleton, a third generation Washington government employee who's father was once an ambassador to China and a Congressman from Ohio, "Are you sure your agent Danny McLean is accurate as to his account of the 'amber' material in Iran"

"Danny McLean is one of our most dedicated and highly trained operative. He would not send this information to us unless he was one hundred percent sure it was correct and also extremely urgent" CIA director Stapleton answered. President Baker then asked his CIA director "Do you think the Iranian Presidents brother Abdullah could have been lying or maybe boasting to avoid punishment from the agents?"

"Based on McLean's account and the methods used by the Russians on Abdullah unfortunately I believe this problem to be totally accurate, Mr. President" as the Presidents intercom beeped and his aide announced that General Vitus Baranov the acting President of the Russian Federation is waiting to speak to him.

"General Baranov, I wish we could be speaking under different circumstances but I just received a briefing about the 'amber' situation in Iran". After the translator relayed the message in Russian to General Baranov he replied "I know in the past we were enemies, but now we have a common enemy that threatens the very existence of both Russia and the United States"

"You are right about the Iranians General. Their government cares nothing about killing Russians or Americans or even their own people for that matter" President Baker added as he was thinking how much to trust the Russians. The President was raised in a cold-war environment and spent time guarding a border between the communist East Germans and democratic West Germany, but the US President felt a connection and trust with General Baranov unlike the Russian government of a few months ago. General Baranov continued "We must help each other either get the 'amber' material and experiments back from Iran or we will surely face devastation never before witnessed by mankind". President Baker assured the Russian leadership that the United States would help in any way possible both financially and militarily if needed. Before both Presidents secure transmission was terminated between Moscow and Washington, D.C., General Baranov told President Baker that if Iran makes the Russian countryside resemble its own Iranian desert, he would turn Iran into a nuclear wasteland.

After the conversation with the new Russian leader, President Baker ordered an immediate and urgent meeting with the Joint Chiefs of Staff at the White House in thirty minutes. The President turned to CIA director Joe Stapleton and quietly told him "Joe, tell your man McLean to find a way no matter what he has to do to find the Iranian scientists and the missing 'amber' material and experiments before World War III erupts"

Once the Joint Chiefs were gathered at the White House's secure conference room also known as the War Room, the President gave them a quick rundown of the current events taking place in Russia and in Iran. The President then asked the Joint Chiefs what military options and assets they had near on in the area of Iran. The Army Chief stated that they still had one armored division and one infantry division located in Iraq and they also had approximately ten thousand troops located in both Saudi Arabia and Kuwait participating in joint maneuvers. The Navy Chief told everyone that they had a air-craft carrier group within a days sail from the Persian Gulf and that if would take another couple of weeks for another Carrier group to arrive. Then the President was told by the Air Force Chief that they had a couple of B-52's and Stealth Bombers available plus another fifty or so fighter jets operating from Iraq, Saudi Arabia and Turkey. After a few more minutes of discussion between the President and the Joint Chiefs, President Baker cleared his throat and announced "I want one hundred thousand troops deployed in Iraq and I want them heading towards the Iranian border, plus I want whatever number of aircraft carriers, bombers, fighters, whatever is needed to facilitate a full scale invasion of Iran from both Iraq and from the sea"

"This movement could provoke the Iranians into firing the first shot, Mr. President" the Secretary of State announced.

"Yes Secretary Lodge, but maybe this build-up of troops by both the United States and the Russian Federation may force the Iranian government to back down and release the 'amber' and any experiments associated with it" replied President Baker.

"But it could also look like the US and Russia picking on yet another Arab nation to other countries in the region" Secretary Lodge replied.

"That is a possibility we must account for, but I think if the situation if half as serious as our agents say it is, we do not have the time to wait for a political answer" the President said to a stunned group in the War

Room. The President then continued "If there is any kind of incursion into Iran this must be coordinated with any Russian invasion coming from Turkmenistan to the north. I also want any plans to be coordinated with Russian General Baranov – we do not need to be shooting at each other"

To some members of the Joint Chiefs and other high ranking members of the United States military, this latest Presidential decree was a extremely sensitive and scary scenario based on the unknown biological and nuclear capabilities of Iran's military, but to others this would be pay back time for the hostage situation years ago.

Twenty-Four

United Nations Headquarters, New York City – Late June 2005

The Plant Loss in Russia was becoming an economic disaster, but was also becoming a complete humanitarian catastrophe in the Ukraine. Because of migratory animals and insects that had traveled west from the affected fungus area in Russia, the Ukraine crop loss now was estimated at almost a fifty percent level. The President of the Ukraine ordered an emergency meeting at the United Nations and requested that all world leaders be present in the General Assembly. Two days later several world leaders including leaders from the European Union, United States, Russia and China were present for the request meeting by the Ukrainians.

The Ukrainian President Ivan Krymsky addressed the United Nations General Assembly and stated "Ukrainians are a proud and prosperous people We work hard and we work honestly. We had started to finally thrive after almost eighty years of Soviet rule, but now our very existence is being threatened. I will not allow my fellow Ukrainians to go hungry like their fathers and their grandfathers before them". As the Ukrainian President Krymsky paused and pondered his next part of his speech, there was a low murmur between several members of the United

Nations Security Council. Ukrainian President Krymsky then forcefully announced "The people of the Ukraine starved because of Hitler, then they starved because of the Soviet Union – we will not starve again!"

"Also we have had abundant forests and farmlands, once with one of the best wildlife areas in all of Eastern Europe, but the Soviets made most of the forested area a radioactive wasteland because of their nuclear accident at Chernobyl and now the rest of our great country may become a wasteland because of another Soviet accident" the President of the Ukraine roared as he slammed his fist against the podium. This caused a stir amongst the United Nations members, but was pale in comparison to what was coming next from the Ukrainian President.

Ukrainian President Krymsky continued "We demand help from the European Union and the United Nations. We demand an open border with our neighboring countries and we demand an end to the spread of this fungus coming from the Russian Federation. This is a Russian Fungus and should be a Russian problem, not the death of the Ukraine"

"You cannot demand the United Nations or other countries to help. We did not cause this fungus to spread to you. We are just as concerned as you are and would be willing to help as much as possible" shouted the Poland envoy to the United Nations before the Ukrainian President could continue.

"Without your help we will be forced to invade both Romania and Poland in order to feed our people and then we will march through Europe and discharge this devastation fungus on our feet and spread it to the rest of Eastern and Western Europe." The Ukrainian President quickly and calmly told the gathered General Assembly of the United Nations. The Polish envoy shouted out again "You could cause thousands of deaths to Ukrainians, Pol's and Romanians if you try to invade us. Why would you consider such a tragic measure?"

"What do we have to lose, either we starve to death by doing nothing or we die trying to feed our children" The Ukrainian President answered. This caused the entire General Assembly to become very quiet, but then a chorus of voices could be heard discussing how best to help the people of the Ukraine.

After the initial shock of the Ukrainian Presidents speech and threats the United Nations Security Council voted unanimously to offer an amount of five hundred million dollars worth of food and other humanitarian aid to southwest Russia and to the Ukraine immediately. In exchange for this aid Ukrainian President Krymsky agreed to accept the closed borders of the neighboring countries, but was secretly told by a European Union representative that any deliberate act of fungus release would be considered an act of war along with any invasion of Romania and Poland and would escalate into another war within the European continent.

Because of how rapidly the fungus had spread and how it had killed so many crops throughout southwest Russia and now over half of the Ukraine had some members of the European Union extremely worried about the possible spread of the fungus throughout Europe by this time next year. Also becoming very nervous was the Chinese government, especially since tests that had been conducted by both American and Chinese scientists concluded that not only was grain, corn, vegetables and some fruit crops killed by the fungus, but so was rice. With the largest population on earth, China could not afford to loose even one rice field or one acre of its farmlands.

Twenty-Five

By the end of June 2005 almost all travel has been banned from Russia and the Ukraine except for humanitarian and food shipments and some limited diplomatic and scientific travel. Most of the European countries that border both Russia and Ukraine have strengthened their border protection with additional border guards, police and some with full military units, especially Romania and Poland. Both these countries were directly threatened by the Ukrainian President and have stationed as many as twenty thousand troops along their borders with Ukraine.

But the most hostile and active military action has been along the lengthy border between the Russian Federation, China and along its Mongolia border. Within the last couple of weeks there have been some minor skirmishes between Russian civilians and the Chinese Army. Most of the Russia civilians along the Russia-Chinese border are of Chinese descent and have family on both sides of the border. The Russian army's main mission along the Russian-China border is to prevent any theft or black market food to cross the border into China, since all excess food not consumed locally has been ordered to be shipped to the affected areas in the southwest part of Russia.

By late June 2005, China has moved almost two hundred and fifty thousand military troops to its borders and had threatened to kill anyone trying to enter China from either Russia and Kazakhstan or from anywhere else illegally.

Twenty-Six

Washington, D.C. – end of June 2005

Along with the United States troop movement into Iraq and the Russian troop build-up within Kazakhstan and Turkmenistan, United States CIA operative Danny McLean was flown by a Russian MIG to Moscow from a make-shift airfield within Kazakhstan. He was then non-stop from Moscow to Andrews Air Force Base near Washington, D.C. in a US Air Force Cargo plane. Danny McLean was very tired and weary from the last few days and was told by the Air Force commander to get some sleep as best that he could on the plane since he had a special meeting to go to with the director of the CIA and with President Baker at the White House.

Once Danny McLean landed he was immediately ushered into a waiting Marine helicopter that is usually part of the Presidential Marine helicopter squadron. He was quickly seated and was flown directly to the White House landing on the famous lawn area near the rose garden. Upon landing he was greeted by CIA director Joe Stapleton. Danny McLean had only met the director one time in the past and that was during a training operation at Langley where he posted a score of ninety-nine out of a hundred on the training course. This high score was only obtained one other time and that was by a young and ambitious operative by the name of Joe Stapleton some twenty years earlier.

After a quick briefing with the CIA director who had told Danny McLean that the President, the Joint Chiefs of Staff and the Secretary of Defense would be joining them in the war room beneath the White House. Danny McLean was then ushered into the main White House elevator and was taken to the secret basement area of the White House.

Upon entering the war room, quick introductions were made and President Baker told Danny "Mr., Mrs. And Sir are not used in this room – formality and humility are checked at the door, so in here there is no Mr. President, Mr. Secretary, etc. We are usually in this room for very serious business, not politics". The CIA director Joe Stapleton asked Danny McLean to very briefly describe his recent trip and events that occurred in both Russia and in Iran to the President, Secretary of Defense and the Joint Chiefs of Staff.

Once Danny McLean finished his outline of his last few weeks and told them what he had found out, President Baker announced "Gentlemen we are here to find a way to get this 'amber' material and experiments out of Iran as quickly as possible"

"We should be prepared to spend any amount of money needed to either kill or capture anyone both foreign or domestic who stands in our way – and let me remind you that this is extremely top secret and stays in

170

this room, since the United States officially does not kill or capture foreign or domestic citizens. Any mission must not fail and we must find a very quick way to make it happen very soon or I'm afraid we will witness the start of World War III" The President added. As the magnitude of what the President of the United States was ordering and was sinking in to all in attendance in the war room, Danny McLean asked the President "May I put together my own team to make an attempt to extract the 'amber'"

"I think I have a plan that might just have a chance of working" Danny McLean added. President Baker looked at Danny McLean, smiled and stated "You can have whomever you want for your team and I do not care who it is. If they refuse to help you, then I will make them wish they did or they will disappear"

"Danny – get this plan of yours finalized with Joe and his experts at the agency and get it started at once. Get whatever help you need and let me know when you are ready. And to not forget to include the Russians" The President added. He then left the war room to phone General Baranov of the Russian Federation to let him know that the United States is planning another covert mission into Iran to try and recover the "amber" and any experiments and the United States would like the Russians help.

Twenty-Seven

Kopet Mountains, Turkmenistan/Iran Border – July 2005

As the summer temperatures rise along the Iranian and
Turkmenistan border so too do the tempers of the new Russian leadership
under General Baranov and the Iranian President. With Russia and the
Ukraine facing both a humanitarian and environmental disaster, many of the
old hard liners from the former Soviet Union have voiced their opinions
that if Iran does not return the "amber" material at once the Russian
Federation should immediately and without remorse invade Iran, retrieve
the "amber" and then take over their vast oil fields and oil wells. One older
ex-soviet hard liner was quoted in the Moscow newspaper as saying "We
will take their oil to heat our homes and then sell what we do not need to
buy food and clothing for our families". Another ex-soviet party official told
the press "We should take the Iranian oil and then march them right into
the Persian Gulf to drown like the dogs they are".

Despite the grueling one hundred plus degree daytime temperatures
and cold nights, the Russian Army continues to mass troops and set-up
camps within the Kopet Mountain range along the Iranian and
Turkmenistan border. In addition to the Russian troops already in place

along the border, the Ukrainian president has promised an many as twenty thousand infantry troops to help the Russian Army. The Ukrainian troops should arrive at the Kopet Mountain border area within a couple of days. During the Russian and Ukrainian troop build-up, several skirmishes have erupted along this hostile and mountainous border zone, especially within the valley area of the Kopet Mountain region called "The Pass" in the local dialect. Within this region there have been unofficial reports of as many as two hundred Russians and over one thousand Iranians already killed during these localized intrusions and fighting in both Turkmenistan and Iranian territory.

Twenty-Eight

United Nations Headquarters, New York City – July 2005

The United Nations Secretary General with officials from the European Union have once again tried to find a peaceful and diplomatic solution to the looming conflict between Russian and Iran and perhaps the rest of the western world. This latest diplomatic mission towards Iran ended with failure and with a loud and threatening argument between members of the United Nations Security Council and the Iranian Ambassador to the UN. The Iranian Ambassador ended up walking out of the UN Council chambers and walking out of the United Nations. The discussions had started out civilized with some Security Council members voicing their opinion that maybe the Russian, United States and Iranian conflict should be allowed to play out in the hopes of either the Russian Federation or the United States finding the "amber" material and thus ending the fungus devastation and maybe a new world war.

The most vocal United Nations delegates were the members from Romania and Hungary. They had expressed their concerns again over the massive refugee situation that is occurring within its borders from both Russia and the Ukraine because of the continued spread and devastation caused by the fungus. The Romanian delegate very forcefully expressed to the Security Council "Romania cannot continue to feed, cloth and house the ever growing refugee crisis emerging from the Ukraine"

"The Islamic Republic of Iran must return the missing 'amber' material at once and also assist the Russian and American scientists in developing a means to destroy this deadly fungus" The Romania delegate continued.

"We have stated in the past as we do so here today, state that Iran has not had or does not know the whereabouts of this 'amber' material" answered the Iranian Ambassador.

"But Sir, your government has already threatened to release a fungus derived from the missing 'amber' material" the US Ambassador to the UN interrupted.

"That statement was just a harsh reaction to the growing hostility and threats coming from the United States towards the peaceful people of Iran" the Iranian Ambassador stated.

At this point the UN Secretary General had lost almost all control of the Security Council members, especially when the Romania delegate started shouting "The Iranian government is lying and should be held accountable for its actions. We believe the Iranians have been lying to us all. Release the 'amber' material at once"

"Is that a threat from Romania, because the Iranian people have been threatened before and have been attacked before and we have always prevailed" The Iranian Ambassador replied. At this point within the Security Council, representatives of both Romania and Hungary told the UN Security Council that they now plan on sending as many troops and weapons as needed to assist the Russians and the Americans against the Iranians. This recent announcement had created a loud tirade in Arabic by a couple of the Middle Eastern members of the Security Council stating that even though they do not agree with the Iranian governments current decisions, they cannot witness this western assault on the land of Persia. Shortly after this, the Iranian Ambassador quickly left the United Nations building to report to the Iranian President in Tehran concerning the current events taking place within the United Nations Security Council meeting.

The UN Secretary General called on the members of the Security Council to act with restraint and moderation concerning the Iranian situation. He then adjourned the UN Security Council for the remainder of the day. As the ambassadors and delegates were filing out of the Security Council chambers, several ambassadors from Middle Eastern members registered their disgust about the current state of affairs within the United Nations and they then officially resigned their countries membership in both the Security Council and the United Nations.

Twenty-Nine

Tehran, Iran – July 2005

After receiving the news from the United Nations, the Iranian Ambassador was ordered home and before he left New York he told the UN Secretary General that the Iranian government would only deal with the UN Secretary General and not the entire Security Council. The UN Secretary General quickly arranged a meeting between the Iranian President, the Ayatollah and himself in Iran, not New York. When the UN Secretary General arrived in Tehran he was escorted to the Presidential Palace, which was now guarded and staffed with hundreds of troops, tanks and Presidential Guard. The UN Secretary General asked his Iranian translator "What are all the troops and tanks doing around the Presidential Palace?"

"The President has announced that war with the infidels may be upon us very soon" answered the Iranian translator.

Once the UN Secretary General was escorted into the Presidential Palace he was then seated at a very long table, where he was asked if he wanted to try some local Iranian coffee. He declined since he had heard that the coffee in Iran was extremely bitter compared to what he was used to drinking in New York City. A couple of minutes later a group of heavily armed Presidential Guard entered the room followed by the Iranian President and then by the Ayatollah dressed in his usual white robe and white turban. The UN Secretary General thanked everyone for their hospitality and for agreeing to this last minute meeting. He then very softly asked the ruling government of Iran to please for the sake of avoiding bloodshed to let him know the location of the "amber" experiments. He was hoping to make his request sound like they were no in procession of the "amber", but they may know where it has been taken. The Iranian President replied "As we have expressed through our UN Ambassador we do not have and do not know of any such "amber" experiments"

"Is there anything else we could help the United Nations with, since we have been sincere with our diplomacy" the Ayatollah expressed through his interpreter.

"Besides the 'amber' issue, the United Nations would also like to request that Iran resume oil shipments to Russia and Eastern Europe" requested the UN Secretary General.

"We would gladly resume oil shipments as long as the Russians and the Americans stop their hostile intentions along our borders and they go back home" The Iranian President replied.

The UN Secretary General mentioned to the Iranian President and the Ayatollah, that this crisis could escalate and become war and that millions of people would be affected by the war, plus the devastation caused by the fungus. The UN Secretary General also mentioned for the first time in a public forum, that the fungus would not stop at the Russian and Ukrainian borders, but could continue to spread devastation across the entire world. The Ayatollah told the UN Secretary General that their Muslim brothers have suffered devastation like that for hundreds of years living in the deserts of the world and that Europe and the rest of the world has done nothing to help these people, but the good and holy people of Iran will assist the United Nations in anyway that it can. At this moment the UN Secretary General had finally lost his composure for the second time in two days and shouted out "Please stop playing games with the world and give us the 'amber' material or I'm afraid Iran will be held accountable for its action and unfortunately its people will pay the highest price for its leader's mistakes". The Iranian President again denied any knowledge of any "amber" material or experimentation and then told the UN Secretary General that the United Nations has become just another pro-American and anti-Islam surrogate and that the UN Secretary General along with all UN employees, staff and delegates should leave the Islamic Republic of Iran at once.

As the UN Secretary General and his staff were preparing to leave Iranian soil they had been informed by a top secret coded message from the United States that read "CIA informant has told US sources that Iran has talked to several groups and may be planning on giving some of its alleged developed fungus to Al-Qaeda terror cells to use against western and American targets or to simply blackmail the United States and Europe. Please inform the Iranians that if this information is correct the United States would consider this action an act of war and would take appropriate action". The UN Secretary General asked his Iranian escort if he could speak to the Iranian President one more time.

Thirty

United Nations Headquarters, New York City – Late July 2005

Once the UN Secretary General arrived back in New York City he immediately convened an emergency meeting of the UN Security Council without Iran's Ambassador or the missing Middle Eastern members. Once most of the Security Council active membership or their delegates of the Security Council were present, the Secretary General announced "The Iranian government has again denied any knowledge of the 'amber' material or any experimentation associated with it". This caused a murmur amongst the gathered council members.

"They have also demanded in exchange for resumption of oil shipments to Russia and Eastern Europe, that the Russians and Americans pull their troops back from the Iranian borders and then vacate all Muslim land or they will not only continue with no oil shipments to Eastern Europe, but would also discontinue oil shipments through out the world". This caused the room to fill with loud shouts and frenzied calls on cell phones.

"The Iranian government has also denied any involvement with terror cells or Al-Qaeda and said how could they give a fungus to someone that they have never seen themselves" added the UN Secretary General. At this point within the Security Council meeting all diplomatic courtesy was abandoned and people were becoming angry and scared. One Security Council member could be overheard shouting on his cell phone "I say Nuke the bastards".

As the UN Secretary General called for calm and quiet it took another few minutes more for the Security Council to quiet down and the UN Secretary General announced that he was resigning as Secretary General, affective immediately and then he told the Security Council "I cannot continue as the United Nations Secretary General anymore because I have failed to find a solution to the current crisis and I feel this is probably the end of the United Nations Charter as we know it and this could possibly be the start of World War III.

A couple of hours later at the White House and after reading his report from the US Ambassador from the United Nations headquarters in New York City, President Warren Baker requested a another meeting with the Joint Chiefs of Staff and then sent a urgent message to CIA director Joe Stapleton and to the acting President of the Russian Federation General Vitus Baranov. The Presidents message to both stated "Please proceed with the Russian and United States joint military operation called "Operation Amber" and please proceed at once".

Thirty-One

Persian Gulf (near the coast of the Saudi Arabia) – late July 2005

As the United States, Great Britain and other western European troops continued to mass along the Iraqi/Iranian border in conjunction with Russian, Ukrainian and know troops from Romania and Poland that continue to build-up and continue to arrive along the Iranian/Turkmenistan border, a non-military outcome looks bleak.

In addition to a massive ground build-up of troops, the United States Navy had started a complete naval blockade within the Persian Gulf to cut-off all Iranian shipping both to and from Iran. The blockade orders were given as a direct response to the Iranians decision to halt all oil exports worldwide and the intelligence gathered about possible threats of the Iranian releasing the fungus worldwide.

The US Navy's 5th Fleet located out of Norfolk, Virginia has now essentially blocked off the mouth of the Persian Gulf in the narrow section where the Persian Gulf meets the Gulf of Oman called the Strait of Hormuz. What makes this area so dangerous is the narrow width of the waterway, the proximity to both Iran and the United Arab Emirates and the fact that Iran has claimed the International waters as belonging to Iran.

The US Navy's 5th Fleet's main objectives for this naval blockade are to stop and board any incoming or outgoing vessel to determine whether its origin or destination is Iran. The Navy was ordered to refuse passage of any ship with goods either coming from or going to Iran with the exception of humanitarian goods like food or medicine. The other mission for the Navy's 5th Fleet was to ensure a safe shipping route for Iraqi, Kuwaiti and Saudi Arabian oil shipments. This mission is absolutely essential now that Iran has discontinued oil exports worldwide and especially to China. Because of Iran's oil export decisions, any other Middle Eastern oil-producing countries have increased both their production and shipping amounts of oil to help make up the short fall created by the Iranian government. Both Saudi Arabia and the United Arab Emirates have pledged substantial oil exports to both Russia and China, but by pledging this oil, they may have cast their leadership as pro-Western and allies of Russia and the United States. Many radical Islamic fundamentalist leaders in anti-Western nations believe the policy of Saudi Arabia and the U.A.E. will hurt Iranians and will hurt Islam.

Just two days after setting up the naval blockade the US reported an incident between the Iranian Navy and the United States Navy. According to President Baker's daily security briefing, several small Iranian gunboats approached the US Destroyer "Sea Hunter" and ordered the US Naval ship out of Iranian waters. The US Navy transmitted a message back to the

Iranians to vacate the area, stop your hostile maneuvers and immediately return to your port at once since the US Navy was in what was known as International waters. At that time two of the four Iranian gunboats opened fire on the US Destroyer "Sea Hunter" with a barrage of heavy machine gun fire. The US Navy Destroyer "Sea Hunter" proceeded to fire back with surface to surface harpoon missiles and 40mm cannon fire and proceeded to sink three out of the four Iranian gunboats. The fourth Iranian gunboat was allowed to flee unharmed back to the Iranian port of Banar-e Abbis, but only after having waved a surrender flag. President Baker called his National Security advisor and asked "Were there any US casualties or any damage to the 'Sea Hunter' because of this Persian Gulf incident?"

"There were no US casualties or injuries and there was very little damage done to our Destroyer, but all four of the Iranian gunboats were blown up and sunk with no sign of any survivors, Sir" the National Security advisor answered.

"How many Iranians usually man a typical Iranian Navy gunboat? Basically how many Iranians were killed?" asked President Baker.

"The Navy estimated between one hundred and eighty to two hundred Iranian casualties, Sir" answered the National Security advisor.

"Let me know of any further developments, no matter what time or where I am" ordered the President as he hung up the phone.

Thirty-Two

Washington, D.C. – Late July 2005

Later early the next morning around four o'clock AM the President was awakened by the buzzer of the secure phone next to his bed. Still half asleep the President said "Hello, this better be an emergency, since you woke me from my favorite nightmare"

"Sorry to disturb you sir, but we were told to inform you of any issues relating to the current Iranian crisis," the White House Secret Service Agent said.

"OK, I'm awake now, what is the message" the President asked still sleepy.

"There has been a serious incident in the Persian Gulf earlier today, Sir" replied the Secret Service agent. The Secret Service agent then proceeded to tell the President that under the cover of darkness last evening three Iranian ships were sunk by the United States Navy. Two of the ships were Iranian gunboats, but one was a passenger ferry "Qashani" named after an original member of the Islamic Republican Party. It was carrying Muslim pilgrims en route to Mecca from the Iranian port city of Bushire. The Iranian ships were ordered to stop and return to their Iranian ports, but

189

they continued to travel towards the 5th Fleet's carrier group and that is when all hell broke loose and all three ships were destroyed. The President just gasped and said "Oh Shit, Oh Shit, Oh Shit".

"Are you alright, Sir" asked the Secret Service agent.

"Yes I'm fine. Do you know how many Iranian civilians were killed?" asked the President as he watched a video of floating boat wreckage in the Persian Gulf being broadcast by CNN.

"Well Sir There were two hundred and five people officially killed, but the Iranians are claiming over three hundred, but out of this total about one hundred and fifty-five people were Iranian civilians and the others were civilians from Saudi Arabia and other Arab nations" reported the Secret Service agent.

"And Sir, unfortunately twenty five of the people killed were children" added the Secret Service agent. The President could not speak for nearly two minutes before he asked the White House Secret Service agent to get the National Security advisor, the Secretary of State and the Navy's Joint Chief of Staff on the phone as soon as possible.

The next morning the United States and its allies had already expressed their remorse over the Iranian ferry incident. The United States had quickly labeled the tragedy an unintentional and regrettable accident that could have been preventable had they not been provoked by the Iranian government. Both President Baker of the United States and General Vitus Baranov of the Russian Federation held separate news conferences explaining to the world press how they believe that the government of Iran has continued to defy the world's leaders, sponsored terrorism and have continued to let both Russians and Ukrainians suffer because of the devastating fungus The US and Russian leadership has also claimed that the Iranian government had allowed and maybe even staged this horrible incident with the ferry in order to draw support from other Arab nations to support their aggressive actions and to make the Russians and the Americans out to be Imperial and Tsarist bad guys in the world.

Meanwhile the Ayatollah and the President of Iran had issued a earlier statement condemning the United States and its allies for its unprovoked and ruthless attack on an unarmed ferry heading to pray in Mecca, which resulted in hundreds of Arab lives lost. The Iranian President went on Al-Jezeera television to declare a holy war against both the United States and Russia. He called on all Muslims around the world to help Iran defeat the infidels in the United States, Russia and the rest of the unholy world.

Because of this latest unfortunate incident, massive demonstrations have taken place in Syria, Turkey, Saudi Arabia and Egypt calling on their respective governments to help Iran and many Muslim clerics have condemned the United States as the new Crusaders against Islam. Because of the tensions within the Middle East, all US and other western military bases and facilities have been placed on the highest alert level. This has further escalated tensions in countries like Turkey and Kuwait. So far only Syria, Yemen and Algeria have pledged any public support for Iran. They have only offered support by their governments, pledging help if Iran is attacked by Russia or the United States. Fortunately for now, most of the moderate Arab nations have publicly condemned the attack of the ferry, but have not officially broken any ties with the West, especially since most of the Arab governments believe that Iran had provoked this major stand-off which the Iranian government had started in the first place with the Russians and the Americans.

The following day during the US President's morning Intelligence briefing, President Baker was shown a CNN broadcast of renewed and violent demonstrations in both Iraq and within Turkey against western Embassies. Some demonstrators turned their aggression on any westerner they could find including US troops, the foreign press and even aid workers. As the President was watching one of the violent demonstrations on television, his National Security advisor said "Mr. President, the Middle East has just become a much more dangerous place to be for Americans"

"That is an understatement" President Baker responded.

"What is the situation in Israel, has there been any large scale escalation of violence towards Israel yet?" added the President.

"It looks as if the Arabs have forgotten Israel for now and have concentrated any hatred on the west, not the Jewish state" answered the National Security advisor.

Just as the President's daily briefing was concluding the President had received a call from the King of Saudi Arabia requesting to speak to the President right away.

"Good evening your Excellency" President Baker greeted the Saudi King.

"I am afraid it is not a good evening here in the Arabia Peninsula. I must ask you about a most difficult request" said the Saudi King.

"I must insist that all United States troops including your Air Force jets and Naval ships leave Saudi Arabian soil and Saudi seas" continued the King.

"This is quite a harsh reaction for just an unfortunate accident, especially since the Iranian government had made a deliberate attempt to disguise the ferry boat, which provoked the attack on the ferry" responded President Baker.

"Plus your Excellency, you know how strategic your airfields are to the United States and our allies" President Baker added.

"In just the last few hours several prisons have been overrun and several suspected Al-Qaeda terrorists have been released" announced the

King of Saudi Arabia and before the President could respond the Saudi Arabian king told the President that the government of Saudi Arabia could no longer guarantee the safety of any westerner or any US troops or US property within the Kingdom, especially if the United States continues supporting the Russians and attacks Iran. The President thanked the Saudi King and said he would start the process of leaving Saudi Arabian soil as quickly as possible, but it would take some time. The President then told his National Security advisor to send an urgent message to the Joint Chiefs of Staff to place all our military assets including Naval, Ground and Air Force troops on the highest level of alert status in all Arab and Middle Eastern territory, including Kuwait, Saudi Arabia and Turkey. He then added "And tell them not to get trigger happy, but to defend themselves if attacked". President Baker then shut the door of the Oval office so he could be alone and contemplate what may be next.

During the current crisis with Iran to retrieve the "amber" material, the crop loss in Russia has continued to grow to over twenty percent of the tillable land in Russia. Adding to the crop loss attributed to the fungus, many Russian farmers have decided not to plant this season in unaffected areas fearing the fungus could spread to these areas and could wipe out their farms and any money they spent on seed, cultivation and maintenance on the new crops. With the actual crop loss from the fungus and the loss of native grasses and other plant life, the countryside in Russia in many locations now resembles the dust bowl areas of Kansas and Oklahoma back in the 1920's. The Russian landscape is being eroded by both wind and rain with precious topsoil being blown and washed away.

Thirty-Three

European Union, Late July 2005

As additional land was being devastated in Russia and the Ukraine, additional widespread panic had begun and was spreading through out eastern and Western Europe, especially within the rich farmland regions of Germany's Rhine Valley, France's large vineyards and the large pasture lands of Spain. The mass panic erupting in these regions has led farmers and various government officials to allow the increased use of previously banned pesticides to kill off insects that may have originated in Russia or Eastern Europe. These same governments have also allowed limited hunting in previously banned regions.

Because of the fear and panic brought on by the fungus through out the world, especially within the continents of Europe and Asia, travel has become increasing difficult and in some regions has completely ceased. These travel difficulties are most notable between bordering countries in Europe and especially along the Eastern and Western European borders. Most forms of transportation including trains, airplanes, cars, trucks and even horses have been banned from crossing border areas between Russia, Ukraine, China and several other European countries. This travel ban or "restricted travel" to be more politically correct has also created limited air, train and ferry service to the United Kingdom and only limited flights from Europe to the Western Hemisphere. This "restricted travel" ban has caused additional economic hardships to both Eastern and Western Europe and within some regions of Russia due to the loss of business and vacation travelers. The ripple effects of these travel bans has created major economic losses within the United States with such companies as Boeing and other airline dependent companies experiencing massive decreased sales and have either laid off entire manufacturing plants or a large amount of their workforce. Also the US companies have had to reduce staff for most of their overseas flights.

So far most domestic US flights have continued, but International flights are hard to find and are extremely limited. When a flight is scheduled Internationally there are usually massive delays caused by the increased screening by the Transportation Security Administration. Some of these delays have increased by hours with some flights having delays of over six hours before boarding begins and some flights are being cancelled altogether. The boarding delays have been caused by TSA screening for terror related devices in addition to any accidental carriers of any unknown biological material that may be considered fungus material. Some airlines have already banned all luggage or any carry-on bags.

Besides a almost total collapse of International travel, trade between some countries has either ceased altogether or is very limited. Primary trade with Russia, Ukraine and most Eastern European countries has been restricted to mostly food imports with only select exports of raw materials such as steel, Iron Ore and other non-vegetative and manufactured goods are allowed. These exports from Russian and Eastern European nations undergo an exhaustive screening and inspection by local customs departments. This additional screening has caused massive delays of imported goods and products by days and by weeks. Again this ripple effect of delayed trade has had worldwide economic impacts. The most notable impact has been felt in China, where every square inch of any imported material and shipping container entering China is completely inspected for any type of plant, insect or animal life in any form. This disruptive screening has caused food to rot in waiting warehouses and along quarantined docks, while nearly twenty percent of China's population is under nourished and with many rural Chinese villages partially showing signs of malnutrition.

Meanwhile, the conditions along the Ukrainian border with Romania, Hungary and Poland continue to be headed towards a military and humanitarian crisis With pressure from the United States and what is left of NATO and other Western European countries, the once closed borders have been partially opened and it is now estimated that over a million refugees from Ukraine and Russia may flee into Romania, Hungary, Poland

and other neighboring nations. This potential refugee situation could create another massive economic load on these once Soviet supplied but now fledging democracies. The projected influx of people from Russia and Ukraine would be more than these countries could handle both from an economic and humanitarian side unless large amounts of economic aid and aid workers were not appropriated from the European Union and the United States. If not for this economic and humanitarian aid these governments would surely fail and topple.

Thirty-Four

Baghdad, Iraq – late July 2005

Hidden amongst a group of ordinary Iraqi government buildings near the once US occupied Green Zone rests a secret United States military command center buried four levels below the city of Baghdad. This secret military facility was buzzing with activity as the sun was burning outside. At this secret military facility a command center was set up for the joint United States and Russian military team. This team was preparing a mission to enter Iran through Iraq to obtain the stolen "amber" material along with the secret Iranian experimental data that was obtained from the stolen "amber" material. The US and Russian team is headed by the United States CIA agent Danny McLean and the team also consists of several Russian Federal Police commandos and members of the United States Delta Force that had previously worked with the CIA and with Danny McLean. Along with the commandos was US scientist Max Hamilton and Russian Paleontologist Boris Panov, both of whom had worked with Danny McLean previously. In addition to the scientists and commandos, both CIA and Iraqi interpreters will be going along on the mission to be able to quickly translate and read both Arabic and Farsi, the language spoken by most Iranian academics and government officials.

Once everyone was gathered within a large secure conference room four levels below the city of Baghdad both Max Hamilton and Boris Panov quickly embraced. Their friendship had grown strong, especially since the death of their colleague Dmitri Pochinkov. Once the group was settled in CIA agent Danny McLean thanked everyone for being there instead of spending this crisis with their families. They were then all given a packet of materials marked "top secret" and were briefed on the basic mission parameters and were told of the many obstacles and life threatening situations they may be facing. Once Danny McLean had introduced everyone he asked "Are there any questions before we start the detailed mission briefing and planning session"

"I'm honored to be with this heroic group, but why were Boris Panov and myself chosen for this mission. We are scientists, not soldiers?" asked Max Hamilton.

"This should have been explained to you in your initial briefing before leaving the United States, but in short, we need to properly identify the fungus material and to make sure the Iranian experiments are still viable and most importantly we need to make sure the fungus experiments derived from the 'amber' material stays alive long enough for, Dr. Hamilton to help develop a means to destroy it" Danny McLean told Max with a trouble look on his face.

"The rest of us are here to get you and Boris into the Iranian laboratories, identify both the fungus and the 'amber' and to then get you, Boris and this 'amber' material out of Iran alive as quickly as possible and with as little bloodshed as possible" Danny McLean added.

The group then spent several hours going over the mission plans and scenarios. It was just after midnight in Baghdad and some members of the group that had traveled from the United States and from Northern Russia had very little sleep. The acting military commando in charge of the military part of the mission, a slender but well built US Delta Force soldier named Tom Bechtel announced with the help of his Russian counterpart "Mr. McLean we are all very tired, so I think we should stop for tonight, get some rest for our big night tomorrow"

"You're right Captain Bechtel and Commander Satovsky. We should rest up and meet again tomorrow morning at 0800 hours to go over final weaponry and planning" answered Danny McLean. As the group of commandos and scientists were leaving the conference room, Danny McLean stopped both Max Hamilton and Boris Panov and told them "I would not normally have allowed civilians to take part in such a terrible mission, but you must know that if we are not successful on this mission, this could lead to World War III, not to mention what devastation that would continue to occur because of the fungus"

"Boris and I will do our best" Max Hamilton replied. Boris then made a jester of pointing a gun and firing it. As they entered the secret elevator to go to the surface of Baghdad, Danny McLean quietly told Max and Boris "Please stay close to me and try not to get yourselves killed, since we have no other experts with this much knowledge about the fungus or the 'amber' material".

Later the following evening a group of freight trucks with the name "Akmed Hauling" painted on the side of each truck entered Iran from the Iraqi border without any border incident. This easy border crossing took place mainly because of some earlier bribes and the fact that the trucks bore the company name of the Iranian Presidents own hauling company. A rumor had also been spread amongst the Iranian border guards that the trucks were carrying secret military parts and weapons systems needed for the Iranian nuclear missile system. What the trucks were really carrying consisted of CIA agents, US Delta Force commandos and a Russian Federal Police commando team complete with sophisticated communication devices, weaponry and a couple of scientists. The truck convoy then traveled a couple of hours before pulling up to a gated and non-descript guardhouse outside a heavily guarded Iranian military based located west of Tehran, Iran.

So far the joint United States and Russian covert mission had been completely successful and without any major complications. Again, with some luck and without any complications the truck convoy was ordered into the Iranian base and directed to proceed to Building Number Seven within the Iranian military complex. The truck drivers were also told that someone at building number seven would direct them where to unload their cargo. Once the US-Russian team had arrived at building number seven the commandos quickly and quietly secured the garage and loading dock areas of the building with the precision termination of two Iranian guards. They quickly moved to an area within building number seven that was supposed to contain the laboratories, Iranian scientists, experiments and the "amber" material per the CIA's latest intelligence report the Danny McLean had received from Langley, Virginia prior to arriving in Baghdad. This CIA intelligence report was supposed to be based on information they thought was very reliable and highly paid for from their Iranian informant.

As the US-Russian commando teams scoured the offices and laboratory areas within building number seven, they found no additional guard or any scientific personnel. It was obvious that the building was empty and deserted, but it had not been deserted too long. It was also ascertained by the interpreters that some very secretive and scientific work had taken place in this complex and it had not been very long since the scientific equipment had been used. After a very quick and quiet meeting in which CIA agent Danny McLean, US Delta Force Captain Bechtel and Russian commander Satovsky had gathered together to discuss their problem. Danny McLean offered "I'm not sure why this laboratory is disserted, if the Iranians moved to a larger or more secure facility or if they were tipped off to our arrival".

"If this is because of a leaked informant situation we must leave this place as quickly as possible in case we come under attack. Everyone fan out and grab as many files and papers as possible, we must leave in ten minutes" added US Delta Force Captain Bechtel.

"Stay in the trucks with the interpreters. I will come and get you if needed" Danny McLean told Max Hamilton and Boris Panov. The commandos completely scoured the laboratory building including shower and bathroom facilities.

The US-Russian commando team was successful in taking most of the Iranian files and loose paperwork that was left behind. The teams then loaded up the truck convoy with the confiscated files, then the commando's left building number seven. As they drove out of the Iranian military complex west of Tehran towards the Iraqi border, each passing mile made the commandos a little more comfortable that a leak, bad informant information or finding the dead Iranian guards did not compromise the mission yet. As the truck convoy crossed the border back into Iraq, CIA agent Danny McLean ascertained that the Iranians were not tipped off, but had simply moved to either a larger or more secure laboratory facility. This assumption was proved correct after the interpreters read some of the

Iranian scientific memo's that were left behind within building number seven back at the Iranian military complex.

Although the joint United States and Russian mission to retrieve the "amber" material and the associated experimentation in Iran had failed, the confiscated files and paperwork had given the CIA a probable location of the new Iranian laboratory and the papers left behind had shown them enough data that the Iranian scientists had not only been able to replicate and develop the fungus from the stolen "amber" material, but had also successfully developed a means to kill it. If the findings from the found paperwork were accurate, this would most likely bring on war between Russia and Iran and would probably start World War III.

The acting president of Russia, General Vitus Baranov along with United States President Baker has sent word to CIA agent Danny McLean to verify the information about the Iranian "amber" experiments. If true, General Baranov announced "We will get the information to kill the fungus from the Iranians or I will personally guarantee extinction of the Iranian people before they have a chance to make the Russian people extinct".

In addition to the confiscated files and letters taken from the Iranian laboratory, a group of Iranian dissidents with the help of the United States CIA and Russia's Federal Police had been able to detain or kidnap to be more accurate, one of the Iranian scientists who had worked on the "amber" experiments. The United States CIA and Russia's Federal agents had been able to persuade the scientist to talk about the "amber" experiments and to collaborate the findings from the files and paperwork taken from building number seven. The questioning or persuading of the Iranian scientist became more difficult when the interrogators asked the Iranian scientist where the current laboratory had been located. The Iranian scientist had then started shaking and speaking rapidly in Farsi before telling the interrogators he would rather be killed by the Russians then deal with torture that would be imposed by Iran's Presidential Guard. After some additional persuasion and just before the Iranian scientist got his wish from the Russians, he had told them that the laboratory was hidden three levels below Iran's Presidential Guard building in Central Tehran. He had also told them that they move the laboratory every couple of weeks and that the laboratory was guarded by both Presidential Guards and by a company of Iran's version of the US Special Forces.

Thirty-Five

Washington, D.C. – last week of July 2005

Once President Baker of the United States and General Baranov of Russia were notified of the latest intelligence from Iran they quickly phoned each other and proceeded to set up a video conference between the two world leaders and their respective military staffs. Once the US and Russian leaders talked about the latest developments they had both agreed to contact the Iranian government immediately, especially since the United Nations had become almost totally useless now except for humanitarian aid. President Baker and General Baranov wanted to notify Tehran of their ultimatum and terms.

Since the United States has had no formal diplomatic relations with Iran since the hostage crisis in 1979 and because the Russian ambassador and his staff had been officially expelled and ordered to leave Iran a few days ago in addition to no viable United Nations support, the two leaders of Russia and the United States still needed to communicate with the Iranian government and to get an urgent message to the Ayatollah and the President of Iran. The Russian and US leadership proceeded to give a secret sealed message to the Saudi Arabian government to transmit to the Iranian

President and the Ayatollah. The message from both President Baker and General Baranov simply read "Return the 'amber' material along with the developed fungus and fungus cure immediately. If you fail to comply with this message, the sovereign nations of both the United States and the Russian Federation will have no choice but to enter Iranian territory and will retrieve this material. Any attempt to destroy the cure, the developed fungus or any of the 'amber' related material will create grave consequences for the nation and the people of Iran. You have forty-eight hours to comply with this request"

After three hours of waiting for a response from the Iranian government, both President Baker and General Baranov were told to turn on their televisions and were quickly shown what appeared to be a news conference with the Iranian President being shown on Al-Jezerra television. The Iranian Presidents speech was not translated until a translator was brought to the White House. After a few minutes of listening and viewing the previously televised Iranian press conference from Al-Jezerra television, the translator told both President Baker and General Baranov through the video hook-up, the in a short version, the Iranian President had said "The great nation of Persia has been invaded, raped and plundered in the past by the infidels. This will never happen again to the great and proud people of Iran. The great Satan the United States along with its puppets from Russia has brought the wrath of Allah on to themselves in the form of this so-called prehistoric fungus. Because of this they blame the great people of the Islamic Republic of Iran for the punishment they have brought on to themselves. Because we are so blessed, Allah has bestowed on us his mighty power. Allah has given us this fungus – not by killing our date and palm trees, but as a weapon we can use to defend Islam and ourselves from the great Satan and his minions. If the United States Satan or its Russian puppets try to take Allah's gift from us or attempt to invade, rape and plunder us again, we will use Allah's weapon and release this fungus to destroy the great Satan the United States and any other country that dares to challenge Iran ever again"

After hearing the translated version of the press conference, President Baker and General Baranov agreed to speak again later after conferring with each others staff and digesting what had just happened and what was said. After switching off the video link with General Baranov, President Baker told his group of military advisors along with the Joint Chiefs of Staff "My God – This could not only be the start of World War III, but the start of the end of the world". The President asked everyone to leave, have a drink, see their families and to meet back at the White House in a few hours.

Thirty-Six

Meanwhile back in the southern portion of the Russian Federation near the fungus affected region south of Volgograd, a group of Russian farmers have resorted to killing to try and stop the spread of the fungus. Just a few months ago the city of Volgograd was a bustling trading city located on the main highway between the countries of Ukraine and Kazakhstan with oil wells to the south and rich farming areas north of the city. This area is also the main migratory route of the endangered Siberian Goose and is also a favorite resting spot for the Siberian Goose on its migration from the Caspian Sea to Siberia. The Siberian Goose is a rare relative of the abundant Snow Goose of North America. Siberian geese are similar to their Snow geese cousins except the Siberian goose is slightly larger with a size averaging thirty-two inches, it flies much slower with a chased speed of only forty miles per hour, it has a slightly longer beak and only has a small amount of black feathers along their wing tips. The Siberian goose is usually found within the northern regions of Siberia and during the summer months they nest along the Artic coast. They then migrate south from their Artic nesting grounds to the Caspian Sea region during the harsh Siberian winters. It is during their migration to and from Siberia that the geese will often stop in the southern farm belt region of Russia to rest and eat. One of the Siberian geese current favorite resting areas is located outside of Volgograd, Russia.

It is within these fields outside Volgograd, that farmers have turned to hunters and have started killing the endangered Siberia goose. The Russian farmers fear that the Siberian goose could spread the fungus to the delegate tundra area of Siberia and other northern plant life located within the Siberian area and other farm regions. Both Russian and European scientists are not exactly sure how the fungus is spread to each plant, but they all agree that insect, animal and human life may have helped spread the fungus besides the effects of wind and storm run-off.

In addition to the Siberian goose, many other endangered birds and animals have been targeted by hunters in both Russia and China and even within some Western European and other Asian countries. Many environmental groups and wildlife experts along with leading scientists from the United States have been preaching that even if the fungus is stopped or dies out tomorrow, it would already be too late for most of the already endangered animal species and many threatened species may become extinct by next year regardless of the fungus spread.

What the farmers and scientists did not know was that the fungus had already started to affect the Siberian plant life. The fungus was already transmitted by humans to Siberia, not by wildlife almost three months earlier and the killing taking place today of the endangered Siberian goose and other endangered species was basically for nothing.

Thirty-Seven

Russian/Ukraine border – August 2005

With over forty percent of Russia's farm crops lost by the killer

fungus, from farmers unwilling to plant in already decimated areas or from

farmers not wanting to chance the expense of planting in fear their crops

would be killed off by the spread of the fungus. This combination of events

has created a crop shortage never before witnessed in Russian history. Even

the Russian farm devastation looks better than what has happened through

out the Ukraine. Over eighty percent of the countryside of the Ukraine has

been decimated and some areas resemble a wasteland. Millions of

Ukrainians have left the Ukraine and have been living in refugee camps

located in Hungary, Romania and other European countries. These refugee

caps or "tent-cities" have been maintained by United Nations aid workers,

the Red Cross and other aid groups. This mass exodus from the Ukraine has

essentially ended the democratic government of the Ukraine which had only

been set up a short time after the fall of Communism and the government

of the former Soviet Union. This exodus has also created hundreds of ghost

towns and cities within the Ukraine. So far the only law and order left in the

Ukraine is along the border regions with Hungary and Romania. Many other

areas within the Ukraine are home to looters, gangs and other organized crime members. The land of the Ukraine was once part of the Soviet Union, and then became an independent sovereign nation is now a land of criminals and lawlessness.

In addition to the loss of the nation of the Ukraine, plus a large amount of southern Russian farmland, the fungus has spread to parts of Siberia despite efforts made by farmers and hunters to eliminate the migration of many bird species including the endangered Siberian Goose. Despite valiant efforts by both environmentalists and scientists to stop the fungus to both northern and eastern Russia, the fungus has been reported in both native plant and crop species in both Kazakhstan and western Mongolia. Officials in Kazakhstan have quietly accused the Russians of bringing in the fungus because of its military incursion through Kazakhstan towards the border with Iran. The Kazakhstan government has not protested too loudly because of the large Russian and Ukrainian military force located along the Turkmenistan and Iranian border, plus the fact that they originally allowed the Russians access into Kazakhstan and did absolutely nothing to prevent or stop the Russian's further military advance when it first occurred.

Thirty-Eight

China/Russia border near Bekatova – August 2005

With the confirmed spread of the fungus within western Mongolia, China has begun a massive defoliage project along its borders with Mongolia and Russia. The defoliage project has consisted of large scale clear cutting of timber, removing and burning thousands of acres of virgin forested land and also applying the use of a newly developed insecticide which is believed to be ten times more potent and deadly than some of the original DDT chemicals that were developed in the United States back in the 1950's. This new DDT is one hundred times more deadly to bird, fish, wildlife and humans then previous developed insecticide chemicals. One scientist working for an European environmental group was quoted in the American Journal of Environmental Science "That the use of this new insecticide in conjunction with the massive loss of wildlife habitat due to the spread of the fungus along with the clear cutting development along the Mongolian, Russian and Chinese borders could wipe out thousands of species of insect, plant and animal life within the next few years if not stopped now.

Thirty-Nine

Volgograd, Russian Federation – late August 2005

Meanwhile back along the migratory route of the endangered Siberian Goose, the farmers and hunters in the southern regions of Russia near Volgograd have resorted to mass capture and killing of the Siberian Goose along with many other species of bird and animals, despite efforts by world wildlife scientists and environmentalists to stop the killing. According to visiting European and American environmental scientists to the area around Volgograd "The estimated numbers of Siberian geese went from an endangered amount of approximately five thousand birds to an extremely threatened number estimated to be less than five hundred birds. This loss is attributed to the mass panic amongst the Russian farmers, the loss of food in nearby farms that the geese feed on and the loss of habitat created by the spread of the fungus". It is believed by many environmentalists and scientists that the Siberian Goose in addition to several other smaller species of bird life could become extinct by wintertime.

The fungus has now started the extinction of plant and animal life just like it had over 65 million years ago.

Along with the possible future extinction of several species of birds and other animals, the world still faced a possible World War and a global economic and humanitarian catastrophe never before witnessed by mankind. At the now useless United Nations headquarters in New York City, last ditch diplomatic efforts were being made to try and convince by bribing and begging the Iranian government to release the "amber" material and all of its scientific data relating to the original "amber" sample. At the same time, Russian troops and armored tanks have continued to mass along the Iranian and Turkmenistan border as additional troops from the United States and now joined by what is left of NATO. These troops have moved to forward military positions along the Iraqi/Iranian border. United Nation diplomats that have been trying to speak with the Iranian President consist of United Nations diplomats and ambassadors from the embassies of Saudi Arabia, Switzerland and Canada. The UN diplomats know that if their efforts fail, military conflict will surely erupt in Iran and perhaps the rest of the world.

Forty

Iran/Turkmenistan Border – late August 2005

Shortly after contacting the Iranian government, the United

Nations diplomatic mission was deemed a failure. Not only did the

diplomats fail in buying more time before the possible military conflict, but

also the Iranians refused to talk to the United Nations diplomats nor would

they even allow them to enter Iran. Before the UN diplomats could try

talking to the Iranian government again, both Russian and Ukrainian

infantry troops along with columns of Russian tanks have begun entering

Iran from several different staging areas along the Iranian/Turkmenistan

border. Coinciding with the Russian and Ukrainian assault from the north,

fighting has also erupted between United States and NATO troops against

Iranian troops along the south western border between Iraq and Iran. In

addition to infantry and armored attacks within the Iranian border regions,

several naval skirmishes have taken place between US Navy war ships and

Iranian gunboats within the Persian Gulf. And in a unprecedented show of

military cooperation and coordination, both Russian Migs and US F-18

fighter jets have targeted and bombed many selected Iranian military targets

including anti-aircraft and communication sites outside Tehran. These air

assaults were assisted with the help of US stealth bombers and high altitude

AWAC support aircraft. Just prior to the coordinated assaults from United States, Russian, Ukrainian and NATO troops, the US Navy had launched over one hundred cruise missiles to try and weaken Iranian anti-aircraft and radar facilities just like the US did during the start of the Persian Gulf war in the early 1990's.

Despite a massive air assault on Tehran and surrounding areas, the Iranian government has continued to defy world requests and has continued production of the active fungus and has continued development of a means to safety kill it. This work is taking place in a secret laboratory facility hidden deep below ground, underneath a school and a children's hospital, which is located along side the main roadway through Tehran. The laboratory was located under the Presidents complex and President Guard quarters just two days earlier.

During a brief cease fire from both the United States and Russian Air Forces to allow the Saudi Arabian government to meet with the President of Iran. The Saudi ambassador arrived at the Iranian Presidents temporary office located within the Al-Takiri Mosque located in central Tehran. This mosque is considered one of the oldest and most holy sites within Iran and within the Muslim world and the Iranian President thought the United States would not dare bomb this site for fear of upsetting many other Muslim nations. The Ayatollah has also been moved from his palace and has been hidden in another secret location. Since the start of hostilities,

224

all diplomatic communications have been cut off between Iran and most of the western world including the United Nations. Only a few Arabic diplomats have been allowed to speak with any Iranian government diplomats and the Iranian President. The Saudi Arabian ambassador waited outside the Iranian Presidents temporary office until he was escorted into the President's office a few minutes later.

"Please sit down and have some coffee" announced the Iranian President, as he carefully poured two cups of steaming hot, bitter Turkish coffee in front of his desk.

"You must be here to give information from the Great Satan and its puppets – am I correct Mr. Ambassador"

"Yes Mr. President" replied the Saudi Arabian ambassador.

"So, let's hear what the devil has to say before they start bombing our great cities again" snorted the Iranian President.

The Saudi ambassador then unfolded a statement that he had received from the United States consulate in Riyadh, Saudi Arabia a few hours earlier. He expressed to the Iranian President that this document has been sealed and it has not been read by himself or the Saudi Arabian government. The Saudi ambassador then read "To the Great People of Iran, we have not intended any harm to you or your cities, but the world needs the scientific data and experiments developed from the stolen dinosaur 'amber'. The very future of planet earth may depend on your willingness to cooperate and turn over this information. We have tried many times to reach a diplomatic solution to this unfolding catastrophe, but have been rejected at all times by your government. This is why bombs and missiles have been dropped on Tehran and this is why foreign troops have entered Iranian territory. During this temporary cease fire we wish to peacefully obtain the 'amber' and its scientific information without any more bloodshed. Once we have the 'amber' and the experimental data, all hostilities will cease and all troops will quickly leave the territory of the Republic of Iran". The Iranian President then interrupted the Saudi ambassador as they watched an announcer on Al-Jezeera television start reading the same statement that the Saudi ambassador had started reading earlier to the Iranian President.

"The Devil and his army have not caused much damage and have only advanced several kilometers into our country before they have been pushed back by the mighty army of Iran" yelled out the Iranian President. As the Saudi Arabian ambassador was ready to read again, several muffled explosions could be heard in the distance, somewhere outside the city limits of Tehran.

"Do not worry ambassador, the Pigs would not dare bomb such a historic and sacred Islamic site as this" stated the Iranian President. The Saudi ambassador then continued to read "If the Ayatollah and the

President of Iran continue to disregard the World's plea, then we will have no other choice, but to use whatever amount of force and weaponry that is required to recover the 'amber' and it information. We implore the leadership of Iran to make the right choice and spare the lives of Iranians and the lives of others through out the rest of the world". The Iranian President thanked the Saudi ambassador for this information and then asked the Saudi ambassador to wait outside his office while he conferred with the Ayatollah and the rest of his Presidential ministry.

After a couple of hours of waiting, the Saudi Arabian ambassador was summoned back to the temporary Mosque office of the Iranian President. Once the Saudi ambassador was escorted into the President's office, he was given a letter written by the Iranian President in response to the US letter on official Iranian government letterhead and was told to deliver the letter to the evil Satan the United States and to deliver it at once. He was told to read the letter himself and tell the Saudi Arabian king what was being given to the US devils. The letter simply read "Surrender your weapons and leave the Islamic Republic of Iran, then vacate all Muslim territories and return to the land of the devil in the United States and to its surrogate Russia. You must comply at once. If you disregard Iran's plea, then we will have no other choice but to turn over the fungus to Al-Qaeda and other friends of Islam to spread it in both the United States and in

Europe. We implore the leadership of the United States and Russia to make the right choice"

The Saudi Arabian ambassador then quickly left the Mosque in central Tehran and made his way back to the Saudi Arabian Embassy were he told his superior about the meeting and gave him both the letter from the United States and the reply letter from the Iranian President that both mocked and threatened the United States, Russia and Europe. The Saudi Arabian ambassador told his Embassy chief "That if this fungus is as deadly as they have seen in reports from Russia and the Ukraine, then the Americans, Russians and Europeans will have no choice but to take drastic measures against the Iranians"

"And if Iran gives the fungus to terrorists, this could be the start of a war against Muslims greater then what had happened in the Crusades, including the citizens of Saudi Arabia" added the Saudi ambassador. The Saudi Arabian Embassy chief then called the Saudi Arabian Director of State, which is like the US Chief of Staff on his secure mobile satellite phone. This phone is now required since most of Tehran's power and communications have been damaged by the repeated bombardment by Russian and American air strikes.

The Saudi Arabian Director of State expressed to his embassy chief "The Iranian President must be crazy – why would he risk this war?

"I think he really believes he will beat the United States and the Russians, like he had during the hostage crisis in 1979 and what had happened to the Russians in Afghanistan in the early 80's" replied the embassy chief.

"Does the Iranian President know that he could stop this war now and possible be hailed a hero if they have successfully found a cure to the fungus?" asked the Saudi Director of State.

"Sir, I believe the Iranian President may really be crazy. He has told several members of Iran's Ministry of Defense that once Iran beats the Russians and Americans out of Iran they will announce that in exchange for a fungus cure, each nation will have to offer its government support for Iran and show complete conversion to Islam" stated the Saudi Embassy chief.

The Saudi Arabian Director of State then proceeded to notify both the Russian Federation and the United States of the Iranian government response to its request.

Forty-One

Moscow, Russian Federation – Late August 2005

Upon receiving the letter from the Iranian President, General
Baranov of the Russian Federation conferred with both the US and his
military commanders leading the assault into Iran. He told his military
leaders of the assault force, that a mission to find the "amber" laboratory
would have to go more quickly then anticipated. He told the commanders
that this mission must be completed at once including a possible massive
loss of life for the Americans, Russians and the Iranians.

After the United States President Baker read Iran's reply to his
letter he quickly convened another emergency meeting with the Joint Chiefs
of Staff and all of his other key personnel in the war room located in the
basement of the White House. President Baker immediately issued several
directives including increasing the number of air strikes in Iran and an
increase in the number of targets including some non-military areas. The
President also ordered a wider ranging border protection plan including a
zero entry policy for both the Mexican and Canadian borders and a
strengthening of sea ports. The border plan is being instituted to because of
the Iranian and Al-Qaeda fungus threat. In addition to air strikes within

Iran, air strikes would also be sanctioned on any other world city that knowingly harbored known terrorists and refuses to turn them over to Russian or US authorities. The President also ordered all combat and support troops assisting in aid and relief missions in the Ukraine to immediately leave Western Europe and report to the combat areas of Iran and Iraq to relieve troops that have already entered Iranian territory.

The spreading of the fungus has thrown two previous rivals and enemies, Russia and the United States together against a common enemy like Hitler was in World War II. Except this time the eastern front lies within the Kopet Mountains along the Turkmenistan and Iran border and the beaches of Normandy are now the sands of eastern Iraq.

Once again a Russian and United States joint commando operation is being planned. This operation is a result of the top commanders of both the Russian and US armies believing that an all out war and resulting occupation of Iran would cost thousands of troop loss and would most likely result in the "amber" being destroyed or taken out of Iran along with any experimental data and the possible fungus cure. Another frightening scenario is the fungus being deliberately spread throughout the world by terrorists or by Iranian government agents. With these theories agreed to by both top Russian and US officials, the only course of action is to try another covert mission inside Iran. The new commando unit will consist of both United States Navy Seal, Army Delta Force units and an elite commando unit from the Russian Federal Police. Joining the commandos will be CIA special agent Danny McLean and once again assisted by the US Paleobotanist Max Hamilton and the Russian Paleontologist Boris Panov.

The new mission parameters would be different than before. This time the commando units would be equipped with advanced weaponry along with new orders to use whatever force necessary to obtain the "amber" and associated experimental data. This new mission has been quickly arranged and organized aboard the United States Aircraft Carrier "Providence" located in the Persian Gulf near the coast of Kuwait. The mission has moved from an urgent status to a critical status due to the quick advances already made by both the United States and Russian army units into Iran, plus credible information stating the "amber" along with its experimental data was moved again to a secret Iranian laboratory facility buried with Mount Demevend, a cone shaped mountain outside Tehran.

The US/Russian commando mission has just become more important that both countries realize because unknown to them and most other intelligence networks, a secret letter has been sent from the Iranian President to the ruling communist party of China. The secret letter requests military aid from China to help Iran in exchange for cheap oil and a cure for the fungus that now threatens the rest of the world.

Forty-Two

Beijing, China – Late August 2005

Even before the latest fungus crisis and the war situation in Iran, worldwide travel had been profoundly effected throughout the world, especially farm rich nations such as the United States and many South American nations. With the possible spread of the fungus by insects, animals, wind and most likely by man, most countries have banned all non-essential travel into their nations. For instance, the only travel allowed into mainland China is reserved for high ranking Chinese government officials and invited scientists and diplomats. China has become more isolated now than during the communist rule of Mao Tse-Tung. In addition to China, both Australia and Greenland have banned all foreign travel to and from their territory. An official in the Australian Parliament was recently quoted "Our farms and livestock are extremely fragile along and along with our harsh environment, we cannot withstand any more hardships to our limited farmlands such as drought and any foreign disease, especially this fungus".

Besides travel, world trade has been substantially crippled. The restricted travel and trade have contributed to a near global economic meltdown never before witnessed before, even during the Great Depression in the 1930's. The regions hardest hit and most devastated by the fungus have been the newly capitalized nations of Eastern Europe and western regions of China. Many western nations have restricted trade and refused any imports from Eastern Europe. This trade block has caused these regions to have little or no incoming funds to pay for the essential incoming trade goods such as food and medicines. Several Eastern European and some regions in western Europe have had to accept food aid and rations that were previously reserved for the poorest nations in Africa.

Forty-Three

Moscow, Russian Federation – November 2005

Due to a early harsh winter so far in Russia, scientists have seen a decrease in the spread of the fungus. Most scientists believe that the fungus is still very much alive, but has slowed down due to plant dormancy and the additional loss of vegetation brought on by the sudden and extreme weather conditions sweeping across the Russian countryside starting in the upper Siberian regions and ranging as far south as Kazakhstan. Many global warming advocates have blamed the extreme cold and wintry weather on the sun reflecting off the snow covered terrain that was once covered with vegetation.

The latest estimates by the Russian Agricultural Institute states that as much as fifty percent of Russia's crops and farmland have been wiped out by the fungus. In addition to the crop loss, scientific evidence has been gathered showing over twenty-five percent of Russia's plant life has been altered or destroyed including almost ten percent within the fragile tundra areas of Siberia. The Russians and Ukrainians are not the only nations affected by the fungus. Both Kazakhstan and Upper Mongolia have reported both plant and crop loss with as much as twenty percent since Russia first made the fungus problem public.

The Asian continent is starting to slowly die off due to the fungus with no apparent way of stopping the fungus by natural means. This has been clearly seen by the massive decline of the already very endangered Siberian goose and as many as two hundred other bird and animal species that have been added to the endangered species list each month.

Environmental scientists estimate that only a few Siberian geese remain alive in the wild, while two geese are being cared for at the Moscow Zoo. The World Wildlife Consortium chairman stated "With no additional sightings of the Siberian goose spotted this month and with no additional geese that have continued to breed, we may have to issue an extinction notice by the end of the winter". When asked by a reporter what the impact would be with the loss of the Siberian goose to other wildlife and plant life, the chairman answered "the ripple effect of both the fungus devastation and the loss of the once vibrant bird species, the 'Siberian goose' could trigger a tragic loss and possible extinction of hundreds of bird and animal species throughout the world in just a few months".

Forty-Four

Urumqi, China — November 2005

Unknown to the leadership of China, the fungus has spread to a few areas in the Xinjiang Uygur Autonomous region of China, near the metropolitan city of Urumqi. This region borders Russia, Mongolia, Afghanistan, Pakistan and India and is mostly desert and prairie land with mountains to the north an a region that is mostly uninhabited except for the occasional shepherd or cow herder outside of the city.

The city of Urumqi which means "Fine Pasture" is the capital of the Xinjiang Uygur Autonomous region and is remote by Chinese standards. The area is over a three and a half hour plane trip from Beijing and has kept some of its ancient tribal customs and language. Both Chinese and Uygur, the language of the Uygurs which is the largest ethnic group is spoken and appears on most signs and posters. The city is bordered by snow-capped mountains and surrounding desert and usually sees a little snow starting in mid-November lasting until March. But this year harsher winter weather has brought colder temperatures and snow starting in October. This was bad for what fall crops were still left to be harvested, but had significantly slowed the spread of the fungus.

The population of Urumqi have not noticed the destruction by the fungus, since the early winter weather has diminished the selling of fresh vegetables at the city bazaar. This time of year the vendors at the bazaar mainly sell fish and clothing, but during the summer months this bustling free market of private entrepreneurs sell fish, vegetables, clothing, watches, homemade noodles and breads. The bazaar is usually very loud and bustling with the many vendors and restaurateurs all competing for customers.

Only a few isolated Mongolian families know of the devastation the fungus can cause. They know about the fungus because of dead plant life near and around Tian Chi, which means "Heavenly Lake". Heavenly Lake is a mountain lake approximately three hours of rough off-road driving from Urumqi. The lake lies at an elevation over Sixty four hundred feet above sea level and lies below the receding glacier of Mount Bogda. The lake is also surrounded by mountain peaks with forests of tall spruce trees above a vibrant alpine meadow. This area is in sharp contrast with the deserts of Xinjiang nearby.

This time of year the lake receives no visitors because of the trip is nearly impossible between September and May. Very few people who live near the lake will travel the forbidding roads and bridges to travel to Urumqi for supplies. Most of the residents near the lake stock up on supplies by September and hope they last until early spring.

Forty-Five

Once United States President Baker and Russian General Baranov heard the tragic reports of the additional plant loss and possible animal extinctions, the two world leaders met and decided to rush the start of the next covert mission into Tehran, Iran and to continue to advance troops and armor into Iranian territory. The two world leaders both agreed to take a minimum of another ten miles of Iranian territory starting from the both the Iraqi and Turkmenistan borders. President Baker and General Baranov had also issued orders for all Iranian civilians to be left alone and for the American and Russian led troops to capture but not kill any Iranian army resistance if possible.

But in war, reality is easier said than done, especially when an elite Iranian Guard unit hid in an unnamed Iranian village near the Turkmenistan border and proceeded to ambush a unprepared advancing Russian army convoy. The Iranian Guard units were hiding among the civilian population and were firing grenades and rockets from civilian homes and businesses. This ambush result was the death or injury of over three hundred Russian and Ukrainian troops and the counter attack by Russian tanks and fighter jets created a tragic loss of over two thousand Iranian civilians and military casualties. The unnamed Iranian village has now become a unnamed Iranian cemetery.

Once President Baker and General Baranov received the terrible report from the military commanders in the field, the Iranian government had started airing a looped video showing dead babies still clutching toys and bottles. The Iranian President ordered the video to be played on all Arab television stations and websites including Al-Jezeera TV. The Iranian government had also sent a copy of the video along with the Iranian delegation that was to meet with Chinese officials about Iran's recent letter sent to China from the Iranian President.

Forty-Six

Beijing, China – November 2005

The delegation from Iran arrived in Beijing, China and was escorted to the historic Imperial Hotel in central Beijing to wait for their meeting with China's ruling communist party. The Iranian diplomats planned to meet with members of the Politboro and select Ministers of the State Council.

The Chinese communist government is made up of the Chairman of the Chinese People's Republic also known as the Premier. The Premier appoints the State Council which is formally made of Cabinet members or commonly called Ministers such as the Minister of National Defense, Minister of Culture and nine other cabinet members. The Cabinet members are approved by the National People's Congress which is an elected body according to China's Constitution. The approval of the Ministers is almost automatic since both the Premier and most members of the People's Congress are high ranking members of the Executive Council of the Central Committee of the Communist Party, also known as the Politboro. The Premier by constitution is not a dictator, but he does control the People's Liberation Army or called the "Red Army" by westerners and he also controls the state run television and the "People's Daily", China's largest newspaper.

The Iranian diplomats were to formally submit a deal with China for Iranian oil in exchange for help in eliminating the American and Russian forces from Iran. China has in the past always maintained a diplomatic and trade relationship with Iran, but the two governments rarely speak other than to discuss and negotiate oil and other trade functions.

China's relationship with Iran in the past has bee mixed with distrust and with a general dislike by the Chinese government for both the Iranian President and the Ayatollah. The recent crisis between Iran and both Russia and the United States has not changed how China feels toward the people of Iran. The love/hate relationship between China and Iran had started shortly after the fall of the Shah in 1979. Basically, Iran had bargained with both Russia and China at the same time for its cheap oil in exchange for military imports. Needless to say, Russia had received most of the cheap Iranian oil and Iran had received Russian T-1 tanks along with Mig fighter jets.

Many members of the current Chinese government would like to tell the leaders of Iran to keep their oil and to try and find a way to make the spare parts necessary to keep its old and un-maintained Russian military junk operating. But China needs the oil and they must also find a way to protect their fragile farms and pastures from this devastating fungus.

Everyone in and outside of China knows that China has a lot of mouths to feed.

As soon as the Iranian diplomats had settled down and got comfortable in their hotel rooms, they were summoned by phone to meet a Ministry guard down stairs in the lobby who would escort them to their requested meeting with China's ruling cabinet and councils. They were also told that the Chinese Premier himself would be present at the meeting.

After phony pleasantries were exchanged between the Chinese Ministers and the Iranian diplomats, the Premier was announced and sat down at the head of a large conference table and announced through an interpreter "Let us not waste time. I know what you have to offer, but what exactly do you want from China".

"We will gladly sell China all the oil we have at a fair and reasonable price and of course we would share any research we may develop concerning the fungus or a cure for the fungus" answered the lead Iranian diplomat.

"All we want in return is help from the Chinese government to help remove and keep out the Russians and Americans from all Iranian soil" continued the lead Iranian diplomat after pausing to sip from a glass of water. The Chinese Minister for Energy had started to ask the Iranians about the price they would have to pay per barrel for the oil, but was interrupted by the Premier.

"Exactly what kind of help are you requesting to use against the Russians and Americans" asked the Chinese Premier.

"We would request ships, jets, tanks, troops or whatever threats are necessary to persuade the Russian pigs and American devils to leave our sacred country" replied the lead Iranian diplomat after taking another long drink of water.

"If you are asking for a nuclear threat, the answer is no. We have had many differences with the United States and Russia, but we now have a good trade position with the Americans that now accounts for over fifty percent of our trade surplus" the Chinese Premier softly said as he looked the lead diplomat directly in the eyes so that only himself and the lead diplomat could hear.

"We would never ask for anything so terrible" interrupted the lead Iranian diplomat.

"We will trade you a few attack ships, a non-nuclear submarine, the latest Chinese Mig's and all the small arms you desire and need, but we will not send any Chinese troops to Iran" announced the Premier after a moment of silence.

"Please note that we will not start shipping any military hardware until our Minister of Energy has agreed to an amount and a price for the oil, plus we will want some of the fungus cure along with any applicable scientific data so we may reproduce as much of the fungus cure as we need to" continued the Premier.

"Do not insult me with a story about how Iran does not have the 'amber' material or does not have a cure for the fungus. No fungus – no deal" added the Premier as the lead Iranian diplomat was going to speak.

"Just let me mention to you that China will survive without any help no matter what. We will suffer for many years, but we will regain our status as an important nation once again in the future. We will not be held hostage by anyone nor will we may any ransom" again the Premier added as the Iranian diplomats were about speak again. The lead Iranian diplomat announced that they would need to discuss the deal with both the Iranian President and the Ayatollah, and would give the Chinese government an answer within twenty-four hours.

The Iranian diplomats left and the Chinese Premier looked at his cabinet Ministers and announced "We must look out for China's interests, but I will not trust the Iranians". The Premier thanked all his Ministers for attending the meeting and asked the Minister for Foreign Affairs "Please call the US President and the Russian general in charge and ask them to reconsider their military plans and future advances within Iran".

"And ask them, If they will not leave Iran, what help could the Chinese People's Republic offer – Secretly of course" added the Premier as the Minister for Foreign Affairs was starting to leave.

"Yes Sir" snapped the Minister for Foreign Affairs as he quickly left the conference room to make phone calls to both Moscow and to Washington, D.C. The Premier had a big smile on his face as he left the conference room and told his Minister of National Defense "China can become immune from the ravages of the fungus as it devours the rest of the world and we can give Iran a taste of its own medicine when we start to negotiate not only with the Iranians, but also Russia and the United States at the same time".

Forty-Seven

Niagara Falls, New York – November 2005

While the Iranians and Chinese officials were meeting in Beijing, China, the United States Department of Homeland Security had reported stopping a group of Arabic speaking men trying to enter the United States from Canada across the border in Niagara Falls, New York. The Arabic men were from Saudi Arabia, Kuwait and Iraq and were all on different watch lists of having suspected ties to Al-Qaeda. The fact that the Arabic men were suspected terrorists was not as disturbing as what they had tried to bring into the United States. Each terrorist had hidden a couple of laboratory containers within their clothing with a unknown fungus looking substance within the laboratory containers. The border crossing was immediately closed and a red alert was issued for all border crossings into the United States. The suspected terrorists were taken into custody and the laboratory containers were sealed and were flown to the F.B.I. laboratory in Washington, D.C. for testing and identification. The Department of Homeland Security had already increased the alert status along the borders from a yellow to an orange alert status immediately after the Iranian President threatened to release the deadly fungus in North America by giving it to suspected Al-Qaeda terrorists.

The substance taken from the suspected terrorists in Niagara Falls, New York was quickly tested and was determined to be only a common household mold that usually grows on bread. This border incident was a giant wake-up call for Americans to again get tough on the borders and along our sea coasts and ports before the deadly fungus can be released into the United States. US President Baker arranged a impromptu meeting at the White House with the President of Mexico and the Prime Minister of Canada. President Baker wanted to discuss ways to prevent Al-Qaeda or any other terrorist from entering both Canada and Mexico before being able to travel to the United States borders. President Baker noted that the spread of the fungus would not be limited to United States territory and borders, but would be spread by birds, animals and people to both Mexico and Canada no matter where the terrorists released the fungus. All three North American leaders agreed to toughen up their respective borders and sea ports to try to eliminate any terrorists from entering North America.

US President Baker then met with his Secretary of Homeland Security and the Secretary of State to discuss additional travel and border security measures. The President was hopeful for answers from the leaders of Canada and Mexico, but has decided that Americans must protect America and we also cannot depend on other nations to help, but must only depend on ourselves and can only hope that any fungus released in Canada or Mexico does not travel north or south into the United States.

The President then made a bold and historic decision concerning travel to the United States and the borders. The President scheduled a prime time news conference and appeared on National Television to announce to the country his new and volatile plan.

"Good Evening" The President announced.

"I interrupt your regular television viewing with an important mandate that I have implemented as of Six o'clock Eastern Standard Time this evening. I have enacted this Presidential mandate under the United States Homeland Security act that followed the events of 9/11. As of this evening I have ordered the temporary closure of all border crossings to all foreign travelers, including any United States citizen that is traveling from a known or suspected country associated with Al-Qaeda or other terrorist groups. This President mandate also includes all incoming overseas flights and cruise lines operating from outside our national borders. I have also notified all government agencies abroad of this mandate and hope the effected travelers are taken off these flights and if not, we will order these persons to be either quarantined or sent back on another out going flight. I know this is a hardship for many citizens and to the commercial airlines, but this action is warranted based on recent border events and the threats made by the government of Iran. I know this policy may be a politically incorrect course of action, especially towards our own citizens that originate from or have visited Arabic and Muslim nations. Regardless of the insensitivity and grief this may cause thousands of people, my cabinet and myself agree that these measures are needed to try and prevent the release, either accidental or an act of terror of any deadly fungus which now threatens both the continents of Europe and Asia. I will not take any questions at this time. God Bless and Good night" expressed the President as the television stations switched to their respective anchors to comment on the President's surprise mandated policy.

After President Baker's speech many world leaders had publicly expressed their anger over the United States border closings, especially the government of Mexico and several European nations. Several hundred mass demonstrations were held around the world denouncing the United States and President Baker. As of nine o'clock A.M. the following morning, several European, Asian and African nations had closed their respective borders to all Americans and have prohibited any more travel within their countries by any American citizens. Also several hundred public demonstrations were held in cities across the United States, both denouncing and applauding the President's mandate. In addition to the demonstrations, many prominent American's of Arab descent along with Arabic businessmen and politicians have denounced their United States citizenship and have vowed to leave the United States as soon as possible. To add insult to injury, a couple of organized white hate groups had targeted foreign owned gas stations and convenience stores with vandalism and destruction of property. The most vile act caused by the recent violence was the killing of a Dunkin Donuts manager, not by a known Aryan nation member, but by a group of black Iraqi war veterans because the India born manager had expressed his dislike of the new US travel and border policy mandate by hanging a "no internment for Muslims" sign in his donut shop window.

After the United States had officially closed its borders and issued the travel ban, CIA intelligence officials had reported that Iran had apparently tried to provide fungus specimens to Al-Qaeda and other terrorists. This conclusion was based on several more failed attempted to bring in fake fungus specimens across both the Canadian and Mexican borders and into the United States. The attempted border crossings had coincided with CIA intelligence sources that claimed Iran had proposed a deal with China in exchange for giving China the fungus cure. This information was given credibility when United States and Russian officials received phone calls from the Chinese government requesting that the Americans and Russians stop their military incursions into Iranian territory. The Russian response was an immediate "no" with the Russian General Baranov quoted as saying "We will use more troops and more extreme measures against the Iranians for each day we loose more plant and animal life to the fungus". US President Bakers response was more measured, but the answer was still "no".

Forty-Eight

Tehran, Iran – Late November 2005

When the latest terrorist group was apprehended at the Mexico

border crossing near Brownsville, Texas, a United States F-18 fighter jet had

targeted an Iranian communications facility in central Tehran, but the high

explosive bomb had accidentally hit part of a hospital complex. The death

toll as reported by the Iranian President was over two hundred civilians

killed including women and children. US President Baker had expressed his

concern and sorrow for the civilian deaths, but had also questioned the

death toll that was provided by the Iranian President. President Baker also

told reporters at his weekly news conference "Although we regret any loss

of life, especially civilian casualties, this is combat and sometimes terrible

things may happen during war. Let me remind you that all Iran has to do is

turn over the 'amber' and the fungus cure along with any experimental data

and we will immediately cease all military operations within Iranian territory

and would start the process of leaving Iranian territory at once".

Shortly after President Baker's news conference, the Iranian

President had convened his own televised news conference covered by only

Al-Jezerra TV. The President of Iran had all of the Arabic and Iranian reporters convene outside his temporary offices located within Tehran's central Mosque that he was using for his day to day business. There were only a handful of western reporters at the Iranian news conference, since most of the international media had already left Iran. Once all the cameras and microphones were set up by the Iranian Minister of Media Affairs, the Iranian President stated "The United States and Russia have again threatened Iran, then they have illegally entered Iranian territory, then they have started killing our women and children. All Iran has done was to study and produce scientific experiments using our great and talented scientists to try and help the rest of the world rid itself of this terrible fungus. We did not create the fungus nor did we spread the fungus, but the Americans and the Russians would like the world to believe that we are responsible for all the world's woes including the deadly fungus. The Iranian people believe this fungus is punishment to Russia and other countries for its defamation towards Islam. Because of their impurity, the Americans are now demanding that we help them along with their impure puppets in Russia. They want our help while defaming the prophet Mohammed, then by killing defenseless Iranian women and children. As President of Iran and with the blessing of the Ayatollah, we demand that the Americans and Russians leave Iranian and Muslim lands at once. If they do not start leaving at once, the peaceful government of Iran will offer to pay anyone a ten million dollar reward to help bring the devils fungus to the infidels of the United States"

The Iranian President concluded his speech, but not before making his threat and reward against the United States again, especially calling on the poor people of Mexico to rise up against the imperialist government of the United States. The Iranian President told the Mexican people to rise up and take back your rightful territory and that they had been the door mat for the Americans for far too long.

Forty-Nine

Washington, D.C. – late November 2005

With the United States military on the highest alert status since 9/11 and the military already stretched thin because of Afghanistan, Iraq and now Iran, President Baker has had no choice but to call up all active and inactive military reservists and National Guard. The President has also requested Congress to quickly schedule a bill and a vote to authorize the military to gradually bring back the draft. The additional troops and support personnel would be needed to replenish positions of normal duty military troops with United States domestic bases requested the President. Also since the new Iranian threat the President had ordered twenty thousand troops to guard the Mexican-United States border and another ten thousand troops to proceed to key areas along the northern border with Canada.

President Baker convened another emergency meeting with the Joint Chiefs of Staff, high ranking military personnel and state department personnel. This was the third emergency meeting in as many days since the border closures. Because of the urgent crisis, the President was only operating on a couple of hours of sleep each day and growing more tired with each crisis. After the emergency meeting President Baker officially issued a response to the Iranian President current threat, again going though the Saudi Arabian government and not announcing anything though the media. The US Presidents message read "The United States takes the Iranian threat seriously and again must insist that Iran turn over all the fungus data it has including the 'amber' specimen. The United States considers the current Iranian threat an act of war and will proceed accordingly with all necessary military action needed to neutralize this current threat. We will be glad to meet with the Iranian government to peacefully end this current crisis, but please note that we will not negotiate what is rightfully the world's cure. And again, please note that if any spread or release of the fungus occurring in the United States that may be linked or contributed to any Iranian action, will automatically result in the most extreme consequences that the United States can bring to bear on the entire nation of Iran, not just a few military bases. Please consider your actions very carefully at this time"

As the Saudi Arabian King read the letter from the United States President, he quickly summoned the Saudi Arabian ambassador to Iran. He then asked the Saudi ambassador to relay the message to the Iranian government and then asked the ambassador to proceed to pack up all his work and for himself and his staff to leave Iran as quickly as possible. The Saudi ambassador asked the Saudi Arabian King if everything was OK and asked him what was so terrible in Iran that he should leave at once. The

Saudi Arabian King turned and told his ambassador "I feel this crisis with Iran has gone too far and that soon the sand of Iran may be turned into glass".

Fifty

Beijing, China – Late November 2005

After a brief telephone call with the Iranian President, the Chinese Minister for Foreign Affairs contacted his boss, China's Premier, about the latest Iranian threat to the United States and he also told the Premier about the Iranian military losing both their main port loading facilities and their northern pipeline. The Minister told the Premier that American military forces controlled all port facilities and the Russian's had taken control of Iran's northern oil pipeline. The Chinese Premier was informed that no oil could be shipped out of Iran unless the Americans or Russians permitted it. The Premier told his Minister for Foreign Affairs to immediately call the United States Embassy and have the US ambassador to China come to this office as soon as possible.

The United States Ambassador to China luckily had just returned to Beijing from a short visit back in the United States to visit his family Before he could unpack his luggage, he had received the phone call from the Chinese Minister for Foreign Affairs requesting an urgent meeting with him at the Peoples Palace. The Minister told the US ambassador to be prepared to contact President Baker because he would be meeting other members of the Chinese cabinet along with the Premier himself.

The US ambassador to China had been to the Chinese Ministry building or commonly known as the Peoples Palace before, but he had never been allowed near the tenth floor. The tenth floor contained the Premier's private offices and his Beijing apartment. The US ambassador and the Minister for Foreign Affairs were escorted in the main elevator to the tenth floor by a RSP guard, an elite unit of the military police from within the People's Army. Without words the RSP guard held open the elevator door and pointed for the Minister and the US ambassador to proceed down the hall. The hallway of the tenth floor was highly decorated with ancient Chinese scrolls and artwork from the Ming dynasty along with large jade sculptures inset in wall nooks every twenty feet on each side of the hallway. The US ambassador was impressed with the amount of art and decoration by the head of the Chinese communist government. The Minister for Foreign Affairs was also impressed, since he had only been allowed on the tenth floor one time since becoming a Minister. They walked to the end of the hall and the Chinese Minister knocked on the massive decorative wood door three times until a very large Chinese guard appeared, opened the massive door and asked the Minister "What do you need Minister, The Premier is a very busy man"

"The Premier is expecting me along with our guest the US ambassador" replied the Minister. The massive door shut loudly and then in a couple of minutes they were escorted into the office waiting area of the Premier of China by the same large Chinese guard. After a few more minutes of waiting, the guard opened the inner office door and waved the Minister and US ambassador into the Premier's office which appeared to be an ordinary businessman's office, minus any frills such as a couch or a luxurious desk.

The Premier's office was relatively small and only contained a couple of metal file cabinets, a small conference table and a couple of unmatched chairs along with a large but plain desk. Seated behind the desk was the Chinese Premier dressed in a blue business suit with what appeared to be bifocal type glasses. The Chinese Premier gestured for the Minister and the US ambassador to please me seated into the unmatched chairs. He offered them something to drink and a cigarette, and after they declined he spoke in broken, but good English "Thank you Ambassador for coming on such short notice"

"My job here in China is to speak with you or your staff whenever needed, Premier" replied the US ambassador in perfect Chinese.

"This conflict between Iran with the United States and Russia has gone too far. We are not judging who is wrong or who is right, we would just like to see an end to the hostilities and we would gladly offer any assistance to mediate an end to this war" announced the Premier, wanting to get to the point. The US ambassador reiterated the United States and Russia's stance concerning the return of the "amber" along with all the supporting scientific data, including the alleged fungus cure.

"In all due respect Premier, we are fighting not just for the people of Russia and the United States, but we are fighting for the world, including China. If this fungus continues to spread like it has already, the end of mankind and most of the world's wildlife could be wiped out in a few years" added the US ambassador.

"Mr. Ambassador, your career is based on preventing wars and conflict. There must be a diplomatic way to solve this crisis before more people die and before additional economic burdens threaten the entire world" expressed the Premier as he sighed. The US ambassador expressed to the Chinese Premier that he would pass on the Chinese request to the US President. Then surprisingly the Premier asked the US ambassador to please call the President now and relay this request. The Premier then politely offered the US ambassador his private and secure phone line to make the call to Washington, D.C.

After briefly explaining to President Baker the Chinese Premier's request, the President asked to be put on the phone directly with the Chinese Premier. The Premier then placed the phone down and switched it to a conference call and then spoke in English "I hope we did not wake you President Baker".

"No you did not wake me Premier, but I would take your call at anytime" responded the US President.

"Premier, in response to your request, we have asked the Iranians for meetings upon meetings, diplomacy upon diplomacy and all we have received are threats and accusations from the Iranian President. This conflict with the Iranians could end tomorrow, if they would simply return what is rightfully the Russian's, I mean, what is rightfully the world's 'amber'. We could then begin to eliminated the fungus and we could start to put the effected countries and world economies back together" added

President Baker. The Chinese Premier acknowledged to the US President that in principle the Chinese government was not against the United States or Russia and that the Chinese government also does not trust the Iranians, but the Premier added "But, this conflict has created a great economic burden on the Chinese people, one that could completely disrupt and destroy any of our current gains we have accomplished in competing within the world market place and sustaining our current industry and agriculture".

"As you know we are the largest importers of oil in the world and we receive about seventy-five percent of our oil from the Middle East" announced the Premier as he had started sweating slightly.

"Just prior to your conflict with Iran, we had signed a trade agreement with the Iranian government to buy all of our imported oil from the Iranian state oil company. About seventy percent of the oil would be shipped by tankers loaded at the Iranian port city of Abadan and the remaining oil would be pumped from a nearby pipeline along Iran's northern border" added the Chinese Premier.

The US ambassador was good at reading people and could tell the Premier was lying, but now was not the time to mention it. The Premier continued "We have received news from Tehran that both the oil loading facility in Abadan and the northern pipeline is no longer controlled by the Iranian government"

"What is it you are requesting, Premier?" asked President Baker.

"China needs this oil to survive. We must start receiving the promised oil within a couple of weeks or we face both a economic and humanitarian disaster. President Baker, you must allow our tankers to be loaded at Abadan and you must speak to the Russians to allow the oil to start flowing again within Iran's northern pipeline" requested the Premier as he stood up and started pacing back and forth.

"Premier, Abadan is a very hostile area, a war time area and" President Baker responded before the Chinese Premier interrupted.

"Then the United States must stop the war and allow the Iranians to come back and start loading oil"

"Premier, I wish it was that simple. We have not interfered with any Iranian pipelines, oil fields or refineries, but this port was being used to supply both weapons and ammunition to Iranian troops" President Baker continued.

"You have put me in a very delicate and dangerous situation. We need the Iranian oil to survive and the Iranians have the oil that we need. If we do not start receiving the promised tankers full of oil, we must take action to obtain and protect this vital resource that China needs to survive" responded the Premier after taking a deep breath.

"Are you threatening military action against United States and Russian troops and naval personnel? If so, we would like to continue talks with you to try and prevent any hostilities between the nations of the United States and China. We do not want to enter into a conflict with China, but the United States, Russia and the world needed the fungus specimen, cure and the associated data, no matter what the cost" President Baker asked the Premier.

"Premier, we would open the port of Abadan tomorrow and start loading your tankers even if we had to man the pumps with our soldiers if necessary, but the Iranians have been sabotaging both the port and some of their own oil field areas to prevent the United States from obtaining the oil.

They could also be destroying the oil infrastructure to bring the Chinese government into this conflict. We believe it is the latter, since our soldiers have captured some Iranian saboteurs and they have confessed to destroying enough oil pumping facilities so that China would enter the war and help them destroy the United States and Russia" added President Baker. The Chinese Premier looked as if he was going to pass out and then he asked the President "If we helped persuade the Iranians to stop sabotaging the oil pumps and pipelines, would the United States open the port of Abadan to Chinese tankers?"

"Yes, as long as China does not use the sale of Chinese tanks and aircraft to Iran as a persuasion tool" replied President Baker.

"I assure you President Baker, China is not a friend of Iran and if we can keep the oil supply intact, we can be of great assistance to the United States" stated the Premier as he regained his composure and wiped the sweat from his forehead. The Chinese Premier and President Baker then thanked each other for showing restraint and diplomacy under trying conditions. Before the Premier hung up the secure phone call to Washington with President Baker, he asked the President to hold while he thanked his Minister for Foreign Affairs and the US ambassador to China, and then showed them out of his office. The Premier picked up the secure phone and told President Baker "We will of course pay you what we had promised to pay Iran for the oil, or we could trade the oil for certain scientific exchanges".

The Chinese Premier then secretly told the US President that the Chinese government had been given a small sample of the fungus cure by the Iranians, but before the deal could be completed for the Chinese tanks and ammunition. Now the Iranian government is withholding the data and scientists needed to create more of the fungus cure and a way to deliver the cure on a massive level.

The two world leaders from the only remaining superpowers had agreed to share scientists and scientific data to try and perfect the fungus cure. The Chinese also agreed to assist the United States and Russia with any intelligence gathering they could obtain from Tehran through their diplomats and oil people as long as they were not targeted by US or Russian bombs or troops.

The once closed and feared society of the communist government of China was now in a position to help and become a leader amongst the world nations by delivering the fungus cure throughout the world. Some Chinese communist leaders would be worried about this influx of westerners and western ideas, but some secretly welcomed the western scientists and the western way of life, among the secret officials who wanted to change the communist regime in China was also the top leader, the Premier himself.

Fifty-One

USS Orlando, somewhere in the Persian Gulf – late November 2005

On Board the US aircraft carrier the USS Orlando, a joint Russian and United States commando unit had just finished with all their weapons preparation and had attended their final intelligence briefing before mission readiness. The United States Delta Force commander in charge of US forces had also received a coded message from the Pentagon stating that the US had information that the Iranians may have given a sample of the fungus cure to the Chinese in exchange for weapons. This coded message also mentioned that the "amber" and most of the scientific data was still known to be hidden in the secret Iranian laboratory facility located deep within Mt. Demavend outside of Tehran, but that some of the fungus cure and its data may be with Iran's chief government scientist who now travels exclusively with and stays near the Iranian President.

With this latest intelligence, the joint commando unit's mission was still authorized to enter the secret Iranian laboratory facility outside of Tehran and obtain the "amber" specimen and all related data. Their orders were to shoot any hostile Iranian forces on sigh, but to try and capture any non-combat personnel, especially Iranian scientists. The main mission of the commando's was to capture the "amber", the fungus cure, data and any

scientific personnel. There were informed that both the Iranian military and

scientific lives were expendable to insure completion of the mission.

The joint Russian and US commando unit was once again made up

of several US Delta Force commandos, Russian Special Police, CIA agent

Danny McLean, US Scientist Dr. Max Hamilton and Russian Paleontologist

Dr. Boris Panov. As the commandos checked and rechecked their weapons,

which consisted of a Heckler & Koch MP-5 submachine gun with silencer, a

Beretta 9mm semi-automatic pistol and several knives. In addition to the

weapons, each commando carried a couple hundred rounds of ammunition

strapped and hidden over the United States Army's latest version of body

armor. The commandos and the scientists were all dressed in black uniforms

without any rank, insignia or identification of any kind. This group of

commandos, besides having proved themselves battle ready in previous

combat missions, all spoke Russian, English and Farsi – the official language

of Iran. The only weapons that Max Hamilton and Boris Panov carried were

the latest high speed small laptop computers that had special extended life

batteries and had satellite telephone with internet capability.

As the US and Russian commando unit was being escorted to the

aircraft carrier's main flight deck to their waiting Marine helicopter, a navy

flight deck officer approached the unit and asked to speak to Dr. Max

Hamilton. The remaining commando unit continued onto the helicopter where they loaded their weaponry and gear while Max opened a letter labeled "Top Secret from the desk of the President of the United States". Max read the letter out loud.

"Dr. Hamilton – Change of Plans. We have first hand knowledge that the Iranians have given a small sample of the fungus cure to the Chinese government. They shared this information with the United States because their agreement with Iran had ended before the Iranian scientists could show the Chinese government how to replicate the fungus cure into bulk quantities. The Chinese government was not given enough data and does not have enough knowledge about the fungus to establish a means to apply the fungus cure to the effected fungus areas". The letter then told Max Hamilton that Boris Panov and the commandos would be briefed about his absence and that another helicopter would take him directly to Bagdad, Iraq to a waiting private jet that would immediately take-off for Beijing, China.

Max was interrupted by the US Delta Force commander and Boris Panov, who was just told that Max was not going on the mission to Iran with them, but he was going to China instead. Boris Panov spoke briefly to Max "My dear friend, I hope you have better luck in China then we do. I fear the Iranians may be one step ahead of us again"

"Boris, I have the easy trip. I won't have people shooting at me, so please keep your head down and I'll meet up with you later to compare notes" replied Max. Boris was about to continue talking with Max Hamilton, but was hustled away to the waiting helicopter that would fly the commandos to the Iraqi/Iranian border and then into the unknown. Max then continued with the letter which continued "Max, you will meet up with some of the crew you had previously worked with in Russia when you land in Beijing. We know the Chinese government will assist you with whatever technology, equipment or people you request. Since our meeting and agreement with the Chinese government, they had received information that the fungus may have spread to some areas that surround Lake Tian Chi in the Xinjiang Uygur Autonomous region of China, which is north of the city of Urumqi. China now has many more reasons to help the United States and Russian".

Max then asked the Navy flight officer where he could destroy the letter. The Navy office took Max into the control tower area where he was able to destroy the letter just as he was summoned by another Navy flight deck officer to follow him on deck to his helicopter ride to Baghdad. Max quickly asked the Navy officer if he could call his family to let them know he as alright and that his plans had changed. The Navy officer helped him onto the waiting helicopter and told Max that he could call home once he landed in Baghdad.

Fifty-Two

Along the Mexican/United States Border – December 2005

Once the initial uproar over the United States decision to completely close the borders between the United States with Mexico and Canada, many other countries in both North and South America have also closed their borders and have also limited travel. Mexico had also reciprocated the United States border closure by placing almost half of its military force along Mexico's northern border and several thousand more troops along its southern border with Guatemala and Belize. This military border situation has created a hostile border between the United States and Mexico, not witnessed since the Spanish-American war in the early 1800's.

Some of the recent hostility started when a rumor was spread by one of Mexico's largest drug cartels. In order to create a diversion for its drug runners, the Mexican drug cartel had pad unsuspecting Mexicans to act as decoys for both large sums of money and food. The Mexican decoys were to be paid to enter the United States along the California border. The drug cartel had given each decoy a small metal box containing several clear bags of bread fungus with a letter written in Arabic. The drug cartel's plan would be to cross the border area near the area where the decoys were being detained, after an anonymous tip call was made to the United States military tipping them off of a possible fungus incursion. The hope by the drug cartel would be to create enough diversion and interference so that the drug runners could once again resume drug shipments into the United States. If this did not work, the Mexican and South American drug cartels would be out of business and the United States would be free of foreign drugs from South America for the first time in over a hundred years. This did not stop drug us altogether in the US, mainly because many Americans have started growing drug crops, especially since law enforcement was far and few in these times.

Further escalation of hostilities started when the Mexican decoys with the fake fungus and the drug runners tried to cross into California and were met with heavy US Army action. The Mexicans were picked up by special US radar and a squad of US Army Rangers riding in Humvees arrived at the border crossing just as the first group of ten Mexican decoys crossed into the United States. The Mexicans were immediately told over a PA system to stop, set down their packages and put their hands on their heads. By this time several additional squads of US Army troops had arrived at the border along with the second group of several Mexican decoys. The entire group of drug decoys were told a second time to place their packages on the ground and put their hands on their heads. Just as the second group of Mexican decoys were putting up their hands, a small group of drug cartel runners made an attempt to cross the border several hundred feet away but were spotted by a US Army Ranger in an open topped Humvee equipped with a fifty caliber machine gun on top. In an unfortunate chain of events, one of the Mexican drug decoys with the fake fungus felt light headed and started to sit down at the very same time a couple more drug runners tried crossing the border into the United States. A young and inexperienced Army Ranger officer thought one of the Mexican decoys was trying to open the metal boxes and the shooting started. When the shooting stopped, twenty four Mexicans were dead, seventeen were innocent decoys and seven were drug runners. After a quick response, a Army chemical weapons team arrived and it was determined that the metal containers contained nothing more than common bread mold.

President Baker called the Mexican President and expressed his condolences at the loss of life and offered his assistance to help in fighting these new drug cartel tactics. The Mexican President accepted the United States apology, but some Mexican government officials within the President's own government called for more than apologies including monetary payments to Mexico. Some radical Mexican officials went so far as to call out for military action against the United States and the eventual return of Mexican lands in Texas, Arizona, New Mexico and California. Most Mexican government officials along with most of the general population in Mexico were against such radical ideas and that this was brought on by the Iranian President, but some Mexicans thought the United States was a bully and had been taking Mexican land and had been creating poverty in Mexico for decades.

During the next few days several armed gangs consisting of Mexican military, police and drug cartel members have attempted several raids within the United States along border areas in Texas, Arizona and California. With the help of some of the Mexican border guards the gangs have been able to kidnap several United States troops and have threatened to kill them if the United States did not return the stolen Mexican lands. The gangs have also grown stronger due to the increase in poverty within Mexico along with continuing disapproval of the current Mexican government including the President. It has become common place for several gun fights to erupt each night along border areas between the Mexican gangs, Mexican military and the US Military.

The United States government was requested that the Mexican military take care of both the gangs and it's own renegade military and police on the Mexican side of the border or the United States military will send in both helicopter gun ships and light armored attack vehicles into Mexican territory to hunt down the gangs that are responsible for the attacks and kidnappings in order to keep Americans and the US border safe for all people, Mexican and American.

Fifty-Three

Russian Federation – March 2006

The world has become a much different place in just the last few
months since the discovery of the fungus. Especially hard hit has been the
continent of Asia with Russia and the Ukraine receiving most of the
devastation so far. With the previous farm and crop losses attributed to the
fungus, the loss has grown to nearly seventy percent of all farms within the
recent borders of Russia. Adding to Russia's farming woes is that with no
monetary compensation for farm losses or other relief help being offered to
fungus effected farms and farmers, many farmers have decided not to plant
any crops this year due to the fear that they would spend what money they
had left on seeds & fertilizer, just to have their crops killed off by the
spreading fungus, severe erosion or other mitigating factors. The loss of
farming in Russia was not estimated to be as high as ninety percent with
only the eastern most farming regions of Russia remaining unaffected

Adding to the crop loss in Russia was the loss of other plant life
and habitats in both southern Russia, up to and including many areas within
Siberia. Also included with the loss of plant life was many rare species of
Tundra plant species. Russian scientists believe the plant loss may be as high

as forty percent in Russia alone. Part of the vegetation and habitat loss was a direct result of the fungus killing particular plants, but a lot of the habitat and plant loss was attributed to massive earth erosion along rivers and streams, man made dikes and lagoons that were previously used for farming or were built to try and cut off the fungus spread. Also many plants were destroyed by insect pests that would have normally infested other native vegetation and crops, but now concentrated and consumed what plant life was left. Many species of plant life that is native to parts of Russia have disappeared from the face of the earth.

Besides Russia, the fungus has nearly wiped out all plant life within the Ukraine. In some parts of the Ukraine the surrounding once vibrant farms and forests that surrounded the countryside now resemble an eroded and barren landscape instead of the abundant fields and forests. The fungus has made the deadly Soviet Chernobyl nuclear accident seem like a minor problem.

Two other countries greatly affected by the fungus at this time are Kazakhstan and Mongolia. The country of Kazakhstan before the spread of the fungus had only about thirty five percent of its land to use as farming land and now that amount measures only fifteen percent since the spread of the fungus started killing off plant life. The fungus devastation has also been extremely hard on western Mongolia with nearly twenty five percent of the western grasslands destroyed. This has pushed Mongolian cattle farmers into less abundant grassland areas with cattle losses starting to add up. Some of the Mongolian cattlemen had been raising cattle in these areas for five hundred years. If the fungus continues to spread further east into Inner Mongolia, it may destroy all of the grasslands and farms west of the mighty Gobi Desert and thus adding thousands of acres of once rich grasslands to the already enormous size of the Gobi Desert. If the fungus continues to spread south and crosses the Altai Mountains, China's north western lands could be destroyed all the way to the Himalayan Mountains in Tibet.

Along with the loss of many species of plant life, recent surveys by the World Wildlife Federation have concluded that the once plentiful and lively Siberian Goose has possible become extinct. During the end of the mass killing undertaken by hunters and farmers of the Siberian Goose, wildlife biologists had been able to tag what they thought were the last known wild flock of Siberian geese just before they started their migration south from Siberia to their Caspian Sea nesting areas. Some of the geese were also injected with radio transmitter devises so that the wildlife biologists would be able to locate them with. As of early this Spring the World Wildlife Federation had not been able to locate any radio transmissions from the hidden transmitters and further investigation showed no evidence of any nesting activities near the goose's previous Caspian Sea nesting areas were discovered. The World Wildlife Federation had set up several checking and spotting stations located along the known

Siberian Goose migration route and so far this Spring not a single sighting of a Siberian Goose has occurred.

In addition to the Siberian Goose, as many as two hundred and fifty other bird and mammal species have become extremely endangered including the Siberian Tiger, Tundra Hawk, Russian Brown Bear and the Roe Deer. These birds and animals have previously been killed off by hunters and by farmers fearing the spread of the fungus. Several more animals have become endangered because most of their habitats have been destroyed by the fungus or by the severe erosion. The last estimate given by the World Wildlife Federation showed that nearly two million animals have been affected by the fungus so far and that as many as two hundred and fifty thousand animals could die before Fall if the spread of the fungus continued unabated and unchecked.

In addition to bird species that were not killed off by the loss of habitat or by the loss of food sources in Russia may have changed their migratory routes that once included a migration from western China through Russia or from southern Russia to Siberia. In order to find new food sources and habitats for nesting, many bird species have started to migrate to areas of southern Europe, but most alarming is that some species of birds only seen within Asia have been reported in both North and South America. This may help some Asian bird species survive, but could threaten and endanger may species of birds native to both North and South America.

The Asian birds could also spread new avian diseases, feed on already scare food supplies, inhabit native nesting areas or more horrific, could spread the fungus from Asia to North and South America. The World Wildlife Federation lists these new sightings as a very dangerous problem that is just as dangerous and foreboding as the increase in endangered animal life has been in Russia and other parts of Asia.

The world was approaching a apocalyptic and historic time with the possibility of nuclear war breaking out and the possible extinction of most plant and animal species, just like it was seventy five million years ago, except now the list of extinct animals could contain humans.

Fifty-Four

Iraqi/Iranian border – March 2006

As news crews follow US military forces into Iranian territory,

several news reports have been broadcast live stating that both United States

and Russian troops have advanced into Iranian territory in some cases as

close of eighty miles from the capitol city of Tehran. The quick advances by

Russian and US forces has been attributed to both a decrease in Iranian

counter attacks along with less frequent Iranian defensive positions and

because of the increased isolated and barren desert like territory the US

military now is traveling through on the way along their march to Tehran.

Several CIA intelligence reports given to the United States military

commanders have determined that the already depleted Iranian military

forces have withdrawn to populated cities and may have created a human

wall surrounding Tehran.

One of the prizes awarded to the United States Army during their

latest military advance was the capture of a large portion of oil wells located

in Iran's Karabi oil fields. According to top US military officials speaking to

the media, the only reason the US and Russian troops have not advance any

further towards Iran's capital city of Tehran was the fear that the Iranian government would completely destroy the "amber", fungus cure and any associated data they have if the United States cornered them or the Iranian government had to admit defeat or surrender. Both Russian and US Intelligence sources have been quoted as saying "Iran's President and Ayatollah would rather destroy the world then admit defeat to people they consider to be 'infidels'". Also the Ayatollah may believe that this possible end of the world scenario and crisis would bring the return of the Prophet Mohammed to rule a new Islamic world. On the other side of the world, several Evangelistic churches in the United States have started speaking out about their belief that this is indeed World War III and that the world would soon be over and Jesus Christ would return.

The destruction of the "amber" and fungus cure were not the only reasons the United States and Russian troops had stopped advancing towards Tehran. They were also waiting for a secret commando raid to advance upon Mt. Demavend to retrieve the "amber" and fungus cure and hoped that the mission was successful.

There has been a renewed cooperation between China and the United States, including the arrival of several top US scientists including Max Hamilton who would be helping the Chinese try to develop additional amounts of the fungus cure previously given to them by the Iranians. And if they are successful, they would need to develop a means to apply the fungus cure to the affected areas in front of the rapidly spreading fungus. Also helping fuel the recent teamwork and cooperation with China was the promise of cheap Iranian oil, supplied by the United States, not by the Iranian government. The Iranian oil would now be loaded into Chinese tankers by United States Army troops, not by Iranian oil technicians.

Because of the latest military events in Iran, China has notified the Iranian President that China has been informed that both Russian and US troops now have control of Iran's main port facilities, their only large diameter pipeline located in northern Iran and now US troops have taken control of most of the oil wells located in the Karabi oil fields. In a secret communication issued from China's Premier to the President and Ayatollah of Iran, the Chinese Premier stated "Iranian forces must cease all military attacks on oil facilities and stop any sabotage of its previously owned oil facilities. China's deal with the Iranian government concerning arms for oil is hereby terminated. China has now made a new deal with the United States and Russia for the oil in exchange for China's help in persuading your government to hand over the 'amber', fungus cure and scientific data to either US military personnel or to the Chinese ambassador to Iran. If the government of Iran does not immediately arrange for a hand over of the 'amber' and cure, China will assist the United States and Russia in whatever way that is requested".

After reading the Chinese communication, the Iranian President became so angry and irate that he smashed several irreplaceable and priceless ancient Persian vases that had taken him years to collect. The Iranian President after he cooled down for a moment quickly met with the Ayatollah and his ruling Iranian cabinet and had scheduled a press conference for the afternoon that he hoped would be broadcast throughout the world.

Inside his make shift office which was hidden inside a Mosque located in central Tehran, the President of Iran looked both angry and tired as he read a prepared statement on Al-Jezeera television which had been set-up to broadcast worldwide through CNN. The President of Iran announced "The peaceful people of the Islamic Republic of Iran have been under attack by the infidels of the United States and Russia, yet the world has not come to help the innocent people of Iran nor has there even been any major condemnation against these infidels. No call for arms or even a strong warning has been uttered from the puppet governments of Saudi Arabia or Egypt. And now, the Chinese government has cancelled a previously committed deal for oil that was made in good faith by my government and China. They have now threatened to side with the infidels to help rape and pillage our nation along with our sovereignty for our land and for our oil. The government of Iran will announce for the last time our plea for all foreign troops, especially Russians and Americans to leave the territory of Iran immediately. If not we will commence in the destruction of any 'amber', any cure and all scientific data including the relocation and silencing of any scientists that had worked on the experiments. This is Iran's final warning". In addition to threatening to destroy the world's only hope of stopping the fungus, but the Iranian President had also called Israel and had threatened to launch hidden missiles containing nerve gas into Israel.

If the United States and Russian commando team are not successful in retrieving the "amber" and fungus cure located in Mt. Demavend near Tehran, then the world will like be facing World War III. United States President Baker, Russian General Baranov, China's Premier and another dozen world leaders have linked up by telephone, the internet and by video conference to discuss what to do if the "amber" and the fungus cure is destroyed by the Iranian government.

Fifty-Five

Brownsville, Texas – March 2006

The United States and most of the rest of the western hemisphere have continued a very tight closed door border policy, especially along the Mexican and United States border and along populated border areas with Canada. This unpopular US border policy has been made even more unpopular by and including any travelers who either originated from or may have traveled through so-called terrorist countries or countries with terrorist ties. This policy has created hostilities from Arab Americans who now cannot travel to visit relatives nor can their relatives visit them in the United States.

Because of the Iranian million dollar fungus bounty against the United States, the United States government has completely closed the border between the United States and Mexico. This measure was enacted to try and prevent any attempted release or spread of the fungus supplied by the Iranian government or from other terrorist organizations and also to decrease the amount of violence that has erupted towards US citizens living near the border crossings.

Since the new border closures and security measures, many demonstrations have erupted in at least ten major cities from Miami to Seattle denouncing the new US border and immigration policies. Many demonstrators have accused President Baker of being racist towards people of Arabic and Mexican descent. US President Baker upon hearing the latest news about the mass demonstrations held a press conference at the White House officially announce his new border and immigration policies and try to explain the new policies to the rest of the nation and the world. After a short fifteen minute prepared statement which the President read which he outlined as the temporary border and immigration policy. President Baker then opened the press conference to questions.

"Mr. President – Andy from MSNBC – concerning the entry of travelers from terrorist nations. Is there a list of these countries and/or governments?"

"The list is updated daily. It is published daily by the State Department on its Watch List" replied the President.

"Mr. President, Karen of Newsweek – What is the rule, if a US citizen accidentally enters one of these terrorist countries and now wants to come home?"

"If you are traveling abroad, which is very restrictive due to the fungus, you should educate yourself as to your destinations and travels. Some exceptions will be made, but that is up to the State Department, but generally the door will be closed" responded the President in very serious tone.

"But, Mr. President this hardly seems fair to a US citizen just trying to visit relatives and" the Newsweek reporter continued before being cut off by President Baker.

"Karen, has Newsweek been to Russia or the Ukraine lately. If not, go look at the devastation caused by the spread of the fungus and let me know how else we going to counter the Iranian threats"

"Jim Barnes from CBS Mr. President – Do you think maybe your staff and our other elected officials maybe overreacting to the fungus threat to our own crops?"

"Besides feeding ourselves, the United States still ships massive amounts of food aid to Africa and we now ship massive amounts of food to over half of Russia and most of the Ukrainian refugees. The world cannot afford for the fungus to spread to the United States or to South and Central America by any means" offered the President.

"One last question before I go" announced President Baker.

"Juan from the Mexico Ciudad newspaper. Is the border between Mexico and the United States even able to be entirely protected and patrolled with this new closure policy and what happens to any Mexican nationals that are here now, including myself?"

"I have ordered five thousand troops to be deployed along the border to assist the US border patrol and we will evaluate the number of troops as needed. As far as any Mexican citizen living or working here in the United States at this time either legal or not is welcome to stay or you may go back, but after today the border is closed and I mean no disrespect to you, Juan, but if go back to Mexico tonight, tomorrow you are not welcome to come back" President Baker answered as he thanked the press and quickly left the press conference.

Many large demonstrations have been held in almost every major US city and many worldwide cities since President Baker's press conference about the US border closures. Some of the protests and demonstrations have begun to turn violent with many clashes between anti-immigration groups, pro-isolationists and among both Arabic and Mexican protesters. The violence first started with an increase in rhetoric and an increase of inflammatory language shown on protest signs from all the different groups involved. Many Arabic and Mexican grouped started with signs that read "The United States is racist" and "The US would not be the US without us". The anti-immigration groups started with signs that read "Go Home – This is America" and "If you don't like the United States, then just leave". The tone and potential violence from all the different groups of protesters reached a peak when signs started to read "American's are racist pigs" to "Go Home Wet-Back" and "Go Home Towel Head"

"The protests and demonstrations have seed many minor skirmishes between the pro-isolationist groups which consist of as many black Americans as white member that are clashing with mostly Mexican protesters. These minor skirmishes amounted to little more than a lot of shouting and some minor pushing, each time they were quickly broken up and dispersed by local riot police.

The violence escalated out of control when a large group of Mexican men which numbered around one thousand were protesting near the Astrodome in Houston, Texas. As the Mexican protesters were chanting "Down with America" and other chants, a large counter demonstration of around five hundred black and white protesters were heading for the Astrodome to confront the group of Mexican protesters. Before additional riot police could arrive at the site, a few Mexican protesters threatened the pro-isolationist group with violence. As the words and gestures escalated, a couple of black pro-isclationist protesters approached the Mexican group and told them to get on a bus and go back south to Mexico. At this time a couple of other Mexican protesters shouted back "Go back to Africa, Niggers" and then came the baseball bats, chains, fists and knives as the two groups proceeded to fight in the parking lot of the Astrodome. The pro-isolationist group was out numbered two to one and they had decided to turn back towards central Houston, but the Mexican group had vengeance on their minds and proceeded to fight with death and injury to police, pro-isolationist protestors along with other Mexicans before the violence and rioting was dispersed by the arrival of a mechanized company of Texas National Guard troops. The outcome of the clash between the protestors and police resulted in ten dead including two Mexicans, along with over one hundred people injured. The other outcome was the public outcry towards Mexican Americans within mainstream America and especially from black inner city young people. This incident was the worst deadly public act of disobedience since the Kent State protest over the Vietnam War.

Because of the increased violence between protesting groups, the President had declared a temporary law stating that any protest or demonstration over twenty people would be illegal. The President also declared that the United States government would not stand for any retaliation towards Mexicans, African Americans, Whites, Asian or any other ethnic background and that any racist crimes would be punished to the fullest extent of the law.

The additional fallout of that Spring day in Houston, Texas resulted in many Mexican and other ethnic businesses being boycotted or even burned, looted or both. These acts continued with an increase in violence towards Mexican Americans. This recent violence may have been a prelude to the start of possible civil war in the United States. This new civil war would not be between blacks and whites like many white hate groups had predicted, but between black and white Americans fighting against Mexican and Arab Americans and nationalities.

Fifty-Six

With a heavy concentration of border patrol agents and US Army

troops located along the United States and Mexican border and with only a

slight increase in border guards along mostly populated areas separating

Canada and the United States, another fake fungus attack was attempted by

terrorists. Four Arabic Al-Qaeda linked terror suspects were going to try

crossing the Canadian border with the United States again. This time the

terrorist suspects were going to attempt to cross into the United States from

Canada through an unpopulated and remote wilderness area known as

Waterton Lakes National Park in Canada and Glacier National Park in the

United States. If not for a curious and suspicious Canadian park guide who

had notified authorities, then the four terror suspects may have crossed into

the United States or would been overcome by the rough and remote Alberta

and Montana wildernesses.

The four terror suspects had previously entered Canada through

Vancouver under student visas to study engineering at the University of

British Columbia about a year earlier. The terror suspects had remained

anonymous until a couple of weeks ago when they had all abruptly stopped going to classes, left the university and traveled to the city of Calgary in Alberta. Once in Calgary, they had secretly met with their Al-Qaeda contact in the basement of a non-descript Mosque located in the poor and ethnic area of Calgary. At this meeting, they were given maps along with the fake fungus containers. They then traveled from Calgary to the small town of Cardston in Alberta, where they purchased backpacks, tents and other camping and food supplies. It was when they attempted to obtain backcountry camping permits for hiking in Waterton Lakes National Park that they started to raise suspicion.

When the terrorist inquired about purchasing backcountry permits from a local guide and supply store, one of the local guides started asking them some friendly routine general questions in order to obtain the permits for their trip.

"How long do you intend to hike and camp in Waterton Lakes?" asked the guide. Two of the terror suspects answered at the same time, but with two different answers, one answered three days and the other answered a week.

"Do you have enough winter gear since it is still very cold this time of year and do you have enough supplies for a week?" the guide then asked. The oldest terror suspect replied that they would be just fine. The guide then proceeded to notify them about a couple of trails that were closed due to rock slides and avalanche dangers. During the guide's routine questioning and advise he noticed that the four terror suspects did not look as if they could last one day in the wilderness let alone spend a week, plus they appeared not to pay much attention to his advise until he mentioned the two southern trails that lead into Glacier National Park in the United States were closed and had been blocked and marked with warning signs. The guide also told them that these trails were occasionally patrolled by the US National Park Service along with Border Patrol agents, but those areas were still so remote that you would not know whether you were in Canada or the United States.

As the guide finished his comments about the US trail closures, he noticed the oldest Arabic man, probably the leader of the terror suspects briefly smile and nod to the other three men. The Cardston guide then told them that the permits would be available the following day probably after 11:00 AM as two of the terror suspects then thanked the guide. As the four Arabic men left the store and proceeded down the main street in Cardston, the quick thinking guide ran out of the door and called out to the Arabic men "If the permits arrive sooner, where can I contact you to let you know"

"We are staying at the Cardston Inn" the terrorist leader replied. He did not worry about anyone in this little Canadian mountain town and just thought the guide was being friendly, after all this was Canada. After the four terror suspects were out of sight the guide went back into the store and called the local office of the Canadian Mounted Police located in Fort Macleod about forty five minutes away.

The still and cold night in the sleepy little town of Cardston, Alberta was shattered by a very loud bang announcing the arrival by the anti-terrorist branch of the Mounted Police. The quiet night was broken and the cold intensified by the arrival of a Police helicopter followed by breaking glass as the night was lit up by large light plants located on the bottom of the helicopter. The Canadian anti-terror team repelled from the helicopter and crashed through the window where the terrorists were sleeping. The four terror suspects were totally surprised and were detained without any incident in their upper quest room of the Cardston Inn. When searching the terrorists quest room, the Mounted Police agents found two metal containers about eight inches long and about four inches in diameter with Arabic type writing on them. The writing was later determined to be Farsi, which is spoken in Iran. Within each metal container was a compartment that looked as if it could contain some type of plant or animal life, since the compartment was sealed, climate controlled by batteries and the entire container appeared to be rugged enough to take some abuse. Along with the metal containers, several maps and literature of Glacier National Park and Yellowstone National Park were found in the terrorist's guest room.

The four Al-Qaeda linked terror suspects were then transported to Calgary by helicopter and were then interrogated by an official of the anti-terror branch of the Mounted Police with the help of a United States FBI special agent who had flown up to Calgary from Missoula, Montana. The information the interrogators needed and wanted was the location of their final United States or Canadian target and more importantly whether or not the terrorists had hidden a real fungus sample, had already released some fungus or if this was just another fake fungus attempt. After several hours of questioning and laboratory results of the container contents, the agents concluded that the terrorists had not hidden or spread any fungus and this was just another test run to see if the terror group could make it into the United States through the Waterton and Glacier National Park wilderness to try and make it to the world famous Yellowstone National Park. The FBI and Mounted Police agents hoped that this information was one hundred percent correct and that these terror suspects were not just decoys while another Al-Qaeda group was attempting a fungus attack at this very moment.

After another couple of hours of more intense questioning, the four terror suspects were then locked up in a isolation area within the Calgary city jail, while the Mounted Police and FBI agents went to prepare for a raid of a nearby local Mosque.

Fifty-Seven

Kazvin, Iran – March 2006

The Russia and United States joint commando unit that was made up of US Delta Force troops, Russian Special Federal Police, Boris Panov the Russian Paleontologist and CIA agent Danny MacLean were transported from Baghdad, Iraq to a US forward position located in Iran in a couple of Blackhawk helicopters. The helicopter flights were secretly taken at night to avoid detection by Iraqi Al-Qaeda operatives who had set up a very good spy network within Iraq for the Iranian government. The Russian and American commandos once at the US forward location would obtain additional intelligence reports, get some rest and food while at the US forward position known as camp K near the city of Kazvin, about a hundred miles west of Tehran.

The commandos after a little rest and a light meal were requested to board waiting Blackhawk helicopters promptly at nine o'clock PM, just after dark so they could be transported to their target, the secret Iranian military base located near Mt. Demavend outside of Tehran, Iran. The commando's final objective was not the actual taking of the secret Iranian military base or the eighteen thousand foot summit of Mt. Demavend, but a secret laboratory facility hidden five hundred feet inside the mountain. Through a reliable Iranian informant, the only way into the laboratory facility was through the Iranian military base.

Just as Danny MacLean, Boris Panov and the rest of the commando unit was lifting off the Iranian desert floor, a massive air strike was taking place just ahead of the commando raid. Several stealth bombers, fighter jets, Russian field artillery units and a couple dozen cruise missiles had hit radar and military targets in and around Tehran, including many strikes near the secret Iranian military base. The purposes of the air strikes were to soften any resistance and to take out any remaining radar sites that may have been repaired or were still active around Tehran. The United States and Russian military hit these Iranian sites again so that the Blackhawk helicopters would not be tracked on their arrival outside the Mt. Demavend military base.

During the flight from the US forward position called Camp K near Kazvin, Iran, Danny MacLean told the commando leaders about his latest intelligence briefing that was gathered from CIA and military headquarters. Danny had pulled aside the leader of the US Delta Force, a large but soft spoken African American named Captain Waters. Danny told Captain Waters that their unit should not expect a lot of Iranian resistance once they had arrived at the Iranian military base. Danny MacLean also told him that they had received credible intelligence that the secret Iranian base normally would have no more than thirty to thirty-five troops that were only equipped with mostly light arms, some trucks and a couple of older T-54 Russian made tanks. Danny continued his briefing "the United States had also completed a top secret deal with the Chinese government to help us eliminate the number of Iranian troops at the base. Most of the Iranian troops have left the base about a half hour ago with all their trucks to pick up a bogus shipment of Chinese arms and ammunition that was supposed to be at a secret Iranian airstrip outside the Iranian city of Samnan, about an hour and a half ride from the Mt. Demavend military base. The estimated number of Iranian troops remaining should be about fifteen or less with most of the troops staying in either the troop dormitory or the mess area".

Danny MacLean then laid out a map and showed the commandos the location of both the dorm and mess hall buildings along with the location of the main gate, the laboratory entrance and the most likely guard locations. Danny continued his briefing "The only guards that should be outside should be a couple guards on patrol along the fence line and another guard at the main gate". Danny finished his briefing as the commandos checked their weapons and switched off their safeties. Danny MacLean exhaled and said "We should try to complete the mission in less than two hours, just in case the Iranian truck convoy is not destroyed by our helicopter gun ships that are waiting at the Iranian air strip near Samnan, Iran".

The US and Russian commandos were dropped off at a location about five hundred yards from the Iranian base outside the fence line. The noise of the helicopters was hidden by a coordinated series of air strikes just outside the opposite end of the base. The ten man commando unit was split up into two groups with Danny MacLean and Boris Panov staying with Captain Waters of the US Delta Force as they approached the Iranian military base fence line. The Delta Force captain signaled for everyone to quickly get down on the ground as he carefully sighted and shot a roving Iranian guard in the chest with a couple of 9mm rounds from his silenced H&K submachine gun. Delta Force Captain Waters then received a signal from the other group that they had taken out the gate guard. The commando unit then quickly cut a hole through the fence and quietly entered the secret Iranian base, still unnoticed by the Iranian military. The Delta Force captain then told the US and Russian commandos "Ivan you proceed to the mess area and quickly take out any diners, while I will take care of the troop dormitory building. Danny, please stay here with Boris until I give the all clear with two clicks of the radio transmitter, then we can proceed to the laboratory entrance".

Ivan the leader of the Russian Special Federal Police quietly entered the Mess hall and quietly shot the Iranian cook as the cook was preparing the next days meal of lamb kabobs and cheese. Ivan then shot another Iranian soldier as he was sleeping on one of the mess hall tables.

Delta Force Captain Waters was not as lucky as Ivan nor was it as quiet. As the commandos entered the troop dormitory building they had put on their night vision goggles due to the lights being out as the Iranian troops had gone to bed after the latest air strikes. Unknown to the commando unit was that one of the six remaining Iranian troops was not in bed, but had snuck into the Iranian commanders' office to call his girlfriend in Tehran. As the US and Russian commandos were dispatching the Iranian soldiers to meet Allah, the lone Iranian soldier had cracked open the door to see if he was being spied on by his fellow guards, but instead of seeing a group of his fellow soldiers, he had barely seen what looked like alien beings walking around and killing some of his friends. All he could initially see was the slight muzzle flashes of the silenced weapons as his fellow troops were killed in bed or trying to flee. The Junior Iranian officer had enough training to enable him to think clearly and to quickly call his Iranian Army headquarters in Tehran to report the invasion of the base. The Iranian junior officer then retrieved his commanding officers 9mm Markerev pistol from his desk.

Just as the commandos had finished taking care of the sleeping guards, they headed towards the commanders office to finish their sweep of the dormitory building. This is when things got noisy and when things went wrong for the commando team. When the lead commando, a young Russian Federal Police lieutenant went to open the office door, the Iranian junior officer started firing wildly in all directions, hoping to kill all of the intruders.

Most of his shots went wide and high, but one bullet had made a direct hit in the center of the young Russian commandos head, killing him instantly. Another bullet had hit Delta Force Captain Water's in his chest, but the bullet had been stopped by his body armor. The US and Russian commando's immediately returned silenced fire and sent the Iranian officer to his death with at least ten bullet holes.

Outside of the dormitory building, Danny MacLean and Boris Panov heard the Iranian gunner fire his weapon as they took cover behind a bunch of electrical transformers. Just as Danny was about to break radio silence to ask if everything was alright, his radio clicked twice, signally them that the base was now in control by the US and Russian commando unit. Danny and Boris were then instructed to proceed towards the laboratory entrance where the commandos would meet them in a couple of minutes. Danny was then told that the commandos had taken a casualty and that they would have to hide the body for later removal.

Fortunately for the US and Russian commando unit, the Iranian guards stationed inside the secret laboratory facility along with the scientists working there, had not been alerted or had been able to hear the brief gunfire from within the base. They could not hear much, since they were over five hundred feet in and below Iran's tallest mountain and also because they were behind soundproof and bulletproof doors. The commandos quickly gathered at the laboratory entrance meeting up with Danny

MacLean and Boris Panov to prepare to enter the laboratory, just as a squad of Iranian Presidential guards was preparing to leave Tehran towards the secret base near Mt. Demavend. The Iranian Presidential guards were ordered to check on the base and the laboratory and to report back to headquarters about an alleged incursion and about a report of gunfire heard on the phone.

Fifty-Eight

Beijing, China – March 2006

As the commando team of Russian and Americans along with Boris Panov were entering Iranian territory, the American Paleobotanist Max Hamilton had arrived at Beijing International Airport where he was escorted to a private waiting area where the rest of the scientists from the United States and other parts of the world were waiting. After a short introduction from their Chinese Scientific liaison, the scientists were escorted to a waiting line of Mercedes Benz limousines. They then proceeded to race through the streets of Beijing with full police and army escorts without any interruptions as if they were royalty or a visiting Head of State. The convoy of limousines are usually carrying dignitaries and are noted to be the personal vehicles of the Premier and were almost always used by either high level diplomats or by high ranking Politburo members or by the Premier himself. But today Max Hamilton and a bunch of scientists were as or more important than any Head of State.

The limousine convoy pulled up to the main entrance of the Chinese Ministry of Science, a bare and modern looking concrete building consisting of eight stories of offices and laboratories scattered throughout the building. The Ministry of Science is flanked by the less industrial looking Ministry for Foreign Affairs building and similar looking public housing along the back of the buildings. Most of the government buildings within central Beijing has been built in the last thirty years and are mostly clustered around Tiananmen Square. Besides Ministry buildings around Tiananmen Square, there are Museums and other less impressive ministry housing units.

As the scientists were getting out of the Chinese limousines a light rain had started to fall. The dreary weather of Beijing matched Max Hamilton's mood concerning the latest war time events and the worldwide crisis that was fueled by the spread of the fungus.

Max and the other scientists were then shown a laboratory area within the Chinese Ministry of Science which on the outside resembled a run-down vacant high school hallway, but once inside Max was pleasantly surprised to find a modern and clean laboratory that was nearly new and was comparable to any top notch laboratory in any large US university. Once all the scientists were introduced to each other, the scientists were separated into groups of expertise, such as Botany, Biology, Chemistry and Paleontology. The scientists were then taken to separate laboratories within the Science Ministry that contained specialty equipment needed for each field of study.

After about an hour of getting familiar with his Chinese laboratory, Max Hamilton proceeded to unpack his gear, including a couple of cases of

316

his own specialized equipment that could help them make sure enough of the fungus cure survived while they were testing any results. The equipment Max brought along included a very sensitive and secret devise that was originally developed for the United States military to both collect and to also disperse chemical weapons agents. Max surveyed the laboratory and his new scientific team and said out loud "I hope we can develop a way to replicate the fungus cure and find a way to apply it to the affected areas and stop the spread of this fungus".

"I also hope for this cure, because I know first hand what the fungus can do – my town no longer is inhabited or even exists at this time, like your ghost towns in the American West" commented a Russia scientist who had overheard Max.

As the Russians and Americans continued to battle Iran for the fungus cure and while Max Hamilton has begun to try and develop the fungus cure along a means to apply it with the help of the Chinese government, the rest of the world may be nearing a crisis never witnessed before. Worldwide trade has nearly collapsed except for food and medical type supplies. Besides the United States, many other countries in South America have been hit very hard by the trade crisis, especially nations that supply goods to Europe and Asia.

Because of trade restrictions, except of essential goods, no televisions, electronics or cars are being shipped to North America, creating a substantial negative trade balance with the United States. The US previously had a large negative trade balance, but had the capital to compensate for it. Now the US and these countries are facing a worldwide depression that could be fifty times worst then the Great Depression of the 1930's.

The once prosperous European Union that had flourished during the 1990's and the early 21st century has nearly collapsed with many countries electing to leave the European Union and go it alone and re-establishing their own currency and locking down their own borders. Most of the European countries south of Germany have already left or have threatened to pull of the European Union and out of NATO. Some of these southern European nations have already stationed their troops along their own borders and have started printing their own money again.

While Max Hamilton starts working towards a bulk fungus cure and application methods, the Chinese Premier and the ruling communist party of China have barely been able to hang or to power. Many rural areas within western China have reverted back to a frugal type of local government and have not acknowledged the ruling communist party. In some Chinese Villages near the western edge of the Gobi desert, the local communist party leaders have either been driven out of town or they have been found murdered. Many local party officials have been replaced with local tribal leadership wearing ragtag and makeshift uniforms and armor that resembled the look of ancient Mongol warriors like in the time of Genghis Khan.

Fortunately at this time, both North and South America have not been physically affected by the fungus. Both North and South American supplies over sixty percent of the food supply to the rest of the world. Also, Africa is still unaffected by the fungus, but still relied on and continues to receive food aid from the United States. Many ecologist and scientists agree that if the United States and parts of South America get effected by the fungus, most animal species and most of human life would be dead within a couple of years.

Fifty-Nine

Fungus affected areas, Russian Federation – late March 2006

For the first time in modern civilization, a civilized country has experienced an almost total crop loss. Even considering volcanic island nations and most the arid African nations, Russia would be the first. But now in the 21st century, not one, but two civilized nations have experienced such a cataclysmic event. In almost ninety nine percent of Russia's farm belt and in most of the Ukraine, there have been no new crops planted or harvested since last summer. In areas where the fungus has been spreading, farmers chose not to plant any new harvests or had simply abandoned the fields that were already sowed at the approach of the fungus or to erosion, animal or insect infestation. The only remaining Russian farms known to exist and that may be planted late spring are located along the eastern part of the country near the Pacific Ocean and China and a few small isolated farms scattered in extremely rural areas of southern Siberia and isolated areas along the border with China.

Even though Russia's farms and its crops have been killed off by the fungus, the most devastating result of the fungus has been the loss of over fifty percent of Russia's flowing and fruit bearing plant life. The area that the fungus has also claimed includes a large portion of the delicate spring Tundra flowers and fruiting plants in northern Siberia. The ripple effect this has created includes lack of food for many animal species including the once large Elk herd population that had once roamed throughout Siberia.

Most of the woody type plant life including Oak and Pine trees have not been affected by the fungus, but other large sections of forest have been gobbled up by landslides and flooding caused by the massive erosion of the surrounding topsoil after the fungus has moved on. The erosion and flooding cannot be fixed or stopped within Russia or the Ukraine as long as any stabilizing vegetation is eliminated by the fungus or wiped out too soon by flood waters.

Without farming or cattle raising, Russia along with its neighbor the Ukraine along with the refugee nations such as Romania, Poland and Hungary have been receiving large shipments of food from South American, the European Union and especially the United States. Even with the large amounts of food aid, Russia has had to implement severe food rationing which has created substantial black market opportunities for the Russia Mafia, which in turn has left many families struggling with starvation and forced slavery to the local Russian Mafia members. Many mass protests have had the unenviable task of both issuing the food rations and the task of trying to keep limited food supplies from getting into the hands of the Russian mobsters and onto the black market.

Besides Russia and the Ukraine, most of the remaining fertile farm areas within Kazakhstan have been affected by the fungus, especially along the Irgiz River region, stretching from Russia to the Aral Sea and eastward to the mountain valley region just east of Lake Balkhash. These regions have been decimated by the fungus and by landslides and erosion which usually follows the fungus devastation.

Another Asian region hit hard by the fungus is the grass and grazing lands of western and parts of the central plains region of Mongolia. Some fungus affected areas may be viewed just outside of the city limits of Ulan Bator, which is home to the largest and most modern dairy facilities in Mongolia. Ulan Bator is also one of Mongolia's most populated cities with almost one-quarter of the regions population living there. These areas can be seen westward toward the Orkhon River valley as far as the eye can see. This area was once the ancient capitol of Genghis Khan. A local Chinese communist official was recently quoted as saying "I estimate that nearly ten thousand head of cattle have either starved to death or were brought to the market in Ulan Bator too soon"

If the loss of income, food rationing, mafia violence and the massive loss of vegetation in Russia was not enough, a group of European scientists working with the World Wildlife Federation, known throughout the world as the WWF have not be able to register a single sighting of the Siberian Goose in several months. This confirms the extinction status previously placed on this once mighty bird.

The WWF scientists have also notified other scientists around the world that at least another one hundred additional animal and bird species have either moved somewhere else or may have joined the Siberian Goose onto the extinction list. The list of possible recently extinct animals and bird species that the WWF scientists have not been able to see or track for the past two months includes the European Bison, the Snow Leopard and the Siberian Tiger.

Sixty

New Brunswick, Canada – late March 2006

Another species of bird life that has not been seen by the World

Wildlife Federation since January was the Eastern European goose. The

Eastern European goose's normal habitat includes a winter breeding area in

southeast Greenland, then they go on their long spring migratory flight from

Greenland across the Norwegian Sea, over northern Europe, Poland to the

farmlands of western Russia and the Ukraine.

According to the WWF the Eastern European goose had not been

spotted anywhere along its normal migratory route and that the geese had

left their winter nesting area in Greenland. As the European scientists of the

WWF were considering adding the Eastern European goose to the extinct

list, several reports had been sent from weather monitoring stations in

Canada reporting seeing what looked like the Eastern European goose. The

Eastern European goose has been spotted flying west over the north

Atlantic Ocean and flying over coastal areas of Newfoundland.

Another report was later received that read "several hundred

Eastern European geese were spotted feeding on wild blueberries near a

unnamed pond located in eastern New Brunswick, Canada". Canadian and

US wildlife experts believe the Eastern European goose has completely changed its migratory route in search of new food sources and nesting areas. The US Department of Fish and Wildlife estimates that the Eastern European goose is just a few days away from flying over Maine and then continuing south in the United States interior.

The Eastern European goose is similar to the native Canadian goose except for a shorter body and a larger head with a much darker grey coloring and a white underbelly. Since altering its historic migratory route, the Eastern European goose has alarmed many North American wildlife experts who believe the Eastern European goose could spread foreign avian disease to the native Canadian and Snow geese populations and would certainly eat already scarce food supplies.

Sixty-One

Tehran, Iran – late March 2006

By a special envoy to the Saudi Arabian King, the Iranian government had announced that the Ayatollah of Iran has ordered the immediate destruction of all "amber", its supporting experimental data and the fungus cure that they had previously developed. The Ayatollah then appeared on mostly Iranian and Arabic television stations where he publicly announced the destruction of the fungus cure and added "The Islamic Republic of Iran has suffered throughout the centuries by the hands of foreign invaders, especially the infidels. The Iranian people will not suffer along with the rest of the world once the planet is made into a vast desert by Allah's gift of this fungus". The Ayatollah then proceeded to read a few passages from the Koran and again announced "All Iranian and Islamic people should start preparing for the return of Mohammed so that they may join with Mohammed to battle against the infidels, where we will be victorious and once again the planet will be an Islamic planet, Praise be to Allah".

After the television broadcast of the Ayatollah's message, most of the Arabic television stations switched to a live broadcast from somewhere else in Tehran, where the Iranian President and members of the Islamic ruling cabinet were being filmed what appeared to be, the Iranian President destroying laboratory experiments along with setting fire to various papers and folders.

What the Iranian government failed to realize in their convoluted isolation from the rest of the world was that the spread of the fungus without any cure and way of slowing it down, would destroy mankind before anyone including the Prophet Mohammed could battle anyone else.

Besides the Ayatollah's religious views that mark the rise of Mohammed and the fight against the infidels, many American religious fundamentalists also believed that this would be the end of the war and the return of Jesus. Some radical religious groups in the United States claim that the Bible's Book of Revelation predicts the plague of the fungus, while some people say the Nostradamus had also predicted this end of the war scenario.

Sixty-Two

Washington, D.C. – late March 2006

In the oval office of the White House, US President Baker was watching the live Arabic broadcast as an Iranian translator started speaking "As ordered by our supreme leader the Ayatollah, we have commenced with the destruction of the fungus cure and all of it's supporting scientific data". The US President knew that some of the fungus cure was in the hands of American, Russian and Chinese scientists in China, but what he did not know was whether this public spectacle was indeed the actual destruction of the Iranian fungus cure of if it was just another staged production by the Iranian government.

Both President Baker and Russian General Baranov waited for word from the joint commando unit located outside Tehran near Mt. Demavend. They waited for word whether the commando unit had made into the secret military base alright and if they had found the fungus cure and data. And if they did find the fungus cure were they able to safely take it away from the Iranians without any loss of the cure. The United States, Russia and China were waiting impatiently for a reply from the secret commando mission. As President Baker stood up to stretch he said out loud

"It should not be taking this long" as his Chief of Staff just nodded in agreement.

Just as President Baker switched off the television that showed a large group of Iranian's celebrating in the street while chanting down with the infidels and death to America as the Iranian President destroyed the fungus cure. President Baker then issued a written statement to his Chief of Staff to announce that the Iranian broadcast had been a fake and that there is still hope that the fungus can be stopped.

President Baker then received a phone call from Russian General Baranov asking the President if he had seen the Iranian television broadcast from Tehran. President Baker replied "Unfortunately I had to watch the Iranian spectacle, but I hope we hear from our commando's soon, telling us this was just another Iranian propaganda stunt"

"I hope you are right comrade Baker, but if our commando mission has indeed failed and the Iranians have truly destroyed the fungus, the "amber" and its cure, we will not stand by and wait to become extinct like so much of our plant and animal life has" expressed Russian General Baranov.

"I think we should at least wait a few more days for word from our commando unit before we consider our next move and any harsh reactions" added President Baker.

As President Baker was ready to wish the Russian General a better evening, General Baranov asked President Baker if he was alone and he then told the US President, "I will wait seventy two hours to hear from our commandos, but if the mission has failed or the fungus cure has been destroyed in the process, then I must warn you to immediately redraw all your military units and any other American citizens from Iran and the surrounding area. Then within thirty six hours after my word, a Russian submarine located in the Arabian Sea will launch a small nuclear strike against Iran and the first target will be Tehran"

"Please General, let's not take such drastic" replied President Baker before being cut-off.

"I hope there is a God, because we only have a few more days left, goodnight Mr. President" announced General Baranov before he hung up the phone.

As President Baker slowly set the telephone receiver down, he just stared out of his window at the White House lawn contemplating what may be about to happen. He knew that a nuclear strike against Iran would destroy their oil infrastructure and could possible contaminate the Iranian oil supply for the next one thousand years. If this were to happen even with a very limited nuclear strike, China would surely attack Russia for Russia's own oil reserves and supplies, since most of the oil supplied to China now comes from Iran. The Iranian oil is pumped and the refineries are not primarily operated by US military troops and civilian technicians. President Baker know that China would not hesitate to take oil from Russia and place the world on the brink of a nuclear holocaust along with the probability of mass extinction caused by a pre-historic fungus.

Sixty-Three

Los Angeles, California – late March 2006

Along with the continuous and ongoing fighting in Iran and with US military forces located in both Iraq and Afghanistan, the already stretched US military must now mobilize and be able to cope with additional requests for both active duty and National Guard troops. Because of the current military circumstances, the US Congress and House of Representatives have scheduled a debate concerning the Presidents request to reinstate the military draft.

Some active duty Army troops are being sent to the border areas to replace National Guard troops that are being sent to help local police departments deal with the increasingly large and more violent groups of demonstrators. The demonstrations have mostly consisted of proponents of the new US border and immigration policies clashing with both Arabic and Mexican Americans. Some of the demonstrations have quickly escalated into full blown rioting with massive amounts of property damage, injuries and even some deaths.

Violent demonstrations and riots have mostly occurred in the more ethnically diverse larger cities. In addition, large gangs of young mostly

Mexican with some Arabic men have started robbing both innocent citizens and opposing demonstrators. The targets of the large groups have been mostly black and white victims. The violence has also included car jackings, home invasions, muggings and in some cases, innocent people have been shot and killed while just waiting for a bus. The attackers and attacks have so far been clustered in already high crime areas and poorer neighborhoods that have either large Mexican or Arabic populations. With the gang violence from all ethnic gangs reaching a level almost too large to handle by local law enforcement, the National Guard has been called in by some states to take care of limiting and dispersing demonstrations and rioters. Some demonstrations had turned even more violent and took a tragic twist when some members of a local Mexican gang started joining up with other demonstrators and this has contributed largely to more violence being attributed to the demonstrators.

One demonstration outside of Los Angeles City Hall was going along peacefully when a band of Mexican gang members started to shoot at innocent bystanders, Police and National Guard troops. Several bystanders and police were injured along with the murder of a National Guard troop. The National Guard and Police were unable or unwilling to shoot back, since the gang members would shoot at them and then hide behind bystanders or behind other non-violent demonstrators. The National Guard troops feared killing the innocent demonstrators or innocent bystanders.

Because of the recent violent demonstrations and riots, several large cities including Los Angeles, New York, Houston and Atlanta have banned any form of demonstration or large gathering regardless of size in addition to any already established federal bans. Some major cities have also enacted a nighttime curfew for all citizens with some curfews starting at sundown. The curfews have been put into effect to help stop the recent and growing number of fires being set and the random number of shootings that were on the rise in almost every major US city each day.

Sixty-Four

Toronto, Canada – late March 2006

In addition to the Mexican threat of an intentional release of the fungus, the porous Canadian border still posed a more likely area of infiltration of Al-Qaeda or other terrorist or radical organizations. Because of the increased threat and a number of previously captured terrorists with fake fungus, the United States and Canada have agreed to allow not only US border guards into Canada, but to also allow US military troops. In an unequalled show of unity and support not seen since World War II between the United States and Canada, the Canadian Parliament and the White House have agreed to allow US military troops to be sent to help the already over worked and under staffed Canadian custom and border guards. The US military troops primary duty will be to patrol the many miles of coastline along both the Pacific and Atlantic Oceans.

Sixty-Five

United States/Mexican border near Laredo, Texas – late March 2006

The increase in both border guards and military troops along the US and Mexican border was a welcome sight by United States citizens living along the border, especially since there has been such an increase in both the number of Mexican gangs and the amount of violence directed towards both United States citizens and US military personnel coming from the Mexican side of the border.

Since the hostilities along the US and Mexican border began, over a hundred Mexican gang members have either been killed or driven off by United States military patrols, except for a group of highly organized and heavily armed Mexican gangs that have recently surfaced. The new Mexican gangs are made up of ex-Mexican drug cartel members, Mexican police and now many regular army troops. These new gangs have launched a few attacks against US military troops and border guards and have even tried a larger scale attack against the city of Laredo, Texas. The new Mexican gang in this attack had used a combination of small arms fire, mortar attacks and even a few light hand-held rockets. With these larger and well armed Mexican gangs increasing attacks on United States border towns, the area along the US and Mexican border in many locations resembles a war zone similar to areas of fighting in Iraq and Iran.

Along with the current military skirmishes along the United States and Mexican border, the United States and Canada have had to deal with some isolated cases of attempted sabotage. The sabotage attempts have been directed at power plants, government factories and other public works facilities. The suspect's criminals behind the attempted attacks are believed to be both Arabic and Mexican Americans. The suspects may have been battling with police and US troops at protests and demonstrations, but with military troops and police breaking up and outlawing most protests, the violent members of these gangs have now begun to spread violence to other suburban areas and have been linked to many cases of attempted sabotage.

Because of the this new threat against the governments of both the government and the citizens of the United States, the Congress and House of Representatives have allowed a new and hopefully temporary "Stop and Search" policy for all police and military personnel. The new "Stop and Search" policy would suspend the old probable cause law and allow both police and military troops to stop and search anyone thought to be acting suspicious or strangely, especially Arabic or Mexican Americans. This new policy does not need to have any warrants or any "probable cause", just a suspicion. This temporary stop and search low has further outraged and angered the Mexican and Arabic population in America and has further fueled more violence and hatred towards black and white Americans.

Many Mexican Americans who had previously spoken out against the recent Mexican gang violence and protests have now expressed their outrage at local police and some have openly encouraged more violence towards the police and military personnel.

Sixty-Six

Mt. Demavend, Iran – late March 2006

Once the US and Russian joint commando unit stormed the outer door of the secret Iranian laboratory they were met with only minimum resistance from the remaining Iranian guards. Once the commandos entered the tunnel entrance under Mt. Demavend they quickly subdued the two Iranian guards by a couple of silenced H&K submachine gun rounds to the head of each guard. After a quick inspection of the tunnel entrance by the US Delta Force commander Captain Waters, he turned to CIA agent Danny McLean and quietly asked him "Where do we go from here Mr. McLean"

"I think we need to go about a hundred yards down the tunnel where it should come to a dead end intersection" answered Danny McLean.

"Once at the tunnel intersection, the commando's should split up into two groups and investigate each tunnel section. The right tunnel should lead you to the living quarters for the scientists and the left tunnel should bring us to the laboratory" added Danny McLean. The US Delta Force commander Captain Waters relayed the instructions to the other members of the joint commando unit and then turned to Danny McLean and instructed "You and the Dino doc wait at the tunnel intersection along with one of my men and wait until I give you the all clear signal". The commando unit then quietly and methodically made their way down the tunnel to the intersection where they quickly split up into two groups and then disappeared into each of the adjacent tunnel areas.

After most of the commandos were gone Danny McLean asked Boris Panov "What are our chances of finding a viable cure for the fungus?"

"I feel that if we find the 'amber' or any form of the fungus cure, that my friend Max Hamilton can find a way to kill the fungus" Boris answered after thinking for a moment.

"I hope you are right Dr. Panov, but I do not share your optimism" added Danny. After a few minutes of silence, Boris stated out loud for Danny McLean to hear "I hope the commandos do not shoot the Iranian scientists, we may need them". Danny McLean's radio then crackled with a garbled all clear signal followed by US commander Captain Waters asking them to proceed down the left tunnel about a hundred yards where they will enter the laboratory.

The only set-back that Boris, Danny and the commando unit has had so far , was the intermittent and lack of radio reception and transmission within the mountain compound.

Once Danny McLean and Boris Panov entered the laboratory, they quickly realized that the Iranian laboratory was working and had in deed existing and that they may have developed a fungus cure here or were close. As they entered the laboratory, Boris noticed several computers were running along with four frightened Iranian scientists lined up along one wall in plastic handcuffs. The remaining commando's that had investigated the right side tunnel then entered the laboratory with two additional Iranians, one a possible scientist and the other appeared to be a cook or a janitor. The other commandos quietly told Captain Waters that they had to shoot another guard who had apparently snuck down for a quick bite to eat.

Boris Panov then made a quick inventory of laboratory logbooks and journals, just as a large and mean looking Russian commando was asking one of the Iranian scientists to help in the inventory and cure collection. After a little encouragement, the scientists were more than eager to help. Boris realized from talking with the Iranian scientists through one of the Russian commandos that the "amber" experiments had been successful and they had created a small amount of fungus cure, but the problem that they had encountered was that some of the developed amount of fungus cure was missing according to the Iranian logbooks and that Boris's entire "amber" discovery was destroyed. Again, after speaking with one of the Iranian scientists who spoke some Russian, Boris had learned that the experiments to develop the fungus cure had required all of the "amber" material, but since then the Iranians had been working on a way to replicate the fungus cure artificially.

After taking all the computer disks, selective files and making sure the "cure" specimen was gathered and secured, the commando leader Captain Waters announced that they must leave at once to make their rendezvous with the waiting US helicopters located in the Iranian desert. He also announced that they would take the Iranian scientists along as prisoners and maybe future consultants.

Just as the commando team was planning to exit the laboratory facility under Mt. Demavend, a group of Iranian Presidential Guards had arrived at the secret base from their post in Tehran to investigate the reported incident of a gunshot at the laboratory. The Iranian Presidential Guard troops had been able to quickly ascertain what had happened or was currently happening at the base and had radioed their headquarters in Tehran for further instructions.

During the delay from their headquarters in Tehran, the Presidential Guard troop leader caught a glimpse of a Russian commando exiting the tunnel entrance. The Iranian Presidential Guard leader then ordered his troops to open fire on the tunnel entrance and the Russian commando. The Russian commando had no chance and was shot and killed with over a dozen bullets. Once the shooting had started, US Delta Force commander Captain Waters ordered the commando unit to fall back into the tunnel and take up positions at the tunnel intersection on each side and be prepared to protect the fungus cure specimen and Dr. Panov at any cost. The shooting from the Iranian Presidential Guards stopped as they approached the tunnel entrance from each side, but they did not enter the tunnel. Once the Iranian Presidential Guard troops were in position to storm the tunnel entrance, the Presidential Guard commander in Tehran announced over the radio "The Ayatollah and the President have personally commanded you to move all of your troops away from the tunnel to the front gate of the base and proceed to initiate a 'Code Allah'".

Unknown to CIA agent Danny McLean and the rest of the joint US and Russian commando unit was the fact that the tunnel entrance was already rigged with high explosives in case the Iranian government needed to quickly eradicate any evidence of the laboratory or anyone working there. Once the scientists were finished with their work or they had somehow compromised the fungus cure and experiments, the laboratory would then become their tomb. This Iranian government scenario was known as a "Code Allah" in Farsi. Just as the US and Russian commando unit was preparing a counter attack and a way to exit the tunnel, they first felt the rumble, then they heard, then saw the end of the tunnel disappear into a pile of rock and a cloud of dust as they took cover not to get hit with any flying rock fragments.

The US and Russians had finally been able to obtain the fungus cure, the supporting data along with the actual scientists who had developed the cure, but now they were trapped a hundred yards inside Mt. Demavend.

The commandos, Danny McLean and Boris Panov have the fungus cure, but were trapped outside Tehran under a mountain without any exist, an unknown amount of air, food, electricity or contact with the outside world.

Sixty-Seven

Beijing, China – late March 2006

As Max Hamilton and his scientific team were just finishing another sixteen hour work day at his laboratory in Beijing, China, a courier from the Chinese Information Office arrived and asked for the American Max Hamilton. Max stood up and said "I'm Max Hamilton is there anything wrong".

"No Sir, I have an urgent message from your government and the Premier said to make sure you personally received the message" answered the courier.

"Thank you" Max said as he took the envelope and opened it immediately and started reading "The US and Russian commando unit with Boris Panov have not checked in with either US or Russian authorities and have not arrived at the designated rendezvous point given for the mission in Iran. Russian and US government officials fear the mission has failed and that the members of the commando unite have either been captured or killed". Max felt like a great weight had been placed on his chest as he set down the letter and then had to sit down himself before he fell down. "Are you OK Max?" asked his young and talented assistant from England's Oxford University.

"I'm afraid not, My friend Boris along with the hopes of the rest of the world may have died in Iran" Max answered with a crack in his voice as he struggled to control his emotions. Once Max had regained his composure he read the remaining part of the letter which simply stated "Please go see the Chinese Premier and call the President as soon as you read this message".

Max was ushered into the private study of the Chinese Premier within the Premier's private offices to call the President of the United States. Once Max was seated, a Chinese official dialed the number to the United States White House using the secure and encrypted communication line of the Chinese Premier. Max hoped he was not waking the President, then he realized that with the time difference, the President would be awake because it was actually the previous day in Washington, D.C.

"United States Presidential Secret Service Agent Forsner, How may I help you" answered the White House Secret Service.

"I have a secure connection from the Chinese Premier wishing to speak to President Baker" the Chinese official requested in perfect English.

"One moment, Sir" replied the Secret Service Agent after checking to make sure the call was legitimate. About a minute later a voice came on the line and said.

"This is President Baker, good morning or I should say good evening Premier".

"Sir, this is Max Hamilton as you requested" as he picked up the phone.

"Thank God you called, I have been expecting this call all morning" the President said.

"I know the Russian scientist Boris Panov was, or I mean is a very good friend of yours Max, but I hope you can continue to concentrate on the critical work you are doing during this time" continued the President.

"Yes Mr. President, Boris is a good friend and also a brilliant Paleontologist that without his help so far we would have no chance at all. But I'm sure the commando unit is also a group of brave and good men" Max said as he began to feel the pressure on his chest again.

"They are all good men Max and I still think that if they have even a remote chance of survival, they will make it, But…" The President said resignedly and paused.

"It looks as if their mission has failed anyway and the very existence of life on earth may come down to that small gift of the fungus cure given to the Chinese from the Iranians" continued the President after hesitating.

"We will work twenty-four hours a day if necessary Sir to develop the cure, but the danger we face is destroying what little amount of the fungus cure we have in order to try to reproduce it" Max said.

"I know you'll do your best Max and God knows you have done more than your fair share in this crisis, especially traveling all over the world, going to Russia, Iraq and now China, leaving your family behind in New York and Montana – Godspeed Max" President Baker said as he hung up the phone. Max just stood looking at the phone then told the Chinese official "I was supposed to be on the mission to Tehran and I should have died also".

After speaking with Max Hamilton in China, US President Baker notified most of the world leaders that the commando mission to Mt. Demavend in Iran may have failed and that any help they could offer would be appreciated. He also told the United States friendly allies that they must help persuade the Iranians to give up the fungus cure, tell us the fate or whereabouts of the joint Russian and US commando team is at once. If not, they fear that the United States may not be able to prevent the Russians from completely destroying Iran.

Several world leaders from Europe, Asia and South America have asked President Baker what they could do about the Iranian situation that the United States and Russia have not already tried. President Baker told several world leaders that the US and Russian militaries were already stretched to the limit because of the ongoing Iranian attacks and because of the domestically threatened release of the fungus across the US and North American borders. The President had expressed a request for a worldwide military invasion of Iran that would make the World War II "D-Day" invasion of Europe look like a beach party. The President also confided with these world leaders that this may buy time from a possible Russian non-conventional assault. President Baker explained his plan that would literally start at the Iranian border, and he meant all the Iranians borders, then they would go house to house until they all reached Tehran, leaving no brick unturned, no well, tunnel, shed, shack or tent unsearched or unchecked. When asked about what they should do about the Iranian people and any attacks or reprisals, President Baker replied coldly "They will either help us or they will be destroyed".

As the month of March ends, most of the 20th century world has changed, but not progressively and not in a good way. Since the continued spread of the fungus and with war escalating with Iran, the European Union has now totally collapsed and now most of the former European Union countries have re-established their own currencies and have initiated closures of their own borders.

The most volatile world changes have occurred in the Ukraine and Russian, with a almost total collapse of the Ukrainian economy and government along with the massive plant loss in both the Ukraine and Russia and now the fledging democratic government of Russia has been replaced by military rule.

Besides Russia and Eastern Europe, the future could digress very rapidly in China due to the effects of the fungus on Russia. With China's massive population and import needs for both food and oil resources and with a worldwide supply of food and oil already stretched beyond capacity, the Chinese communist government has been barely able to control an underlying mass panic within the Chinese population. So far the United States has been able to increase food shipments to China and has increased supply of Iranian oil, just so the Chinese can barely survive. Even though the US government would love to see an end to communist rule in China, now would not be best time for that to happen. For the first time since the original Cold War at started, the US government was in a position to help prop up a communist type government.

The United States and Canada have not had it much easier. Both unemployment and inflation rates have reached levels greater than that of the Great Depression of the 1930's. With many layoffs contributed to the decrease in manufactured goods supplied in the United States and abroad. This was especially due to the lack of imports coming into the US and Canada, such as televisions, cars and other electronic devises. The only saving grace for the American and Canadian work force was the extra workers needed by farmers and farm related companies such as John Deere and Caterpillar to keep up with the high demand for food crops. These new farm workers were needed to replace previous Mexican migrant workers, who have either joined protestors or gangs or have fled back to Mexico. The farm pay is very low, but since President Baker had frozen retail food and other prices, the inflation rate has started to come down. The US unemployment rate may rise again after the fall harvesting in the northern latitudes or if the Midwest farm areas do not see any significant rainfall in the next few weeks.

Sixty-Eight

Moscow, Russian Federation – early April, 2006

Marking the end of March and the beginning of April in many areas of Russia and the Ukraine was usually observed by a wide range of spring festivals and celebrations to mark the start of the farm harvest. The festivals were usually smaller versions like Germany's fall festival "Oktoberfest" but with vodka and local beer, but this year there were no celebrations and no festivals. This marked the first full season without any productive farming within either Russia or the Ukraine. In addition to the elimination of most Russian farmland, scientists have estimated that almost two-thirds of plant life within southern Russia and the Ukraine has been affected because of the fungus and that another one-third of the plant life within the delicate Siberian tundra has been eliminated.

To add to Russia's and Eastern Europe's growing shortage of food was a decrease in the normal amount of food imported from the United States. The US food exports have been dramatically reduced due to a very dry and warm winter along the American west coast and southern farming regions. This end of winter drought has affected the US spring harvest and has caused a decrease in food shipments to Russia, Eastern Europe, Africa and Asia. Because of the already reduced food rations and shortages, some cities within Russia and Eastern Europe have started to experience food riots, especially within the city of Moscow and in some of the refugee cities located in Romania and Hungary. Because of the growing hostility and violence within their own borders, Russia along with the Ukraine and Hungary have had to reassign troops headed for Iran to stay at home and help control the growing food crisis by dispersing crowds and stop riots. In some areas surrounding Moscow, many people have been hurt and some have been killed while attempting to find enough food just to survive. In other areas like the once wealthy farm settlements in Russia, several deaths have been contributed due to starvation, mainly among the young children and elderly pheasants.

In addition to Russia, many other countries have been affected by the fungus and many others are also threatened. The once and only fertile farm valley within Kazakhstan has been destroyed by the fungus and the land is now being reclaimed by the high desert which now threatens the entire region. In the southern region of Kazakhstan near the border with Uzbekistan the once harvested poppy plants have also been affected by the fungus. Now exports of heroin shipments from Kazakhstan have been almost eliminated, which has affected over twenty percent of the heroin drug market in the United States.

Also in western Mongolia, over twenty thousand acres of grassland has been eradicated by the fungus. Many Mongolian cattle ranchers have been pushed into much smaller grazing areas, which have created hostility amongst the ranchers who are fighting for both land and water for their cattle. Many Mongolian ranchers have given up and have ended up dispersing their herds of cattle along the western edge of the Gobi Desert. This loss of cattle ranch grasslands has now decreased the amount of an already devastating food shortage within China, threatening a crisis in China similar to the red-Chinese take over, but without food and with the largest population on earth.

Sixty-Nine

New Brunswick, Canada – early April 2006

Since the winter and the confirmed extinction of the Siberian goose, the World Wildlife Federation has listed another one hundred different species of animal life that may become extinct with another one thousand plus additional animals being placed on the endangered species list.

Beside the extinction of the Siberian goose, additional sightings have been confirmed of the Eastern European goose in Canada, plus a flock of Eastern European geese were photographed using a Canadian goose nesting area along the eastern shoreline of New Brunswick, Canada. The larger and less docile Eastern European goose had taken over the nesting ground and had killed many young Canadian geese and had also displaced hundred's of others. The environmentalists and scientists watching this extreme species deviation of the Eastern European goose migration have become very concerned with the threat to the native bird populations in northern Canada and the northeastern United States. In addition the environmental scientists fear that the Eastern European and Canadian geese could possible mate and could create a less diverse and less disease tolerant species of waterfowl.

Other scientists studying the affects of the fungus on plant life in Russia and the Ukraine fear that the Eastern European goose could possibly transport the fungus from Eastern Europe to North America. Environmental groups have been able to keep this information secret so far, for fear that if this information was made public, it could doom both the Eastern European, Canadian and Snow geese just like the Siberian goose. The environmental groups know that the geese would be hunted down in Northern Canada in massive numbers like the Buffalo were hunted in the American west.

Seventy

Babol, Iran – early April 2006

Without any contact from the joint US and Russian commando unit in Iran and the refusal of the Iranian government to comply with any of the demands to turn over the fungus cure and data, the Russian military proceeded to unleash one of the largest and deadliest military attacks since World War II. The severe Russian actions had persuaded the Iranians to partially admit to not having destroyed the fungus cure and that they may be willing to negotiate a deal, but not with the United States or with the Russians. The Russian attack had occurred after repeated pleas by Russia, the United States and as many as forty other nations for the Iranian government to turn over the fungus cure and it supporting data or tell the world leaders where it was hidden.

The Russian Army and Air Force had then commenced an attack on the Iranian city of Babol near the Caspian Sea. After nearly twenty-four hours of aerial and artillery attacks, the Iranian death toll amounted to over three thousand people including women and children. Besides the death toll, most of the buildings in Babol have been damaged or destroyed. Russian General Baranov held a news conference where he expressed remorse for the loss of children's lives, but had stated in his news conference that Russian children were also dying everyday, but by a slower death that was caused by starvation. During the worldwide broadcast of the Russian press conference, General Baranov had directly appealed to the Iranian people to overthrow the current Iranian President and oust the Ayatollah or next time Russia may launch a non-conventional attack against the city of Tehran. General Baranov purposely did not use the word "nuclear" because the US President had almost begged him not to. General Baranov further added that Russia will inflict an equal amount of death and destruction on the lands and people of Iran for every acre and death that is lost in Russia as a result of the fungus.

The Russian news conference created another crisis situation throughout the world, especially in China. Shortly after hearing the Russian news conference, China's Premier consulted with his ruling communist cabinet members and had then issued an urgent communication to both the Russian and American governments. The Chinese Premier stated "China both abhors and regrets the circumstances of the destruction and death within the Iranian city of Babol. We understand the urgent need to obtain more of the fungus cure and especially the corresponding fungus data, but Russia must refrain from these deadly attacks and must not under any circumstances launch a nuclear strike into Iran or severe consequences will follow". The Chinese Premier knew what "non-conventional" meant and he

364

also figured that Russia and the United States would know that his reply was solely based on the availability of oil for China and not the well being of the Iranians. The Premier has always distrusted and disliked the Iranian people, especially the Religious leaders such as the Ayatollah. The Chinese government would not utter a word if Russia nuked them all if it was not for the oil.

Following the communication to Russia and the United States, several members of the Communist cabinet had met with the Premier to give him some erroneous scientific information that they had mistakenly received that showed that radiation may kill the fungus. With this false and erroneous information, there was some talk within high levels of the Chinese communist government to allow and encourage Russia to launch a nuclear strike against Tehran and then for China to defend Iran and retaliate by launching a nuclear counter attack against Russia. But the Chinese would not target the Russian city such as Moscow, but target affected areas of active fungus attack. Some members of the Communist cabinet wrongly believed that if they were successful in killing the fungus, they would likely be hailed as heroes and that Russia or the United States would not strike back at China with nuclear weapons.

Seventy-One

Eagle Pass, Texas – early April 2006

Since the massive rioting and demonstrations in the United States at the end of March, most of the small US towns and rural areas of the country have settled down somewhat, but some US cities are still experiencing armed Mexican gangs who have been committing robberies, vandalism and attacks on both black and white Americans. In Los Angeles, Phoenix and Denver, Marshall Law has been declared along with strict curfews. These curfews are in effect to try to prevent and stop Mexican gangs from starting fires and other vandalism and to stop retaliatory white and black gangs from shooting both innocent Mexicans and Mexican gang members.

In addition to the large cities like Los Angeles and Phoenix, Marshall Law has also been declared in almost every United States border town along the Mexican/US border from California to Texas. Some towns like Eagle Pass, Texas and Douglas, Arizona have been completely taken over by US military forces with most of the civilian population either having already moved out or they were relocated to new homes further into both the interiors of Texas and Arizona. These towns have been nicknamed "Fort Douglas" and "Post Eagle Pass" by local US law enforcement. The large US military presence has been in response to previous attacks across the border by armed Mexican gangs made up of drug dealers, Mexican police and the Mexican Army. Some areas along the US/Mexican border have been literally at war with each other with Mexican Army patrols firing mortars and small arms across the border into the United States which then is immediately followed up by a retaliatory air strike by US Army helicopter gun ships.

While tensions have been escalating along the US/Mexican border the situation in Canada after a couple of weeks of US troop deployment has been quiet and well received by the Canadian people. Because of this cooperation, both the Canadian Prime Minister and United States President Baker have agreed to suspend all border guard duties along the US and Canadian border. This agreement has essentially eliminated any border between the United States and Canada, thus freeing up valuable border guard and military troop resources. These resources could be used to strengthen both the US and Canadian coastlines along with adding troops to the already volatile Mexican border.

Because the escalation violence has resumed between the United States and Mexican militaries, President Baker, Mexican President Cortez and Canadian Prime Minister Winters have scheduled an emergency meeting in Montreal to discuss a way to stop the increasing and more deadly violence along the US/Mexican border.

The meeting with the leaders of Canada, Mexico and the United States ended with an agreement to pull back all military forces at least one mile from the two borders to help eliminate any spontaneous fighting and attacks and to help calm down the current border situation. After the meeting, President Baker and Prime Minister Winters along with members of both the Congress and House of Representatives to set up a new military cabinet of this new joint US/Canadian military alliance between Canadian and American military forces. In addition to the military alliance, the North American leaders had agreed to merge several border police forces, the Mounties and the F.B.I.

One of the first measures enacted by the new joint Canadian and US police forces was the implementation of an even stronger non-warrant type search and seizure laws. These new laws enabled law enforcement personnel to stop and search anyone they thought was acting strangely, especially Arabic and Mexican nationals and citizens. The new F.B.I. was now authorized to detain people without warrants or probable cause and was allowed to detain them up to forty-eight house without cause. This angered almost every civil liberties lawyer who vowed to fight these laws and it has further angered the Mexican-American population who had thought that their Miranda rights were protected by the US constitution, but were told that in these terrible times and during national emergencies, the government had the right to suspend or temporarily change both freedom of speech and other civil liberties. Also the Mexican-Americans were harassed by racist advertising and other radical journalism, proclaiming that they had no right to be in American, so American law could not be offered to them. The President tried to counter all the negative feedback by promising once the fungus and the threat from terrorism was over, the United States could once again protect all civil liberties. This fueled another round of protests and riots that quickly escalated into massive violence and vandalism throughout Mexico, Canada and the United States. The violent demonstrations may have been responsible for as many as five hundred deaths and thousands of injuries throughout North America in just a few days.

Seventy-Two

Mt. Demavend, Iran – early April, 2006

Meanwhile buried under tons of rock and soil, Boris Panov and the joint United States and Russian commandos were going to attempt to blast their way out with grenades from the collapses tunnel under Iran's Mt. Demavend. But because of the limited amount of oxygen and the inability to move the injured troops away from the impact area made a large blast impossible without risking more injuries and maybe depleting an already low oxygen level.

One hopeful sign was during an exchange with one of the captured Iranian scientists who spoke some English. The Iranian scientist told them that they heard that a secondary shaft was originally constructed in the mountain during the laboratory construction and that the shaft may still be there, but may be hidden behind a wall. The Iranian scientist also told CIA agent Danny McLean that he had seen drawings of the shaft on old blue prints and that if they could locate the plans, they could locate the old construction shaft. Danny McLean and the commandos split up into separate groups to look for the blue prints and the construction shaft, while

Boris and the commando medic attended to the injured soldiers and to listen for any signs of rescue at the collapsed tunnel.

While Boris, Danny and the commandos were buried under Mt. Demavend in Iran, United States President Baker had convinced Russian General Baranov not to launch a nuclear strike against Tehran at this time. President Baker said "General, the commandos may still be alive and in possession of the fungus cure. You know the Iranian government would either attempt to try our soldiers as criminals or would herald them as heroes if they had them. If you launch a nuclear strike on Tehran now, the fallout would surely reach Mt. Demavend and would totally eliminate any chance they have of bringing us the fungus cure".

Another reason the Russians held off on any nuclear strike was based on an increasing global diplomatic and military alliance brought on by the economic and environmental disaster blamed on the fungus. The number of countries that pledged diplomatic and military help far exceeded the number of coalition forces of the original Persian Gulf War against Iraq. This new coalition not only consisted of NATO and neighboring Arab countries, but also included China and many South American countries including anti-American nations such as Venezuela. The leadership of this new international coalition consisted of Generals from the United States, Canada, United Kingdom, France, China, Russia, Egypt, Turkey and Brazil.

If Iran did not heed the latest international diplomatic warnings, then the international coalition expected to start a massive military deployment of troops and support personnel along every border with Iran and would start fighting to find the fungus cure and to possible rescue the US and Russian commandos from Mt. Demavend and maybe remove Iran's current government.

Seventy-Three

Beijing, China – Early April, 2006

Because of the expected failure and the dwindling hope the commandos would be found alive or for the fungus cure to be handed over by the Iranian government and with World War III about to begin, Max Hamilton had doubled his scientific staff in China and had been working eighteen hours a day to try and replicate the small amount of fungus cure obtained by the Chinese.

Just as the new International coalition was formed to help make Iran give up the fungus cure and hand over the commandos or their bodies, Max was working with renewed energy as they discovered a way to replicate a small amount of the fungus cure in his Beijing laboratory. Max quickly notified the Chinese Premier and President Baker of their latest scientific advance, but warned them not to celebrate just yet. Max told the Chinese Premier and President Baker "We have only replicated a very small amount of the fungus cure so far. We need to find a way to replicate much larger amounts of the fungus cure before we start any effective fungus elimination program. We also need to find a viable method of dispersing the fungus cure over large areas of land. Without these solutions, I believe we can not eliminate the fungus".

"Good work so far, Dr. Hamilton, Whatever or whoever you need to complete this tremendous task, I am at your disposal at any time or at any cost" replied President Baker.

"I second what President Baker just said" announced the Chinese Premier.

"Thank you Mr. President and Premier" Max offered.

"I hope you can find the commandos and my friend Boris Panov alive, because even if the Iranian fungus data and cure is gone, we may need Boris's expertise with the original amber experimental data to try and figure out a way to disperse the cure and kill the spreading fungus" added Max Hamilton.

"We are doing everything we can to find them" President Baker assured Max, then wished Max and the Chinese Premier good luck and they ended the call.

With World War III looming in Iran just a few weeks away, the economic meltdown in Europe and Asia has surpassed the spread of the fungus. Most of Europe and parts of Asia are now almost entirely dependent on US and South American food shipments and aid. The once prosperous and now dependent Europe has caused most European countries to fall into a deep recession with high unemployment with some countries reaching levels just under fifty percent.

So far the United States economy has been limping along due to the large amount of farming within the United States and Canada. But most high paying factory and office work has now bee replaced by lower pay farming and farm related manufacturing jobs. The average United States worker's pay has decreased in half, but the President has imposed price regulations and Congress has helped curve any major spikes of inflation so far. One major change happening in large portions of the United States was the once popular idea of developing farmlands into housing developments reverting back to farming. Now some older buildings and housing projects are being demolished to provide additional land for farming, even in some larger cities.

Seventy-Four

Russian Federation – April 2006

The Russian people had not faced such extreme food and fuel

rationing during this cold spring, even during the darkest days of World War

II. Adding to the Russian's misery was this spring has been on the coldest

springs in over twenty years so far. Some moderate to warm regions in

southern Russia have seen several weeks of below freezing temperatures

with above normal amounts of late snow and ice. The only good outcome

attributed to the cold and snowy weather this spring in Russia and the

Ukraine was a slowing of the fungus spread. The only evidence of the

fungus still spreading this spring was in extreme southern regions of Russia

and in Afghanistan. Even with the fungus having slowed, almost two-thirds

of all plant life in central and southern Russia and within the Ukraine has

been effected. Thankfully the cold spring temperatures in Siberia have

delayed the spread of the fungus within the delicate Tundra regions, at least

for the time being.

One of the main reasons for Russia's severe food rationing, besides

the loss of crops and the severe weather was due to a sharp decline in food

shipments from the United States. The US food shipments were dramatically reduced due to a late winter and early spring drought within the Midwest and southern states of the United States, plus a large increase of food also needed in China. Some additional shipments of food was expected from South America, hopefully before severe malnutrition and starvation starts occurring within Russia, like it has been affecting Central Africa for many years.

Because of the additional rationing in Russia and because of a violent black market organized crime activity, the Russian military has had to increase troop levels in most major Russian cities along with a form of martial law and curfews. If the Russian Army cannot get control within the large populated cities of Russia, the Russian government could melt-down and anarchy would soon follow. The Russian domestic troop needed have temporarily stalled the Russian military invasion forces and the number of attacks within Iran, at least for this spring.

In other countries affected by the fungus, one good thing that could be attributed to the fungus spread was the almost complete elimination of poppy plants and the large scale poppy growing operations located both Kazakhstan and Afghanistan. Many Afghan tribal leaders and former Taliban supporters have stopped fighting against the American and coalition forces in Afghanistan and have started requesting food and other supplies in exchange for their weapons and terrorist information.

In China, the fungus has slowly continued to spread within the Mongolian plains, creeping slowly towards the western edge of the Gobi desert. Unfortunately large herds of Mongolian cattle have either starved to death within the Gobi desert or have been prematurely slaughtered because of the now limited and continuing death of the grazing land still found west of the Gobi desert.

Besides the terrible economic and human toll the fungus has created in Russian and neighboring countries, the toll to plant and animal life has been catastrophic. Because of the lack of food, nesting areas, and loss of habitat, many species of birds and mammals have either been listed as extremely endangered or have been placed on the Extinction List. Most scientists in the late 1990's would have bet that large scale animal and plant loss would have been attributed to global warming or because of a massive nuclear attack or nuclear accident, not because of a pre-historic plant fungus. Even with a drastic increase in global warming in conjunction with a nuclear accident, the effect on wildlife and plants would not have had this sudden or this severe.

Seventy-Five

Newcastle, New Brunswick, Canada – April 2006

Since establishing a nesting colony that was once used to nest by the native Canadian goose, the northeastern shore of New Brunswick near the town of Newcastle had been the new home of the Eastern European goose and they have prospered while the local Canadian geese population has declined. Many scientists and environmental experts have arrived in the town of Newcastle to study the Eastern European goose and the study the reasons for their new migration. Also arriving in the town of Newcastle were large numbers of hunters who have been hired by both US and Canadian farmers to kill off the Eastern European goose or to drive them back to Greenland. The environmentalists had tried to keep the Eastern European goose new migration secret, but word still out to the general public.

Spurred on by the media and the many unsubstantiated and false rumors that had surfaced about the Eastern European goose, the stories and rumors have created fear about and toward the geese populations. One of the frightening rumors going around amongst the farming communities stated that Canadian scientists had confirmed that both the Eastern

European and native Canadian goose populations were carrying the deadly fungus into Canada and the United States and the two governments knew about it.

Another false rumor that surfaced had local residents believing that the Eastern European goose had also brought a deadly bird virus which could wipe out all of North America's waterfowl including ducks and geese and would eventually affect poultry. So far, the Canadian and US scientific community has maintained rumor controls and has found no evidence of any bird virus on many test geese. They also know that the Eastern European goose could not possible be carrying the fungus because of its long migration journey and the many stops they made along the way. Besides an assurance by the onsite scientific team located in New Brunswick, Canada, both local and hired hunters have started shooting geese on private and public lands, creating a hostile environment between scientists, environmentalists and hunters. The looming hostility could become violent, towards the geese and towards each other.

Seventy-Six

Tehran, Iran – April 2006

After Russia had launched another surprise and deadly attack in Iran, Russia had given the United States and other coalition members another month to either get the fungus cure or find the commandos or Russia will begin a series of attacks on Tehran that would make the attacks of 9/11 look like a minor incident. In addition to discussing the future of Iran with the United States and other coalition countries, Russia had sent a secure message to the Iranian President and the Ayatollah, stating that if the Iranian government did not turn over the commandos from the United States and Russia along with the fungus cure in one month, the Russia military would severely punish both the government and the people of Iran like Russian troops had in Babol. The message to the Iranian government ended with the following frightening statement "If you do not comply and the fungus continues to spread throughout Russia, we will launch a massive nuclear strike against multiple targets in Iran, including your capital city of Tehran and we will wipe out the Persian people from the face of the earth".

The Chinese government which had previously pledged both military and diplomatic help to the Russians and coalition countries was first to respond to Russia's latest threat to Iran and China had sternly condemned the latest Russian threat. China's Premier stated on the Chinese National television channel "China cannot stand by and allow nuclear destruction of another country and another race of people because of the rogue and insane governments of Iran and Russia". What the Chinese Premier was actually thinking and would have liked to say was that if it was not for the oil from Iran, they would love to fire a couple of their own nukes into Tehran themselves for all the trouble the Iranian government has caused. Russian General Baranov very quickly sent a private reply to the Chinese Premier and a copy to other world leaders which stated "The Russian people are starving to death and we cannot tolerate any more losses due to this fungus. We now have nothing to lose, and we will fight and attack anyone or any country that stands against us. We will fight to kill the fungus and again return Russia to prosperity or we will die trying".

The Chinese communist cabinet again debated whether to launch a pre-emptive nuclear strike against Russia to protect China's oil supply from Iran and to possible kill the fungus in the process before it spreads further into China. After consulting with leading Chinese scientists and other world experts including the scientific team lead by Max Hamilton, the Chinese government had decided not to consider a nuclear option into Russia, since the radiation may not kill the fungus, plus they would now have to nuke themselves since the fungus has spread into rural areas of western China.

Seventy-Seven

Washington, D.C. – April 2006

With World War III a possibility within a few short weeks, the United States has had many additional instances of violence from armed Mexican gangs within it own borders and now within the combined military border with Canada. The attacks from Mexican gangs towards white, black and other citizens have become increasing more violent and have been increasing in numbers even with an increase of heavily armed police and National Guard. The gangs have been continuing to violate strict curfews and have even defied the US military in the cities that have been placed under select elements of Marshall Law and have been patrolled by both active military and National Guard troops.

Because of the increased threat by armed Mexican gangs, President Baker has reluctantly ordered National Guard troops to immediately take any arrested Mexican gang members and transport them to border outposts along the Mexican/US border and force the arrested gang members to leave the United States or Canadian soil immediately. President Baker believed his actions were severe but warranted, since most of the current state and federal maximum security prisons have become so overcrowded they have been walled in with outside guarded facilities similar to the movie "Escape from New York". These prison facilities have large numbers of heavily armed guards patrolling outside the prison grounds with strict orders to shoot on sight any prisoner attempting to climb a fence or any other attempt to escape. Food for the prisoners is usually transported into the prisons by newly arrested prisoners entering the prison property. Because of the uncontrolled and violent situations within these new "prisons", non-violent prisoners have been already been allowed to leave the prison and have been released from the prison facility.

If any Mexican gang members refuse arrest and continue their violence and destruction, the President has authorized the US military and all local law enforcement personnel to use deadly force with or without a visible gun or knife visible. This temporary use of deadly force was also rumored to be used for any arrested gang member unwilling to leave the United States or Canadian territory.

With the US President's new policies taking affect immediately concerning the growing Mexican gang violence, President Baker must now consider what the United States must do if the meetings with Mexican President Jimenez along with the Canadian Prime Minister are successful and approved by Congress for a new North American military alliance. Since the last meeting with the Mexican President and his government leadership, violence along the US/Mexican border has slightly decreased.

With the prospect of a new North American military alliance filtering down to the individual border regions, the number of border clashes has also been reduced along with both the severity and duration of the skirmishes.

Since the merger between Canadian and US military and other law enforcement personnel in the newly formed US-Canadian military alliance, the number of attempted Al-Qaeda like attacks or attempted border crossings has been significantly reduced or stopped altogether for the time being. Also local police in conjunction with the new joint FBI have noticed a large reduction of suspected Al-Qaeda and other militant phone and internet communications.

Within the new US-Canadian military alliance, tension still remain high since the United States had enacted temporary "non-Miranda" rights laws that were initiated at the end of March. These new laws have created a divide between Americans that has not been witnessed since the early days of the Civil War. This time the divide between Americans was not due to slavery, but due to a division between the ethnic Hispanic populations and black and white Americans.

Besides the division and hostility towards Mexican Americans, the border problem has now spilled over to other Central American countries. Many so-called freedom fighters from El Salvador and Nicaragua have traveled through Mexico to help the Mexicans fight the imperial Americans along the US and Mexican border.

Based on this new intelligence, the new joint US and Canadian military command has carefully reached out to Mexican President Victor Jimenez to discuss forming a new North American military alliance. President Jimenez of Mexico has agreed in principle to the initial plan, but the Canadian and US leadership is asking President Jimenez for assurances of complete cooperation between the Mexican military and police along with the current US and Canadian military forces. The US Congress also wants assurances from the Mexican government that the new drug border will be along the Central American border not into Mexico. In addition to these requirements, the US-Canadian military leadership would expect a very harsh and swift removal of all know Central American militants and freedom fighters before this agreement could be finalized.

Seventy-Eight

Mt. Demavend, Iran – April 2006

Meanwhile back under Mt. Demavend outside of Tehran, Iran, Boris Panov along with the United States and Russian commando team was unsuccessful in an attempt to use a small amount of explosive to blast a way through the blocked tunnel entrance. But they were able to locate a small functioning fresh air intake shaft using an old building blueprint that was found and then interpreted by one of the Iranian scientists. Even during the messy and mostly dark laboratory prison that they were confined in, the Iranian scientists had continued to try and work on the fungus cure and their experiments and vowed to help even if they were rescued.

Once the air shaft was located, the commando unit started working with the Iranian scientists to try to find a way to build a make shift radio antenna that they could use to send up the air shaft and then possibly call for help and to let the outside world know about their situation.

While the trapped commandos and scientists continued working on the fungus cure and a means of escape, the world's leaders have taken advantage of Russia's new pledge not to strike Tehran with nuclear weapons at least at this time. Over twenty countries have sent in search and rescue.

military and construction experts racing towards Tehran and the region near Mt. Demavend, Iran to help look for the missing US/Russian commandos whether they were dead or alive. Another military convoy consisting of coalition members from China, America, Russia, France and Egypt have left their northern desert outpost and airfield located in Kuwait and started heading north through Iraq on the way to Iran. There mission is to find and overthrow the current Iranian government including the ruling religious leader, The Ayatollah.

Seventy-Nine

Beijing, China – April 2006

After what seemed like another long disappointing day, good news was finally delivered to Max Hamilton as he was again struggling with sleeping no more than an hour at a time. Max was also struggling with the constant disappointment of failing to reproduce the fungus cure, plus he missed his wife, kids, his parents and his hometown in Montana.

As Max's thoughts returned to his tiny sleeping area in the dingy dormitory area of his Chinese laboratory, he was given a message from one of his assistants that the scientific team had been able to both successfully replicate the fungus cure again and that the sample has remained viable for the last few hours. Max then quickly dressed and joined his assistant Adil in the laboratory where he examined their laboratory results and then examined the living specimen of the fungus cure. As he was gazing through a microscope at the molecular makeup of the fungus cure, his assistant Adil, a highly recommended, intelligent and hard working scientist on loan from a large global pharmaceutical company located in India reminded Max that this breakthrough had only replicated a very small amount of the fungus cure again. Max told Adil "Even with such a small amount produced, this is still a major breakthrough worthy of notifying the world leaders".

"Won't this give Russia and the world hope the may never happen?" replied Adil in his heavily accented English.

"Any hope is better than no hope and maybe this little bit of hope may prevent a global catastrophe and possible prevent World War III" Max said as he clasped Adil on the shoulder as they left the laboratory.

Max left the laboratory and immediately woke up their Chinese scientific liaison who then woke up the Chinese Premier. From within the secret confines of the Chinese Premiers residence at the Politburo, Max had called the US President Baker and Russian General Baranov and told them with the Chinese Premier about their small ability to replicate the fungus cure not at two different times. Max also told the world leaders "This is only a small breakthrough so far, hopefully with larger amounts of fungus cure replication taking place in another two months or longer. Hopefully we can then begin testing the cure by summer".

President Baker, General Baranov and the Chinese Premier expressed their gratitude to Max, the scientists and the many workers who have worked so hard to end this fungus catastrophe and then wished them good luck and a quick result in creating a larger scale production of the fungus cure.

"We may be able to replicate the fungus cure, but we still have not been able to develop a method to mass disperse the fungus cure on a large scale even if we had large amounts of the cure" Max told the world leaders. It was during Max's conversation with President Baker, General Baranov and the Chinese Premier that he started to think that a smaller scale deployment of the fungus cure may not be able to eradicate the fungus, but could buy some time before either World War II breaks out or before the fungus destroys mankind.

As warmer temperatures and weather approaches most of Russia and Northern China along with new plants and flowers, the fungus has actually started to slow down its destructive path. Along with the warmer temperatures and spring flowers, the world has now been officially told of the efforts being waged in China having the top scientific minds of the world headed by the US Paleobotanist Max Hamilton. Along with this knowledge also comes the realization of limited food and other resources throughout Eastern Europe, Russia and Western China.

Many world leaders now fear that if the fungus continues to spread even though it has slowed throughout China, Europe and Southern Asia, a worldwide economic collapse would be certain and many so-called civilized nations could revert back to a primitive life similar to life before the Industrial Revolution. The only difference between now and pre-Industrial Revolutionary times would be that the generations before were based on agriculture to survive, but now most of the farms would be gone with no

chance for any continued harvest periods. This would mean global

starvation.

Eighty

Russian Federation – May 2006

With the temperatures starting to rise along the Russian and Chinese border, the deadly plant fungus has again started to spread its deadly destruction in all directions. As the middle of May approaches the plant loss in southern Russia and the Ukraine is estimated to be now at close to seventy-five percent.

Not just the temperature are rising in the once communist country of Russia, but so is the impatience of the people mainly due to the country's growing unemployment rate which has know gone over fifty percent.

In addition to the plant and animal life destroyed by the fungus in southern Russia, almost fifty percent of Siberia has been affected by the fungus or by the recently relocated farmers and Industrial workers trying to make a living in the harsh regions of Siberia. The destruction of the forested and farms areas of southern Siberia has migrated northward destroying large portions of the delicate tundra region.

As deep desperation was setting in with most Russians, the current ruling government led by General Baranov has ordered military rule in most of the medium to large size Russian cities from St. Petersburg to Moscow in an effort to help distribute food aid, help disrupt civil and food riots and try to maintain calm amongst the citizens enough to delay a total collapse of the current interim government of Russia.

Russia and the Ukraine are not the only countries affected. There have been reports of massive plant loss in large remote areas of Kazakhstan and Afghanistan. One good outcome previously reported out of Afghanistan stated that most of the large fields of poppy plants and drugs that were destined for drug shipments to Russia and the United States have been completely wiped out.

In addition to areas of Kazakhstan and Afghanistan, the fungus has also been reported in areas of western China. The communist government of China has kept most fungus reports to a minimum, but a Chinese source working with Max Hamilton and his scientific team suspects that now almost ten percent of western China has been affected by the deadly fungus.

Eighty-One

New England – May 2006

With the spread of the fungus continuing, animal and bird populations have been declining rapidly and more species may be placed on the Extinction List in parts of Russia, Kazakhstan and now western China.

Besides any recent extinction list, global nesting and migratory patterns have been dramatically altered and disrupted, especially the Eastern European goose. Since establishing a new nesting colony in Canada, the Eastern European goose has now started migrating further south into Maine and other northern New England areas. This new migration has started a bloodbath of animal killings not seen since the slaughter of the Buffalo in the American west during the 1800's. United States and Canadian hunters have teamed up with local farmers and have started killing off the Eastern European goose along with the native Canadian geese as they try and fly further south into the United States.

Since the Eastern European goose and the Canadian goose look so similar, hunters have not tried to distinguish between the two geese and have tried to kill all of them. The mass hunting of the geese population has been fueled by many rumors that the geese may be able to spread the fungus that may have been carried over the northern Atlantic Ocean from northern Europe.

It was this same type of rumors that started the mass panic, loss of food and loss of habitat that led to the extinction of the once prosperous Siberian goose in Russia. Since the rumors have surfaced and the killing has spread, many environmental groups have staged peaceful rallies and have tried to educate and inform both the hunters and farmers that the geese do not carry the fungus and they should stop killing off the geese before it's too late like the Siberian goose. But the wholesale slaughter of the geese has continued and now some hardcore fanatical environmentalists have brought military style assault weapons to New England and Canadian fields and have threatened to kill hunters and farmers and vice-versa.

This hostility and fear between the Environmentalists and hunters abruptly became a reality within a chilly northern Maine cornfield. Instead of corn being planted in spring, the old cornfield has been littered with the bloodied bodies of geese, hunters, farmers and environmentalists. All told, over thirty people were killed and eighty were injured. This was the worst American on American battle since the Civil War. This deadly scenario had played out several more times in other field until the joint US/Canadian Army was brought in to stop the violence and disperse the hunters, farmers and environmentalist.

Eighty-Two

Moscow, Russian Federation – May 2006

Meanwhile, several thousand miles away, Russian General Baranov had grown tired of watching his people starve, fight for handouts and slowly die as a nation. General Baranov has told all the world leaders including US President Baker that "Russia has given the world and especially Iran, more time then we have, and would not hold back any means to destroy Iran"

"Russia has run out of patience. We have ordered the largest search and rescue mission in Russian history to find the US and Russian commando team and to find the fungus cure. Once we have our people safely home and the fungus cure in scientific hands or we find our forces dead, we will destroy Tehran including every living soul whether we find the fungus cure or not" continued General Baranov with a sigh.

Fearing a nuclear war between China and Russia, the United States and other foreign leaders had called Russian General Baranov and begged him to reconsider his latest comments. But the United States and world did not need to worry about Russia and the Chinese this time since the communist government of China has issued a immediate reply to General Baranov's statement, "We have now observed some possible fungus spread in Mongolia and fear that a spread of the fungus inside inner China. This would be too much for our large population to bear, and we would like to offer any assistance to Russia and other world leaders that may be needed". Not only has China backed down from a possible fight with Russia, but has admitted the spread of the fungus inside of China, and has now offered help in fighting the Iranians and the government within Tehran.

Eighty-Three

Denver, Colorado – May 2006

Since President Baker had ordered instant deportation of any
Mexican national or other non-US citizen that gets arrested for any type of
gang or other activities related to rioting and other crimes, the number of
riots, attacks and acts of violence has decreased. But also since the
Presidential mandate, the severity of attacks has increased along with their
brutality. One such attack occurred in a suburb outside of Denver, Colorado
where three white families were brutally murdered after being robbed, raped
and tortured. One of the houses where the bodies were found was sprayed
painted with the words "Death to the Yankees, Vive New Mexico".

In addition to the violence taking place within and around major
US and Canadian cities, the violence has continued along the US and
Mexican border, but the attacks have decreased slightly due to the high level
meetings taking place between joint US/Canadian officials and the Mexican
government. But again the number of attacks may have decreased, but the
amount of force and weapons being used by the Mexican forces have greatly
increased. This escalation has been attributed to new weapons being sent to
Mexican forces from the anti-American governments of Libya and

Venezuela. Along with the increased effectiveness of the new Mexican attacks, the US and Canadian border forces have also been increasing the harshness and size of their reprisals. These attacks along the border have killed almost two hundred US and Canadian troops, but have accounted fro the deaths of over five thousand Mexican Police, military and unfortunately some innocent civilians.

With no new attempts by Al-Qaeda trying to either enter North America or any attempts to bring the fungus to US or Canadian soil has helped President Baker decide to suspend the new "anti-Meranda" laws. This suspension of these controversial laws was to try and quell a potential civil war between Mexican Americans and other ethnic groups. The new "anti-Meranda" laws were considered very harsh and anti-American by most Mexican and Hispanic Americans and the law was deemed unconstitutional by many other people including some US Congress members.

Again the US and Canadian governments have reached out to Mexican President Victor Jimenez to again try to talk about a united North American Military Alliance consisting of Canada, Mexico and the United States. The US and Canadian governments have been seeking assurances by the Mexican President and his cabinet of complete cooperation between Mexico's police and military with the new joint US/Canadian border forces. Even though President Baker and the Prime Minister of Canada were strongly for this new North American military alliance, they still faced a nearly fifty-fifty split among Americans. Some people were pro-North American military unity and some were for a complete border closure and isolation from Mexico. President Baker believed that with assurances from Mexico, the American and Canadian people would rally behind the plan, since they all agreed that American, Canada and Mexico would be stronger with this alliance then without it.

After a week of scheduling and arrangements, Mexican President Victor Jimenez met with President Baker and other US/Canadian military commanders. President Jimenez had then assured them that Mexico was onboard with the alliance plan and would like to sit down with all the joint US and Canadian military leadership to discuss implementation of the alliance plan and to discuss his and other Mexican military officials future role and positions in the new North American Military Alliance.

Eighty-Four

Mt. Demavend, Iran – May 2006

Meanwhile buried several hundred feet inside a mountain outside of Tehran, Iran, Boris Panov and the joint US/Russian commandos have been able to fabricate a pole and pulley system to raise the commandos communications antenna and were able to communicate with United States and Russian forces inside of Iran. Once the situation was known to the US and Russian forces in Iran, a quick response force of US Special Forces was immediately sent to the Iranian base to deliver food, water and other supplies including urgent medical supplies along with canisters of oxygen. These supplies were sent down the Fresh Air Shaft in which the trapped commando force was able to communicate.

As the promised large scale Russian search and rescue effort sponsored by Russian General Baranov had started to arrive at the Iranian base, several worldwide military forces had also arrived and were already busy starting work at the collapsed area of the tunnel entrance under Mt. Demavend. During the initial raid of the Iranian base by the US Army Special Forces, it became very clear that they would have no military attacks from the remaining Iranian military guards at the base.

Once the US troops entered the Iranian base, they were surprised to find no resistance at their arrival and were again surprised to find out that the Iranian guards had helped to set up the commandos' make-shift antenna system and had also shared what remaining meager supplies of food and water rations they had with the trapped scientists and commandos. The US troop leader had found a crude, but effective system of transporting food and supplies down baskets into the air shaft.

Eighty-Five

Beijing, China – May 2006

Once the euphoria wore off from the discovery of limited fungus cure production headed by Max Hamilton and his team working in Beijing, China, they had realized just how little fungus cure they had created. Max knew their hope of creating large scale production of the fungus cure was dimming as he watched as the scientific team began to lose hope.

Max's feeling of dread was short-lived with the news that his friend Boris Panov had not only survived at the Iranian base, but had been able to possible secure viable amounts of the fungus cure along with supporting data that was hidden at the secret Iranian base. Even though Max was concerned for his friend Boris's safety during the tunnel excavation and rescue, he was more concerned with getting the Iranian fungus cure and supporting data sent to China.

Max immediately called the White House and asked President Baker "Mr. President, What do we have to do get both the Iranian fungus cure samples and data from under Mt. Demavend to Beijing as quickly as possible"

"I will call General Baranov and we will get the fungus data and specimens to you within a couple of days. Max, do you think this will help create large scale amounts of the fungus cure" asked President Baker.

"With the Iranian data and seemingly how close we are now, I truly believe we can get it done in a few weeks, Mr. President" Max answered. The President ended the phone call by assuring Max that the Chinese government would do anything within their powers to help him.

In addition to the good news from outside of Tehran, Iran, good news was coming from Beijing, China in the form of a viable fungus cure. Once the second trial of experiments were successful and confirmed, Max Hamilton quickly informed the Chinese government and then phoned Washington, D.C. to announce that they may have figured out a way to mass produce the fungus from the Iranian scientific data that was just received. Max also announced that they may have also developed a means to apply the fungus cure. Max's scientific team had figured out a way to mix small amounts of the fungus cure with an ordinary soybean oil solution which could be dispersed by an air activated spray system. This method of applying the fungus cure has so far killed the fungus on an isolated test section of fungus affected plants within a controlled and measured section of plant life located in southern Russia.

The world was now in the process of exhaling a cautionary sigh, since the news was broadcast about the Tehran rescue and the scientific results from Max Hamilton's laboratory in Beijing, China. World leaders still understood that worldwide economic and social collapse could still occur and would most certainly happen if the fungus continued to spread late spring into summer. Another sign of some good luck, was that the spread of the fungus was slowed considerably by the massive expanse of the Gobi desert in Mongolia and the semi-arid regions of southern Russia, Kazakhstan and Afghanistan.

Max Hamilton knew the burden on his and his teams' shoulders, but he was mostly isolated from most of the gloom and doom shown on television in the western countries, due to China's limited and government controlled television programming. President Baker, General Baranov and other world leaders were hoping and praying that Max and his scientific team could kill the fungus before it was too late.

Eighty-Six

Russian Federation – late May 2006

The fungus has again started to spread very rapidly. With the fungus now spreading again, most edible plant life in southern Russia and the Ukraine has been destroyed, along with thousands of acres of the delicate Siberian tundra.

In addition to a northward spread into Siberia, the fungus has continued to spread south, east and west into parts of China, Afghanistan and now into parts of eastern Poland and Romania.

Many additional species of animal and bird life has been either pushed to the brink of extinction or have been added to the Extinction List. Estimated range as high as two hundred species of birds have become extinct and almost as many animal species have vanished.

Eighty-Seven

New England – late May, 2006

Since the joint US/Canadian Army troops have enforced measures to stop the killing of geese by farmers and hunters, the confrontations between hunters and militant environmentalists have stopped. Most of the farm fields in northern New England have again become quiet. The geese are still rumored to carry and spread the fungus, but scientists have pointed out that there is no scientific evidence or any reported fungus to support these rumors and everyone should direct there efforts in helping others in the world effected by the fungus.

Once the slaughter of the geese had diminished, the Eastern European goose has started to settle down and co-exist with the native Canadian goose and the snow goose in some northern nesting areas. Some scientists believe the two species will ultimately breed and possible create a new hybrid goose between the Eastern European goose and the Canadian goose, creating a whole new species.

Again the flocks of Eastern European and Canadian geese have started their migration again venturing further into the interior and eastern areas of the United States.

Eighty-Eight

Mt. Demavend, Iran – late May 2006

A large scale rescue mission had begun by one of the largest
mobilizations of men and machine ever undertaken by any multi-national
force in the earth's history. Large earth and rock moving equipment and
machinery was airlifted to Iran from the United States, Japan and China.

The hope of getting the joint US/Russian commando unit out from
under Mt. Demavend alive was now a certainty more than a hope.

Eighty-Nine

US/Mexican border – late May 2006

With Mexican, US and Canadian officials continued talks to form a new joint North American military alliance, the domestic chaos involving groups of rioting Mexican nations has almost completely stopped along with a big decline in violence by Mexican gangs directed at blacks and whites and vice-versa.

In addition to hostilities declining within the interior cities of the United States, so have border clashes along the US/Mexican border. This is partly due to both Mexican and United States military forces being pulled back a minimum of one mile from the border area as directed by President Baker and President Jimenez.

Once final negotiations were hammered out, the US, Canada and Mexico have agreed to terms on a new combined North American Military Alliance. The new military alliance will start with a slow transition in about four months. The interim military alliance of North America will consist of a three-way Presidential panel consisting of President Baker, the Canadian Prime Minister and Mexican President Victor Jimenez. The military commanders and troops from each country will be slowly integrated to avoid any possible logistics and accidental incidents.

Epilogue

Present Day

Since the spraying of the fungus cure has been going on non-stop from May 2006, most areas of fungus development has been completely eradicated and no new areas of fungus devastation have been detected anywhere within the world. This new data has added stability to a world economy that has started to rebound and shows signs of reaching pre-fungus growth and vitality.

Since the eradication of the fungus a new democratic style government has been established in Russia. The new Russian government has been established with the newly elected General Baranov, who had won the election by a landslide due to his effective leadership during the fungus crisis and his diplomatic skills dealing with other world leaders.

Many plant, animal and bird species have been placed on the Extinction List, mainly attributed to the fungus, but also due to increased pollution and the effects of global warming. But some very endangered species have begun to reproduce and show signs of re-habitation within previous effected fungus areas.

Some of the success of the world economy and saving of animal species is due to a massive global effort to re-vegetate all of the effected areas of the fungus devastation. With help from all of North America and from China, farmers have transformed the once rich poppy fields of Afghanistan into productive and profitable vegetable and other crops.

Once all illegal hunting of both the Eastern European and Canadian goose was eliminated, the geese were successful in completing their north and south migrations throughout North America. In addition to the migration, a new species of goose has been confirmed between the Eastern European goose and the Canadian goose. The new species of goose was simply named the "Eastern Canadian goose".

As for Iran, the anti-western and anti-United States government of Iran, including both the President and the Ayatollah were quietly replaced with a new interim government which was more moderate and was based on Sectarian law, not religious laws. The new Iranian government was assisted and watched by a panel of world delegates made up of members from North America, Russia, China and several Arab nations. This panel was like the panel set up to watch Germany after World War II.

Max Hamilton and Boris Panov were reunited in New York City where Max was again working at the world renowned New York Museum of Natural History. This time Max was not in charge, but was a part-time lecturer and exhibiter. In his free time, he spends his time with his wife

422

Monica, his kids and his family in Montana while not out working with Boris. Boris and Max had started a private company to scour the world looking for new pre-historic finds and other adventures.

Terrorism and Al-Qaeda still exist with attempted attacks still occurring. All of the attacks have occurred outside of North America and have been small an unorganized. Most of the attacks have taken place in and around Israel, which was left alone during the fungus crisis, but is now the center of attention again.

In addition to a new North American military alliance and the new Russian government, talks have been going on to combine individual nations of Eastern Europe into one large common Eastern European Union.

The fungus has now been completely stopped with no new outbreaks reported for twelve months. Most scientists conclude that the deadly fungus has been eradicated and that the current plant life show no signs of the fungus.

With scientific research and money now being directed to stop global warming and other earth friendly matters, most scientific research about the fungus has declined or completely stopped. Even with the world having been able to rebound from the fungus, most scientists agree that the fungus is dead, but Max Hamilton cannot stop the feeling that the fungus is not dead, but maybe it has just went dormant again like it did after destroying the dinosaurs. Max's last scientific writing about the fungus crisis ended with his theory that the fungus may have just went dormant again.